Doc Holliday's Woman

What the literary experts are saying about
Pulitzer nominated
DOC HOLLIDAY'S WOMAN:

"A terrific biographical novel."
~ Rocky Mountain News

"One of the finest works of literature written by an American . . . and one of the ten greatest love stories of all time."
~ Council Fires

"The story of an incredible woman by an incredible writer."
~ El Paso Herald-Post

"Spellbinding."
Benjamin T. Traywick, Tombstone, Arizona Historian

Doc Holliday's Woman

Jane Candia Coleman

Ravenhawk™

Books

Ravenhawk™ Books
A divison of the 6DOF™ Group

Printed in the United States of America

Library of Congress Cataloging-in-Publication Data

Coleman, Jane Candia
Doc Holliday's Woman / Jane Candia Coleman.
p.cm.

ISBN 1-893660-02-8

CIP 2004099911

Book Design by Hans B. Shepherd, Jr.

*Cover photo of "Big Nose Kate" courtesy of
The Boyer Collection*

Dedicated respectfully in loving memory of

Mary Katherine Harony, "Big Nose Kate"
May God grant her eternal peace.

More books by Jane Candia Coleman

Historical Fiction

Moving On
I, Pearl Hart
The O'Keefe Empire
Doc Holliday's Gone
Borderlands
Country Music
Matchless
Tombstone Travesty

Women's Literary Fiction

Desperate Acts
The Italian Quartet
Wives and Lovers

Poetry

No Roof But Sky
The Red Drum
forthcoming title; The White Dove

Memoir

Mountain Time

Acknowledgments

Without the guidance and early research of Professor A. W. Bork, who interviewed Big Nose Kate in the Arizona Pioneer's Home in Prescott in the 1930's, and Glenn G. Boyer, the world authority on Wyatt Earp and the editor of *I Married Wyatt Earp*, the memoirs of Mrs. Josephine Earp; this book could not have been written. Mr. Boyer is also the author of *Wyatt Earp's Tombstone Vendetta*. Professor Bork shared his recollections of Kate with me, and Glenn Boyer turned over to me his personal collection of taped interviews with Kate's relatives, her letters, photographs, and autobiography. He also checked the manuscript for accuracy. In addition, Juanita Speake, district clerk, and Crystal Shook, deputy clerk, of Stephens County, Texas; Cheri Hawkins and Lana Clift, deputy clerks of Shackleford County, Texas; and J. Richard Salzar, chief of archives, and Al Regensberg of the New Mexico State Archives in Santa Fe all assisted with my research. Diana Stein of the Galeria de los Artesanos in Las Vegas, New Mexico, helped me find books I needed for information.

Special thanks to Buddy Fincher of Albany, Texas, who showed me where old Griffin used to be.

Last but not least, thanks to my Appaloosa gelding, *Jefe* (Spanish for "Boss"), who carried me diligently up the Western Cattle Trail during the course of my research.

"This is the story. Some is sad and some is quite laughable, but such is life any way we take it."

~ from a letter written by Mary K. Cummings, "Big Nose Kate," to her niece, March 18, 1940.

PROLOGUE

1876

"Wake up, Kate! Get dressed and we'll go buy you that brooch you've been ogling."

Doc sounds like a boy. He is leaning over me, his grey eyes with a hint of sky in them wide, his cheeks flushed, not with fever but with success. He's had a run of luck at the tables and wants to celebrate, and his excitement finds an answer in me. I reach out my arms and, laughing, pull him close. "Don't ever go away again," I say. Without Doc I'm like the land with a drought upon it - useless, grey, blowing away, the wind's plaything.

1935

"Wake up!" The harsh voice shatters my dream.

She has rough hands, this nurse, this woman without a shred of kindness. The Pioneer's Home can't afford to hire ministering angels. I push her away. "Let me alone," I say, torn between dream and reality; between what was and what is.

"You have company," she says. "That writer."

"That buzzard! He just wants to pick my brains and me not dead yet." There's so much to tell, but he'll hear only what he wants and leave out the important things.

He'll write about Tombstone and Doc and Wyatt Earp forgetting they were people with bodies and feelings that made them what they were. And if he puts me in at all, he'll do what the rest have done. He'll make me a bad woman, wicked, scheming, rowdy. I was never any of those things, regardless of what's been said. But I was a lot else.

And what about the others ~ Mattie, Bessie, Allie, Lou ~ the Earp women ~ who'll tell about them? Not this man. He's only interested in the shooting. Maybe I'll tell him that part. I was in Tombstone, after all, that afternoon in October.

As for the rest, I'll write it myself. It's my life. I lived it, and I remember it all as clear as I remember Doc's eyes and the touch of his fingers.

It takes so long to move nowadays,to dress and make myself presentable though clothes are so much simpler. Lord, I've lived through hoop skirts, bustles, and basques; through yards of tulle and lace, ruffled petticoats, those dreadful whalebone corsets, but I fumble with the buttons on my blouse, do them up wrong and start over.

How is it possible I'm this wrinkled old lady in the mirror when only a few days ago it was 1862 and I was twelve wearing a dress made of tiers of starched white muslin and a bonnet lined with pink satin curtseying to Ferdinand Maximillian, Emperor of all Mexico?

I was as reluctant then as now, homesick for the Hungary where I was born, for the golden plains, the house with its high ceilings and Turkey carpets, its glitter and its comforts. I missed

3

Rella who ran the schoolroom and the nursery and who sang the old songs to us; I missed the gypsies and my white pony. And most of all I missed my grandmother, that indomitable woman who oversaw the estate, rode a horse like a man, and who always had time for me even in the midst of harvest or the making of the wine.

I wanted to be there among the loved, the familiar. Instead I was in Trieste in a castle called Miramar that overlooked the sea, in a room the ceiling of which was a vast aquarium filled with plants and multi-colored, darting fish, and the man responsible for this marvel was bending over me, his blond mustaches sweeping his chin.

He took my hand in his large pale ones. "Are you excited to be going to Mexico with us, Katya?" he asked as if I were four years old to be distracted by sweets.

Frustration shaped my answer. "No, your Excellency," I said. My words rang through the vast reception room silencing the low voices of those who had come to reaffirm their allegiance to the Hapsburg prince and his wife, the new rulers of Mexico.

My mother clicked her tongue in horror and poked me, hard, between my shoulders.

The Empress Carlotta drew in her breath with a hiss of disapproval and glared at me with her burning dark eyes.

Unrepentant I stared back at Maximillian who was, for the moment, wordless. Then surprisingly, he laughed. "Why not?" he asked.

"I miss my horse," I told him. "And my grandmama. I want to go home." I disregarded my mother's hand clamped like iron around my arm. Oh, I was in for it! But I didn't care. Not about emperors, not about punishment. I had already gone through the worst, uprooted, taken away from Hungary and all

4

that I held dear. And I was as headstrong at twelve as I would be all my life.

Who, after all was this person? A man like any other, and not nearly as handsome as my Papa in his gold-braided uniform.

"Humph!" he said, taken aback. I noticed he had bad teeth, another mark against him, but to his credit he wasn't nearly as pompous as his Empress who seemed about to explode.

Abruptly he patted the top of my bonnet. "You will love your new home too," he pronounced. "I promise. And, who knows, perhaps there will be a new pony. I understand that they are fine horsemen in Mexico."

He gave a little nod, and I curtseyed as I had been told, catching a blurred glimpse of myself in his highly polished boots as he moved on to my mother, soothing her apologies with what was, I had to admit, considerable charm.

"How could you! How could you!" My mother pounded her fists on her knees as the carriage carried us away from the castle. "You've disgraced us all! Wait till your father hears."

My earlier courage had deserted me. I felt a child again and miserable. "But it's true," I blurted. "I want to go home. Don't you miss it, too, Mama? Don't you?"

A beam of sunlight entered through the window and struck her face, and I saw, for a moment only, a deep sadness in her blue eyes. Then she looked down and smoothed the green silk of her gown. Her fingers trembled. "I go where your father goes," she answered finally. "We do what we must, Katya. Now ~ no more talk of home. Our home is with Papa in Mexico. Do you understand?"

I nodded. I have felt alone many times since, but never as badly as then, never as helpless. On the verge of womanhood I thought how dreadful it was to relinquish happiness simply at the desire of one's husband. Was my Papa right, following the young Hapsburg into the wilderness? I didn't know, nor it seemed did my mother. Probably she had not been asked.

I looked back at Miramar castle perched like a white bird on its hill above the ocean, and I made a vow. Never, I thought, never would I go against the yearnings of my heart at the whim of a man - or a woman. Never would I compromise as if I were no one, nothing, a piece of furniture moved here and there, an ornament packed and un packed, placed on a shelf.

And, with one exception for which I never forgave myself or the man responsible, I have kept that vow.

Times were different then. Men and women did what they had to do to survive, as I did. But there's no need to go into all that with this writer who wants to talk to me, this skinny creature who thinks he knows it all. And no need to confess that I, Mary Katharine Haroney born in Hungary, am not even a citizen of this country except in my heart where these things matter.

On my application here, I lied. I said I was born in Davenport, Iowa, and in a sense I was. After Davenport I was never Mary Katharine Haroney again.

I was sixteen when my life changed a third, and irrevocable time. Hungary lay in the past, and Mexico, that dream turned nightmare for all of us.

Beaten, uprooted again, my family made its final pilgrimage to Davenport, fleeing the heat, the fevers, the violent and changing whims of a country in upheaval.

1865
We fled the revolution in Mexico, carrying with us only our clothes and a few mementoes. My parents bought a house with a garden, and cautiously entered into the new world of free-

dom, of limitless horizons and opportunity. We children, Mina, Rosa, Alexander, and I were sent to school, the first real school we had attended. A nurse was engaged for baby Louis whose birth had cost my mother her fragile health. The nurse's arrival freed me from the duties I'd shouldered in Mexico where I learned the language and ran the house in, I thought, much the same way that my grandmother had run the estate, with a mixture of kindness and authority. Such a little dictator I was!

Looking back on that innocent Mary Katharine, I want to laugh. Or weep. She was so sure of herself, her position. She hadn't a hint of the future, its struggles, its pain. If she had, would she have lived differently? Probably not. Who can say?

I pinch my cheeks to put color into them and smooth my hair. "Foolish old woman!" I say to the lined face in the mirror with its long Haroney nose grown more prominent over the years. "Vain as a girl just because there's a man in the parlor, and you old enough to be his mother!"

The old ways die hard. I was never a beauty, not in the way my mother was, but I had something else. A smile brought all the attention I wanted. A smile and a swish of my hips under those voluminous skirts.

I learned to flirt in my cradle the way all girls did when the goal in life was to find ~ and keep ~ a husband. I copied my mother's laugh, that tinkle of sleigh bells men adored - and the way her eyes gleamed bright blue through fluttering lashes. I was an apt pupil, as those who aren't blessed with beauty usually are. Life was happy, exciting, fun! The world lay at my feet, its rules of conduct laid out as plainly as the steps of a waltz. And then everything changed and, unprepared, floundering, I changed to meet it.

Enough! I'll go see this man and tell him what he wants. Then I'll write my own version....

He's not handsome, but he's polite, rising as I enter the parlor, making proper greetings as he leads me to a comfortable chair. Then he looks at me and I see greed in his eyes, a look I learned to recognize over the gaming tables, a commonplace regardless of class or position. Everyone wanting more; more money, more land, one women or ten.

"You're a link with history," he says in a syrupy voice that intends to flatter, but which in his case achieves the opposite. "You were there that day. What was it like? Tell me."

I close my eyes and see it all again; Tombstone glittering in the high desert between the jagged thrust of the Dragoon Mountains and the forbidding mass of the Huachucas. It never slept, that town. It was always alert and ready for trouble. And trouble came that bright morning in October.

I start slowly, feeling my way back. "I got up early that day," I tell him. "I was only visiting, you understand. I never lived in Tombstone. I ran a hotel in Globe, but Doc would write begging me to come, and I would. I couldn't ~ I couldn't stay away."

And that's the truth. I could never make our separations stick. My heart always got the better of my head no matter how much I tried, and I'm glad of it for the heart cannot lie.

"I remember I wanted to make some calls. On Bessie Earp and Mattie. So I got dressed and went out and met Ike Clanton looking for Doc. Looking for trouble. You learn to read the signs. So I went back to our room and said, 'Doc, Ike Clanton is looking for you.'"

Doc was shaving. In the mirror his face seemed carved out of some hard, cold stone, and when his eyes met mine in the glass they looked through me, out into the street.

He ran the blade under his jaw, then wiped it and put it away. He was always neat about his person. Clean. You got to

8

appreciate that in those days when a man smelling of soap and water was rare.

"If God will let me live long enough, he shall see me," Doc said, turning finally.

"Be careful," I said, useless though it was to try and warn him. "I didn't come here to go to your funeral."

"Hell, don't worry. I won't be out there alone. Why don't you go to breakfast?"

He started to dress as if he'd forgotten me. "Damn you!" I yelled. "How do you expect me to eat and you out there with those rustlers waiting to pick you off?"

"Go on," he said. "Just stay off the street."

I didn't go to breakfast. I don't remember eating anything at all that day. About half an hour later the shooting began. I went to a side window of Fly's Gallery that faced the vacant lot. One shot came through the window just two panes above me, but I couldn't move. I was hypnotized by the scene, by the long shadows Doc and the Earps made. As if they were bigger than life. I stayed until the fight was over.

CHAPTER One

It was March, 1866. We stood shivering beside the grave and watched my mother's coffin being lowered, heard the clods, heavy with melting ice, fall upon the lid.

My father stood stunned. "I brought her here to die," he kept saying, like a litany. "To die."

In spite of her tears, my sister Mina tried to comfort him. "It'll be alright, papa," she said, taking his arm. "You'll see."

But nothing was right from that time on. Two months later we were back in the same spot, Mina, Rosa, Alexander, and I, watching our father's coffin being placed beside the other. Lilacs were in bloom. We'd decorated the grave with the opulent purple branches, and the scent lay heavy in the humid air.

"What's going to happen to us?" Mina whispered. She

was pale; the tip of her nose was red. "What will we do?"

I shook my head. "I don't know," I answered, feeling as lost as she did. I was the eldest, but unprepared for the responsibility of keeping our small family together. For all I knew we could be sent back to the old country that, in spite of my earlier longings, I hardly remembered.

I made up my mind then and there that I wouldn't go. I had fallen in love with America on our boat trip up the Mississippi from New Orleans to Davenport. Since then I had spent hours on the banks watching the sidewheelers shoving upstream against the current, white wake spreading behind, splashing at my feet on the shore. I wanted to go on those boats with their lacy superstructures and tall stacks, with their bells and giant paddlewheels that churned the water with a sound like driving rain. I was adventurous, and with no mother to guide me had run wild with my brother and the children from school. I had explored the waterfront, the docks, the furrowed farm fields. And I had dreamed as all children do, of riches and a great love.

The neighbors were kind. They fussed over us, patted us, took Rosa and Louis onto their laps and soothed them in the old language. They took us into their homes, but a farmer named Otto Schmidt was appointed our guardian.

He and his wife had a fine house, a good barn, one hundred and sixty acres of farmland and no children. Rebecca Schmidt was lonely. Otto was filled with greed. Greed for land, for money, for free labor, for women. When he took us in, he got much of what he wanted.

We worked in the house, the barn, the fields. Little Louis carried wood, tottering under the weight of the logs. Rosa and Mina helped with the house and the washing. Alexander and I worked in the barn and the fields with Otto, and I hated it because of how he looked at me, how he sweated and stank like an animal, like one of his pigs.

Sometimes I thought of the Empress Carlotta and my mother, ladies in silken dresses, sweet-smelling and fair-skinned. Even so, I could have been happy if it hadn't been for Otto. He burned with lust. I saw many like him afterwards, men like rutting bulls, buffalo hunters straight off the prairie, cowboys at the end of the long drive up from Texas. I could understand them. Otto Schmidt I hated.

He came at me in the barn one evening, his intentions plain. I fought him with all my strength, even ripping at his hand with my teeth, but in the end he threw me down on a pile of old straw and battered his way into me like a stud horse covering a mare.

When he finished he pushed himself away with a grunt. "Next time it'll be better, eh? Next time you won't fight." His penis that only minutes before had been huge as a fencepost, dangled limply against his thigh. Ugly! It was ugly. Otto was ugly. And so was I for having been infected with it.

"Next time!" I shouted, unable to contain the pain, the shame between my legs and in my heart. "There won't be a next time!"

I struggled to stand, hands flailing. One of them brushed against a heavy object buried in the straw and without thinking my fingers closed around an axe handle.

He put a heavy hand on my breast. "I gave you a home. You and the rest of those brats. If you know what's good for you, you'll shut up and do what I tell you."

I could see my future; full of thrustings and gruntings in a stinking stall, in the rows of the cornfield, my belly swollen with Otto's rotten fruit.

I gave him a push and swung the axe handle. It caught

him just below his ear, and he went down without a sound.

"I hope I killed you," I told the inert body with its parts still exposed. "You son of a bitch, I hope you're dead."

My mama would have died in shame had she heard me. But she did not. Could not. I was alone. I kicked the filthy straw over his face and ran out into the yard.

Mina was struggling with a bucket of water.

"Quick!" I said. "I think I killed Otto. I'm leaving. Help me get my clothes in that old bag of mama's."

Mina wasn't good in a pinch. She dropped the bucket and stood staring at me, her eyes and mouth round o's.

I put my hands on her shoulders and shook her. "For God's sake, Mina! Move! He raped me and I hit him. If he's dead they'll hang me. Now do what I tell you."

Mina blinked. "Raped you?"

Clearly I had to think for both of us. "Take that water in. Then keep Rebecca busy in the kitchen so I can get my things."

She was so helpless, and I was leaving her and the rest of them. I threw my arms around her thin shoulders and hugged her hard. "Kiss the little ones for me, and take care of them. I'll try to let you know where I am. Now go!"

We wiped our tears and looked at each other for perhaps the last time. Then slowly Mina stooped and grasped the handle of the bucket. Slowly she climbed the steps on to the porch and went through the door. She looked like an old woman. She was fourteen.

I hadn't much to take: my good dress dyed black for my parents' funerals; a pair of black kid boots; my black bonnet lined with pleated white satin; my mama's garnet necklace and a small turquoise and enamel brooch that had been my grandmothers'; a silk purse where I'd had the foresight to hide two gold coins. Not much in the way of worldly goods but more than

13

many runaways have had.

So, burdened only by an old carpet bag, I made my way out of the house and through the fields where I'd played, to the docks on the Mississippi where the steamer, Burlington, was tied.

I stood on the bank and looked at her a long time. Then I found an old stable and exchanged my work clothes for black bombazine and button boots.

Otto's stink was still on me and probably would be for the rest of my life. I shuddered at the possibility, the remembrance, then pushed it down into a dark corner of my body where I hoped it would stay.

"May God damn you to hell," I murmured. It sounded like a prayer.

Then I braided my yellow hair into a rope thick as a man's arm, pinned it up, tied my bonnet, and stepped out and onto the gangplank of the Burlington. I was sixteen.

I meant to hide on one of the lower decks, losing myself in the crowd of business men, planters, wives and children en route to St. Louis or New Orleans. But the gambling salon that overflowed with handsome men and beautiful women lured me.

With pleasure I noted the latest fashions on the women, the brilliance of their jewels, the quick fingers of the gambling men, like a dance of wasps.

Just so had my mama swirled her skirts; just so had papa looked in evening dress with starched and studded shirt front and a vest of luxurious brocade; and the Emperor bowing from the back of his prancing horse.

In that crowd I stood out like a guinea hen among peacocks, but starved for elegance and laughter, I lingered, entranced.

The steward who approached me was pinch-faced and

proper.

"What are you doing here? Let me see your ticket."

I looked at him and shook my head. "I thought I could buy a ticket here," I said.

He took my arm. "That's what they all say." He steered me out of the salon with a heavy hand.

We went straight to the Captain's cabin. "Stowaway, Captain Fisher." He pushed me ahead of him into the small room. "Some kind of foreigner."

"Foreigner!" The word jarred me.

"Be quiet. Let the Captain do the talking." He released me with a warning pinch.

"What's your name?" the Captain asked suddenly. "And no lies, please."

What was my name? Suppose they'd found Otto and were already on my trail? What would my mother have said, her daughter a murderess, entrapped between two accusers?

"Katharine," I whispered at last. "Katharine Boldizar." My mother's name, God forgive me.

His eyes narrowed as if he could see my soul. Something more was called for, obviously. I was at his mercy.

"Please." I stepped nearer. "My parents are dead. I have no one. Before she died my mother told me to go to the convent of the Ursulines."

Well, she had said it less than a year before when we'd toured New Orleans on the last leg of our journey and stopped before the high walled convent garden. "If anything happens to me, you must go to the nuns," she'd said. And I, flippant, tossed my head. "Nuns! What good are nuns?"

At this point, however, the convent seemed a haven, an island of safety in a world filled with Ottos.

"Please," I repeated. "Take me to St. Louis. I can pay

15

you. I will pay you."

"No husband after you? No police?"

"I have no husband." Better leave the police out of it. "No family at all."

The Captain sighed. "Alright. But I'll see you to the nuns myself, young lady, and no funny business."

He pushed back his chair and stood, a tall man, lean and quick on his feet. "We'll be underway in a little while. You, Miss, will stay right here until I come back. Is that clear?"

"Yes," I answered. Where else was there to go? Like a piece of driftwood, I was cast on the current of the river and would go where it took me.

He left, locking the door behind him.

I ran to the window and looked out. Had he believed me? Or had he gone to make inquiries about the "little foreigner?" My heart was beating so hard I thought it would choke me ~ the way the hangman's rope would ~ cutting off breath. What an end for Mary Katharine Haroney, dangling like a corn dolly from a tree branch!

On the dock, I saw only the last minute bustle; the loading of boxes and bales, passengers swarming up the gangplank calling goodbyes. There was no sign of the Captain.

From deep in the heart of the boat came the rumble of engines like the breathing of a large animal. Then the whistles blew, ropes were untied, and with a shudder we were underway.

Free! I was free! My legs began to tremble and I sat, suddenly in the Captain's chair, struggling to calm myself before he came back.

On the desk stood a decanter of whiskey and a glass. I poured some and sipped, blinking away tears and the harsh new taste. Slowly, though, it warmed me, spreading along my veins like a golden flood. I was almost asleep when I noticed the bed against the wall; a real bed with pillows and a comforter unlike Otto's straw ticks and harsh blankets. I stumbled toward it unbuttoning my basque with unsteady fingers. Then I sank into its softness and blotted out the world.

I woke screaming, the Captain's hand on my breast.

Quickly he placed his other hand over my mouth. "Hush!" he said. "I'm not going to hurt you. Lie still."

"No! Please!" I pushed away from him and wrapped my arms around myself, back to the wall.

Was this all men thought about? Ramming themselves into womens' bodies? Was this where the elegance led, the flirtation and the dancing? And if it was, why had no one ever told me? Somehow I'd been betrayed, not by men but by women with their giggles and hints of conquest, with their emphasis on the pleasure never on the results.

I lay trembling, watching him, disgusted by it all.

"Don't be afraid." He traced my cheek gently with his thumb. "You looked so beautiful lying there, all that yellow hair." He reached up and released it, running his fingers through it until it lay heavy on my shoulders. Then he leaned forward and kissed me, his tongue lingering on my lips.

Unconsciously, I relaxed. Whatever he was going to do, he wasn't in the least like Otto.

"That's better." He eased himself on the narrow bed, took my hand and placed it between his thighs. I snatched my hand away.

"No!" I said. "I won't do this. It's ugly. It's a sin."

He raised his brows. "Ugly? Come, Katharine. I'll prove to you it isn't ugly, something you should know before you're any older. How old are you?"

"Eighteen," I said, simply to leave the child far behind.

"Old enough." He slid his hand under my skirt and up

17

my thigh where it paused for a moment and then continued until it found its mark. I quivered in spite of myself as he stroked and probed, slowly at first and then, finding what he sought, harder.

I permitted it, my body responding on its own, languorously at first and then with an urgency I didn't understand. I said, "Please," again, meaning something different than denial. I moved against him lifting my mouth for his kiss, arching toward him like the ripe fruit he had made me.

When at last he came to me I had forgotten the terror of that earlier time. I had forgotten everything but the clamor of my body ringing in my ears.

What I learned from the Captain that night and the next stayed with me always, and with it, gratitude. What the women who had taught me had failed to tell, he showed me, and in the showing banished my loneliness.

I remember still, though I am old and supposedly beyond such things. Well, the body has a memory, too; one that can make the heart cry with longing, breasts ache for caresses.

Perhaps I could have stopped him, my Captain Fisher, but something in me refused that notion. My need for comfort was the equal of his, my loneliness as large.

CHAPTER Two

"Get your things together, Kat. We'll be in St. Louis in half an hour."

Neatly dressed and clean shaven, my Captain seemed a different person from the lover of the dark hours. There was a distance between us, a widening gap I tried to close.

"Why can't I stay?" I asked. The little cabin felt like home and I knew I could make it more so.

He sighed and put his hands on my shoulders. "In the first place, it's against the rules. And in the second..." he paused, frowning, "in the second place...I have a wife. And children."

"A wife!" That had never occurred to me. Somewhere a woman waited for him, secure, content, trusting. Yet he had loved me, too. I was sure of that.

It didn't make sense. "How could you? Go from her to

me?"

"For God's sake, Kat! I haven't been home for two months. I'm a man and there you were looking like a little yellow kitten." He shook me gently. "Don't stand there like it's the end of the world. People do what they do. We gave each other something we needed, and what's wrong with that?"

"Nothing," I said. "I guess...I just thought..." I spread my hands, despairing of words.

"I know what you thought. God help you, you're an innocent. But learn this. Life's tricky. It'll fool you just like that river out there will. It'll eat you alive just as soon as you start to trust it."

I turned away. "It already has."

He took me in his arms then and held me, his face in my hair. "No it hasn't. You're young, and the young always feel that way. But life is long and we grow up to meet it. Believe me."

I said nothing, simply stored away the feel of him in my bones, in that place where the screaming was.

"After we dock and I've taken care of things, we'll go out. You need some decent clothes, not that thing you're wearing that makes you look like a crow. Even in a convent you can't wear the same dress all the time. How does that sound?"

Like bribery, I thought but didn't say. "Fine," I answered.

"Good. Then we'll find this convent of yours, and don't worry, I'll come see you now and then. And if you study hard I might even be able to find a position for you. A governess. Something."

A governess! I'd had them. I'd hated them all, poor, simpering little women with no future, no hopes. I nodded, and he was satisfied.

Yet in spite of my disappointment I found St. Louis

exciting. To my innocent eyes it had everything; the bustle and commerce of the wharves and the river, the openness of the West where the town leaned toward the prairies. There were saloons and dance halls, clothing emporiums and general stores, wide streets clogged with traffic, imposing hotels and the gracious houses of merchants, traders, politicians removed from the row houses of rivermen and the darkies, the prostitutes who worked the wharves. It was a city that also never seemed to sleep, that pushed at its limits the way the river in flood pushed at the levees.

The War Between the States was over, and everything, everyone was in a state of ferment, eager to get on with interrupted lives. Only the convent seemed remote, the serenity behind its brick walls undisturbed.

Captain Fisher, acting as my guardian, delivered me to the Ursulines that humid afternoon at the end of June after seeing to it that I had two new dresses, a plain white lawn for the summer heat, a navy blue muslin for every day. He also tucked some money in my pocket before he left me with the Mother Superior in the front parlor.

"Learn all they can teach you," he said, kissing me properly on the cheek. "And behave yourself."

I felt betrayed and couldn't bring myself to do more than say goodbye.

The nun and I assessed one another. She was a tall woman with pale cheeks and steely-blue eyes. I disliked her, rigid and self-righteous, willow-thin beneath black robes.

"I hope you will be happy with us," she said in a thick German accent. The tone of her voice indicated otherwise.

"This was my mama's wish," I said. "She's dead."

"Ah." Something like compassion flickered across her face. "I'll remember her in my prayers."

21

Prayer had never been my answer for anything. I must have betrayed my skepticism because she asked, "You are Catholic?"

"Yes."

"Yes, Mother," she corrected. "You must call me that. My name is Mother Magdalene."

She wasn't my mother. She was an adversary. My mother was gone and I wanted her. As if in a dream I remembered her waltzing with my papa, heard the sound of violins, her laughter fading away.

The nun tapped her foot, a swift gesture of irritation. "Come now, Katharine. There are rules here as in life. You must abide by them. That way lies true happiness."

I knew about rules, having already violated many of them. But for the time being it was better to be here than making my way on unfamiliar streets.

"Yes, Mother," I said.

She gave a quick nod. "Good. Sister Antoine will show you the dormitory. Supper is at five followed by study and prayers. I hope you will be a credit to us. We of the Ursuline order have dedicated ourselves to turning out fine young ladies."

I held back a snort. Young lady! A fine thing it was to say, but what did it mean? I was, however certain of one thing. A young lady I wasn't.

I hadn't noticed the other nun standing in the doorway, her hands tucked into her sleeves. She was plump and rosy, and when she spoke it was with a musical French accent. She began to chatter as we ascended the stairs which branched at a landing, right and left. To the left, she explained, were the nun's rooms and offices. To the right, the classrooms and dormitory. Beneath, the dining room and the parlor we had left. There were ten boarders, daughters of the well-to-do sent to be prepared to take their places as wives of influential men, mothers of leaders. I was lucky, she reminded me, to have so generous a guardian. Not many orphans were as fortunate.

What would she do, this trusting soul, if I told her of how I had spent the last two nights and that my presence here was not due to generosity but was simply payment for services received and expected? I tightened my mouth so as not to laugh. Already I was becoming a cynic.

Each student had a bed, a small chest with a candle, a pitcher and basin, a space to hang clothes. That was all. Elegance and privacy were not part of the curriculum. Even studying was done under supervision, as if we were not to be trusted. Indeed, for the most part, we were treated as potential sinners in need of curbing if not forgiveness.

Outside the window was a garden. My future classmates were there. I heard their voices, their laughter, quickly smoth-ered, as though obvious happiness were forbidden.

"See!" Sister Antoine pointed out the window. "Sister Frances is our gardener. Isn't it pretty?"

"*Oui, Soeur Antoine.*" I responded in French purely out of mischief, having learned that language as a child. Her response was one of delight.

"Oh, you speak French! How wonderful! Perhaps you will be able to help me with the young ones. I try to teach them, but they will not learn."

A teacher already! A governess! I must remember to tell the Captain if I ever saw him again. A glance backwards at my life brought only remembrances of those I would never see again. I sighed, and Sister Antoine looked at me with sympathy.

"Your mother is with God, Katharine," she said. "Believe that. Would you like to rest before joining the others? We have an hour in the garden before supper."

"No, thank you, Soeur Antoine. I'll put my things away and then come down." Her kindness, her eagerness to help, touched me more deeply than I wanted to recognize.

She patted my shoulder. "I hope you will be happy with us," she said, echoing Mother Magadelene but sounding sincere. "And if you would like to talk ~ or pray ~ I am here, child."

But she could just as easily be taken away. I'd learned that much. And I had nothing in common with her or with those tittering girls in the garden below. What could she tell me that I didn't know? The answer was clear. Nothing. I had only myself, and I had run away once before. Most certainly I would do it again.

That, however, proved almost impossible. Rules were piled upon rules and the cracks between filled with prayers. We were watched, shaped, scolded, banished to the church and told to pray for our endangered souls at every infraction. Born in sin, we lived in sin, fearful of dying in the same way. But I didn't want to think about dying. I'd had enough of it. I wanted to live, and so was always in trouble. For talking, for laughing too loud, for writing naughty rhymes about the nuns, themselves. On our chaperoned walks I stared at everything, despite admonitions to keep my eyes down. I dawdled before store windows, smiled at tradesmen and even the darkies, tried to lose myself in the streets.

"Men!" Mother Superior said when my behavior was reported. "Men, Katharine! How could you behave so?" She sounded as if men were skunks; not our future husbands but some alien and repulsive species ready to befoul us.

"I felt like it," I answered.

"Then learn to conquer your feelings," came her inevitable reply. "Men will take advantage of you. Go to the church and think about your soul and say a rosary to the virgin."

I wondered how she knew about taking advantage. Had she, too, been used? Had she, too, been unlucky enough to know an Otto? I didn't dare to ask, seeing the humorless lines of her face.

Relief was granted on those widely-spaced Sundays when Captain Fisher came to check on my progress. He would take me out in a carriage, and we would dine in a restaurant, or window shop in those stores that were so fascinating. And we went, when there was time enough, to the river where the Burlington was tied awaiting passengers and freight. In his cabin we would talk and touch. And love.

Most Sundays, however, I had no visitors, and spent those afternoons reading or helping Sister Frances plant and weed the small garden. Often I looked at the locked gate in the brick wall and wondered how I could open it.

I never knew when the Captain would come. One of the novices would be sent to find me, and she would be breathless, caught in a flurry of grey skirts. His appearance affected them all in one way or another, even Mother Superior.

"You are fortunate to have such a guardian," she told me often. "You must study hard to repay him. It is your duty."

What did she know about payment! About the ribbons he bought me, or the bits of lace. At these speeches I simply bowed my head and agreed with her.

It was through Captain Fisher that I met Silas Melvin who changed my life forever.

I had, one Sunday, seen a pair of white kid boots in the window of a store. They had tiny heels and pearl buttons, and they shone in the display like Christmas tinsel.

"Even Charlotte hasn't a pair like that," I commented.

He smiled behind his beard. "Who is Charlotte?"

"Charlotte Pruneau. Her father's a planter. She's very

25

rich."

"Ah," he said, nodding.

I should have recognized the thoughtful tone of his voice. It hadn't occurred to me that I, although obviously an object of pleasure to him, was also an embarrassment, even a danger. He gambled his marriage every time we were seen together.

The next afternoon one of the novices sought me out. "A visitor for you. A man. With a package. He won't leave, and Mother Superior is furious."

Quite stubbornly he stood in the parlor, his hat in one hand, the package in the other, staring at Mother Superior out of eyes that looked like blue steel.

"Yes?" I said. I smiled at him, ignoring the nun.

He looked directly at me then, a look only I in that place could recognize. Silas Melvin was as reckless as the counts and cavalry officers I'd known as a child; men who took risks, drew swords or pistols over the smallest slight; men like my father who once rode his horse into the house and up the inside stairs, urged on my the rest of us, as wild-eyed as he. But when Silas spoke his words were ordinary.

"Captain Fisher told me to deliver these, Miss. If they aren't right, I'm to bring others."

The boots, of course, were those I had seen in the window. They were as soft as velvet, a gleaming white. My fingers trembled as I lifted them from the tissue.

"How lovely!"

"Try them, Miss." He knelt to help me. His hands were warm on my foot, and his hair shone yellow, so thick I wanted to feel it in my hands like summer wheat. I was sure that he, too, felt the sudden current that ran through me at his touch.

"I think they're a little tight. Is it possible to have a larger pair?"

Our eyes met again, this time as conspirators.

"Why yes," he answered. "I think there is another. I just opened a new store, so I'm not sure. But I'll check and see. Shall I bring them?"

"Yes, please." I let my eyes dance at him. Then I turned to Mother Superior who had been watching us. She was as still, as grey as a piece of carved driftwood. "Is that allowed, Mother?"

She frowned, partly because she sensed an undercurrent, partly because the situation was unusual. "Just this once, I suppose. Because it's Captain Fisher. But..." she turned to Silas, "this must never happen again, young man. We don't encourage salesmen here."

This was said in a tone meant to embarrass. It had the opposite effect. Silas squared his shoulders and then winked at me. "I'll bring them tomorrow," he said.

When I returned to the dormitory it was all aflutter, as if a fox had come to a hen house. Except for relatives and the priests who said Mass and heard our confessions, men never visited. Forbidden fruit that they were, we lusted after them all the more.

"Lucky Katharine," said Charlotte. "Tell us. Who was he?"

She was ridiculous. So were they all, breathless with the stirrings of youthful desire.

"He was the prince with the magic slipper," I said, treating them like the children they were. "It didn't fit though, and so...and so...he's coming again tomorrow!"

What a lifting and falling of arms, legs, and bosoms followed! What excited chatter!

"Unfair!" Charlotte cried when the full story had come

out. "I have never had shoes brought to me, and my papa gave to the altar fund." She had black hair and snapping black eyes like berries. "I shall ask to be fitted, too."

"Why not?" I said. Charlotte's help would make seeing Silas easier.

She, of course, had her way. Mother Superior was defenseless against the reality of coin, even to the point of leaving us alone with Silas while she spoke with another visitor, a grey haired man who seemed vaguely familiar as he stood, hesitant, on the doorstep.I turned away quickly, more by instinct than recognition, sure that he was someone I'd known in Davenport.

Cleverly Silas had brought several pairs of boots and a pair of green satin slippers decorated with tiny bows.

Charlotte seized them at once, and twirled out into the hall to admire her feet in the pier glass mounted in the center of the mahogany coatrack.

I tried to stay calm while straining to hear the conversation at the door. Automatically,I smiled at Silas. "She's very excited. We don't see people very often."

He stared at me sensing something in my manner. "Do you like it here?" he asked.

I seized the moment, as I always have. "No. But I'm an orphan. I have no place to go. Not until I'm married off." I leaned close to him, so close I could have touched his cheek with my lips. "I've got to get away from this place. Can you help me?"

His eyes flared with that wildness I'd counted on, but before he could answer Charlotte pirouetted back. "I'll have these - and those." She pointed to a pair of butter-yellow boots. "And some buckles. Can you bring buckles?"

"Yes, Miss," Silas said, using her prattle as a cover to

whisper back to me, "I'll do what I can."

"Good. Tomorrow then." Charlotte had forgotten that he was young and handsome. All her attention was on herself.

He gathered the shoes and smiled at me, a quick, secretive motion of his mouth. Charlotte wandered back to the mirror, lifting her skirts and admiring her tiny feet.

"I have to get out tonight," I whispered. No matter what, I was leaving.

He frowned a moment, then delved into his pocket. "Come here. I'll meet you." He handed me a card with a printed address, and we followed Charlotte to the hall in time to hear Mother Magdalene's parting words to the man at the door.

"As I told you, this is a school for young ladies. Although we do not lack in charity, we have no runaways here."

Swiftly I turned on my heels, hiding my face from the visitor. It could only be me he was looking for.

I put my fingers to my lips, hearing the door close heavily behind me. "I'll find you," I whispered again.

He bowed, first to me, then to Charlotte. "Good afternoon, ladies. It's always my pleasure to serve you."

On his way past he flashed me a glance, his eyes dancing with blue fire. "The dragon approaches," he murmured.

Once more the world narrowed. Whether or not I was the object of the stranger's search, my position was perilous. Sooner or later someone would discover me - orphan, murderess, adulteress. I would bring disgrace on us all, on my brothers and sisters, on Captain Fisher to whom I owed my life.

As I mounted the steps to the second floor with Charlotte chattering happily beside me, I made my plans.

"So handsome!" she was saying. "And those lovely shoes! Oooh, I can hardly wait to wear them!"

Lost in my own problems, I made no reply. She shook

29

my arm. "Kat! You're not listening. Are you under his spell already? Are you? Confess."

"I have a terrible headache," I said. "I have to lie down."

She was instantly contrite, giving free play to her vision of herself as ministering angel. "Oh, poor Kat. You must lie down, and I'll bring you a cloth for your head."

"Just let me sleep. It'll pass. But tell them I don't want supper. I don't think I can eat."

She came with me to the dormitory where she insisted on arranging the bed, removing my shoes, drawing the sheet around my shoulders. "There," she crooned. "Now go to sleep, Kat." She sounded as if I were a doll upon which she was practicing a role.

What had been a lie moments before was rapidly becoming true. Blood beat in my temples and behind my eyes. I sat up and glared at her. "For God's sake, go away! How can I sleep with you fussing over me?" Then I lay down and closed my eyes.

When I was sure she had gone, I went to the door and listened. The dutiful silence of study hall, a child's voice haltingly reciting the multiplication tables, were all that I heard.

How swiftly I moved then, bundling my dresses, my shoes into the old carpet bag, tiptoeing to the window and dropping the bundle in the soft earth between the hedge and the wall of the building. How quickly I returned to my bed as I heard footsteps approaching.

Sister Antoine laid a cool hand on my forehead. "You have the headache, Katharine?" she inquired as I opened my eyes.

"Yes, Sister."

"I'll bring you a powder," she said, rising. "Then you can sleep. Too much excitement over that young man I think."

She smiled as she spoke, and her rosy cheeks grew rosier.

I smiled back. "Perhaps."

"Lie still, now. I'll be back."

When she'd gone I forced myself to stay as I was though I wanted to run, to be as far away as possible before Mother Magdalene began to put two and two together.

If only my parents were alive! If only we'd never left Hungary! I gave myself over to hopeless thoughts. If only I'd never laid eyes on Otto!

But I had. The actions of emperors and kings had filtered down to me, little Mary Katharine, and because of them, I'd killed a man. I took a deep breath to calm my trembling and pretended to sleep as the nun returned.

"*Pauvre petite*," she murmured from the foot of the bed. Quietly she put the glass on the table, then crossed the room and closed the blinds before leaving me alone again. I wanted to call her back, to lay my head on her starched breast and confess. Let another hear my sins and bear them! I was not equal to the task. I was a child wanting, crying out for comfort. None came. I was alone, the loneliest person on earth.

When the clatter of dishes and silver told me all were at supper, I got up, took my money from the drawer and stuffed it inside my dress. Then, noticing Charlotte's reticule flung carelessly on her bed, I rifled it, shamelessly adding her money to mine.

"Another sin added to the list," I thought, and quickly muttered a prayer for forgiveness before opening the door and cautiously descending the front stairs.

No one heard. Healthy appetites held them all captive at the table even as I opened the front door and stepped out into the early evening light. I retrieved my bag from behind the hedge and fled down the street and around the corner.

31

A striped tom cat prowled there, in and out of shadow. A clever animal. I would do the same.

Chapter Three

The city was still an unfamiliar place. All I knew were the wharves on the river, the streets considered by the nuns to be seemly places for young ladies to walk, and those popular restaurants where I'd been with the Captain.

Worst of all, when I reached in my pocket for the address Silas had given me, it wasn't there. How could I have been so stupid to have lost it! And where? Frantically I searched my other pockets, my bosom where I'd shoved my money. I knelt on the curb and pawed through the clothes and shoes in my bag. But the card was gone. My only hope seemed to be in finding Silas still at his store if I could find my way in the gathering twilight. I walked steadily, purposefully, trying to look as if I had a destination. The route I chose was a long one, and when I

33

finally reached the store it was closed.

Disappointment brought sharp tears which I blinked away. A girl bawling on a street corner was sure to draw attention, the last thing I wanted.

But where to go? Certainly not to the hotels where I might be seen and recognized. And the area near the docks was unsafe at night, filled with wandering rivermen and the prostitutes who lived off them.

Hesitantly, I made my way toward the respectable neighborhood of Benton Place. The night was warm with only a hint of a breeze blowing off the river. With luck I might find a garden summerhouse where I could spend the night, or even a stable.

"Beggars can't pick their bedfellows," my mother used to say. Well, better a stall with a friendly horse than the streets. I turned into the alley behind the imposing houses. Lamps were being lit, and the odor of food cooking reminded me I'd had no supper. Next time, I thought, I'd have the foresight to steal some.

Next time! Dear God, was there to be a next time? "No," I said out loud. "No. No." And fool that I was, I believed it.

Luckily, a careless groom had left a stable door partway open. When I peered into the shadows, two carriage horses turned their heads and nickered at me.

I slipped inside. "Good boys," I said, petting their noses and their silken necks to calm them. "Be quiet now and don't give me away."

I looked around. There were two empty stalls, one with a pile of clean straw. In the corner was a bucket of water and, to my delight, a bag of windfall apples, bruised but edible. I helped myself, giving the cores to the horses. Then I drank some water, burrowed into the straw, and, resolving to find Silas in the morning, fell asleep.

Shortly after sunrise, after a hasty wash in the horse trough and a breakfast of a few apples, I made my circuitous way toward the center of town.

The carpet bag weighed me down, jabbing my knees at every step. I was hot, tired, and so hungry I was dizzy. Slowly I made my way back to Silas, and this time found him.

He was arranging shoes in the store window when he looked up and saw me staring at him through the glass, and he ran outside in time to catch me as I fainted.

"Kat! Kat! Are you alright? Wake up, Kat?"

I came to in the dimness of the back room. Silas was bending over me waving a palmetto fan. My mouth was dry, my lips like sandpaper. "Thirsty," I said and closed my eyes again.

"What happened to you?" he demanded, when I'd gulped the water. "I waited for you till after midnight."

"I lost the address. It just wasn't there. So I slept in a stable." I leaned back in the chair again, fighting dizziness. "Can you help me find a place to stay? I haven't got much money"

"The place I wanted you to come to last night," he said. "It's not for a lady like you, but it'll do till we find another."

I laughed. My life the past few months had eradicated all thoughts of lady-hood. "I'm too hungry to worry about being a lady right now. Where is this place?"

"South of town. A woman owns it. Blanche Tribolet. She's an octoroon up from the French Quarter. Runs a private gambling establishment. Oh, it's respectable enough, invitation only, that sort of thing, but it's not the kind of place you mention to the town gossips."

"What's an octoroon?" I asked.

He explained and I shrugged. Color meant nothing to me or the things women did in desperation. I'd seen and done too much. Only people mattered, and what was in their hearts.

"It'll only be temporary," he assured me. "I'll ask around and find someplace else." He paused on his way out of the room and looked back over his shoulder. "You aren't in any trouble or anything, are you?"

"No," I said. "No trouble." I closed my eyes again to cover up the lie. Then I decided to elaborate. "They were going to marry me off to this old man. Old enough to be my grandfather. I...I couldn't bear it. He smelled like the grave."

"Jesus," Silas said. "Who was he?"

"My guardian. But he just wants to be rid of me. Now he is. He won't come after me, you can be sure."

"I don't care if he does," Silas answered. "Nobody's going to force you into anything. Now sit there and rest."

He returned with his lunch - thick slices of bread around slabs of overcooked beef. At one time I'd have been horrified by such poor cooking so crudely presented. Hunger, however, obliterated my fancy notions. I ate it all.

Blanche Tribolet lived in a tall brick house South of the city. There was nothing to proclaim it a gentlemens' gambling establishment. What made it unique was the mass of flowers in beds on either side of the path, the trees and shrubs that lent grace and a certain privacy.

I liked Blanche before I saw her for the artistry of her eye, for her green thumb.

"It's beautiful!" I was holding onto to Silas's arm, and I squeezed it hard. "Oh, Silas, thank you."

"It's temporary, Kat. Believe me. If you want to be accepted in this town or any other, you'll never talk about this."

"Because of the gambling?"

36

"Of course. And other things I don't have to mention. No scandal. Nothing like that, but the old hens will talk and I don't want you involved."

"Why not?"

He frowned, annoyed. "Because you're a lady, Kat," was all he said.

We went up the walk between the roses, the lavender, the gaudy cosmos, and he knocked at the small blue door.

It was opened by a gigantic negress wearing a thunderous expression that changed to a smile when she recognized Silas.

"Mr Silas. What you doing here this time of day?"

"I want to see your mistress. Tell her it's about what I mentioned last night."

She stepped aside, then ushered us down the hall and into a tiny parlor. "You wait. I'll see if Miz Blanche can be disturbed."

We didn't wait long. Within a minute the most beautiful woman I ever saw stood in the doorway, paused, for effect, I thought, to give us time to appreciate the perfection of her face, her sea-green tea gown, the incredible wholeness of her beauty.

"Silas!" She advanced, her hand extended. "How nice to see you. Nancy said you needed help?"

He bowed over her long fingers but wasted no time in stating our problem. He introduced me as his cousin Kate in need of a place to stay until other quarters could be found.

Blanche appraised me out of large, grey-green eyes, the color of river water in fog.

"Ah, a cousin is it?" she said in her musical English. "What am I supposed to do with this cousin?"

I took the matter into my own hands, sweeping her a curtsey. Her manner deserved one.

"My parents are dead, madame," I told her, wondering if I'd ever be done with that refrain. "I came to the city to find work, but I have no money and no place to stay. If you let me, I'll work hard for you. Silas said maybe you needed somebody."

She raised one eyebrow. "What kind of work can you do, little cousin?"

"I've been running a house for years," I said. "My mother was ill. I can cook, shop, see to the cleaning.." I spread my hands.

"Where did you do this? Not in America."

"Many places. Europe. Mexico." I had her interest now.

She went to a small, gilded chair and sat on it, arranging her skirts to her liking. To Silas she said, " Come back later. Your cousin is safe and we have things to talk about."

He looked at me for confirmation. I nodded. "When will I see you?" I asked. I had the sudden fear that, his promise fulfilled, he would disappear leaving me deprived of his presence.

He leaned over and kissed my cheek. "Don't worry. I'll be back. Tomorrow evening. We'll do the town."

"Oh, yes. Please!" I beamed up at him, into his blazing eyes.

When he'd gone, Blanche motioned me to the chair opposite hers, and for the first time I looked around the room, noticing the dove-grey walls, the green draperies shading the windows. There was a gilt clock on the mantel of the small fireplace, and matching sconces on either side. The chairs we sat in were French and delicately made, the carpet, in pale shades of pink and green, French, too. It was a room out of my past.

"This is lovely," I said.

"And you didn't expect it?"

"Not in America," I answered. In Davenport the houses

of friends, while large and well-furnished, had lacked the taste, the clever hand of a woman like this one.

She sat back, crossed her legs with a rustle of silk, and laughed mirthlessly. "Why should you? Silas must have told you about me. But not all. Not all..." She shook a slender finger. "Later I'll tell you what you want to know. Now...now you tell me. The truth, please. I detest liars."

Whoever, whatever she was, there was a toughness under that lovely face that I trusted. To her I could tell the whole story. I spread my hands. "What I told you is the truth, madame. My parents died. My brothers and sisters and I were sent to a guardian. He got all our money, too. I'm the eldest. The others are little. They couldn't help themselves. But the man....the man...he..." Again I saw Otto coming toward me, felt his fat flesh, the brutality of his thrustings. Speechless, I appealed to her. "I ran away. I couldn't...."

She narrowed her eyes. "They will do it, child. All of them."

"I hated him!" The words burst out.

"Forget hate." Her words shot forth in the wake of mine. "Learn to forget. To look ahead, never back. If you don't, little cousin, you become a stone in the mud. A thing to be picked up, used, thrown away again. Hate makes you ugly. You understand what I say?"

I supposed I did. I wasn't sure. I was more tired than I'd ever been in my life. I smothered a yawn.

Nothing escaped her. She had the eyes of a hawk, the instincts of a hunting cat. "You need to sleep," she said, rising with that silken rustle. "Come with me. Tomorrow's time enough for talk. Tomorrow we'll see what we will see."

"Thank you." I wished I didn't sound so dull, so schoolgirlish. Beside Blanche I felt gawky and unsophisticated, a child, a fool for having made such a mess of so many lives. I wished I were older, more aware of the world.

She turned. "Come along," she said. "And what's your name, little cousin? What should I call you?"

I blinked. My name. The old question. Who was I now? "Kate," I answered, yawning again. "Kate Elder." And with that, I baptized myself.

Chapter Four

I awoke to the sound of a rooster crowing, so close he seemed to be in the room which was at the back of the house.

In the grey light of early morning I lay there and took stock of my surroundings - the small, white bed, the chair where I'd dumped my bag the night before, a carved bureau with a mirror above. Flowered curtains hung over the open window, limp in the absence of a breeze.

I'd been so exhausted by my flight that I'd gone to sleep in my clothes. They were wrinkled and clinging to me, and my mouth had a sour taste like mouldy ground. I wished I'd had the foresight to ask for a pitcher of water. As it was, I'd have to appear unkempt, with grimy fingernails and possibly a dirty face unless there was a pump in the back yard.

I stood up, shook out my skirts, and opened the door. What I saw surprised me as much as Blanche's parlor. Behind the house her imagination had run wild. A mass of flowers, yellow and scarlet, purple and blue, lifted gaudy faces; behind them brilliant tomatoes hung from their vines, and peppers so large they dragged on the ground.

Against the board fence at the far end of the yard stood a hen house where the rooster with irridescent tail feathers and red wattles strutted. Beside this, a pump and a tin bucket.

I hurried down the path, eager for the coolness of water, and as I passed I snatched a tomato from the vine. The juice spilled down my throat as the Captain's whiskey had done, but I'd been too hasty.

At the pump I retched violently until nothing was left in me and I stood steadying myself on the pump handle.

I put my head under the stream of water and came out gasping but refreshed.

"You're up early, little cousin," Blanche said.

In the pale light, in her lavender morning gown, she rose from the tangle of stems like one of her flowers.

"I needed some water."

"I was bringing some, but you were too quick." She plucked off some dead cosmos and crumbled their crimson petals between her fingers. "A nice garden, don't you think?"

"Better than the royal gardens in Mexico," I said.

Her eyes shone. "Since we're up early, get dressed and tell me about them while we eat."

I pulled on the oldest of my dresses, one left from the farm, smoothed my hair, and joined her in the kitchen.

She was slicing a loaf at a long table. The odors of coffee and frying ham repelled me despite the previous day's hunger. Remembering the disaster with the tomato, I accepted only coffee.

She raised her eyebrows. "Eat," she ordered. "Don't be polite."

"Maybe later."

She leaned her elbows on the table and searched my face. "You're in trouble, are you not, little cousin?"

"No, ma'am," I answered, thinking of the furor that must be happening at the convent.

She frowned. "What I mean...you're with child."

I gaped at her. With child! Whose? Captain Fisher's, I supposed. "How?" I exclaimed. "When? How could it have happened?"

She threw up her hands. "*Mon Dieu*, but women are fools. How do you think it happens? How long has it been since your courses? Think."

I couldn't think. All I could do was to sit open-mouthed in astonishment.

"Kate, Kate, you aren't as innocent as that? Ah, I guess you are." She reached across the table and took my hand. "We, none of us bring up our daughters right. But there are things you can do. There's no need to have it. Not the fat one's. I'll help you."

Otto's! She thought it was Otto's. But it wasn't. If, indeed there was a life growing within me, it was the Captain's. If so, I would bear it.

"I can't," I said. "I'd go to hell."

She snorted. "Religion isn't for women. Me, I was raised careful like you, but I'm still a nigger. A thing. Passed from one to the other with God taking no notice. It's up to us to do for ourselves. You hear what I say?"

"Yes," I whispered.

"Then, if you want to keep it, you find yourself a man.

43

Quick."

"Silas," I said, or someone did. Someone who wasn't quite me.

"Ah, yes. Your cousin." She laughed her soundless laugh. "The priest, he won't know."

"Silas," I said again, remembering the electricity that had passed between us.

"You'll have to manage him. He gambles. Unwisely sometimes. There's a wild streak there. But..." she shrugged, "that's what makes him attractive, eh, cousin? Those eyes with the devil behind them."

She took my hand and turned it so it lay, palm up, in hers. "Let's see what's in store for you," she said, peering at my palm for what seemed to be a long time. Finally she looked at me strangely. "*Mon Dieu*, what a life!"

"What? What do you see?"

"Men, places far from here. Too far. I don't know, it makes no sense what I see. Tonight before he comes I'll read your cards. Perhaps there..." her voice trailed off.

Cards. The men on the boat beneath glittering chandeliers. Flicker of hands and eyes and coins changing places. "Can you teach me cards?"

"Why you want to know such things, child?" She sounded cross.

I told her. I told her about the gamblers, the rivers, the trip out of Mexico on the little steamer, Sonora; about the young Emperor facing an army he'd never seen; about my mother and her dying eyes. I told her more than I'd ever told a living soul, and when I finished I felt light, free.

"So. So," she said, as if she'd decided something. "You and me must make our own ways. I'll teach you cards, then, though it's not for ladies."

44

"I'm not a lady. What good does that do anybody?"

She folded her arms across her bosom and looked at me severely. "I know what I know. Your mama raised you up a lady and in your heart you still are one. Where it counts. Don't forget what I say."

"Did you see a baby?" I blurted. "In my hand? Please. I want to know."

"Later," was all she would say. "Here's Nancy come to clean. You help her for now. When my men come for cards in the evening, I put out a supper. That's what you'll do. Make sure they have what they need." She looked at my dress with distaste. "You have something pretty to wear, or only these...?" she made an unflattering gesture.

Once I'd had more dresses than I could count; striped organdy, a pink tulle, a yellow silk like a sunbeam, embroidered shawls and shoes to match them all. Now I had only three. "I have several," I said, hating poverty, hating fate, vowing silently never to be in such a position again.

She noticed, of course. "Ah well, better you don't attract attention here. Cards only, eh, cousin?"

I had no idea what she meant. I was thinking about Silas. Then I remembered. "Oh, I forgot! Silas is coming tonight. I'll have to tell him I'm busy."

"Busy!" she shouted. "*Mon Dieu.* You will not be too busy to catch a husband. Tomorrow you work. Tonight you go with him. Now you help Nancy with the dishes. Me, I go out for awhile. Take the air like a lady." She left laughing and swishing her hips in imitation.

When I went to the parlor later that afternoon I was wearing my white lawn and carrying the funereal black bonnet, unfortunately all that I had.

Blanche rolled up her eyes in horror. "You'll never catch

45

a husband looking like that," she said. "At least not one you'd want." She headed down the hall to her room and beckoned me to follow.

Once there she threw open the doors of a mahogany wardrobe and stood back, tapping a finger on her lips.

"You have more dresses than my mother and the Empress put together," I said, feasting on the colors and materials that overflowed into the room.

"You can never have too many dresses," she remarked, pulling a pale blue satin trimmed with cream-colored lace from its hanger. "Try this one."

"Me!"

"Of course you. We're the same size, I think. And remember, men don't look at scarecrows. Only at women. Now do what I say and be quick."

She helped me out of one and into the other, her hands nimble on the buttons. When she finished she sat me down on a stool, facing away from the mirror though I squirmed to see myself.

"Not now. When I'm through." She loosened my hair, then fastened it into a chignon so heavy it tilted my head. From a collection of intriguing small pots, she rouged my cheeks and darkened my lashes, overriding my protests.

"Hush! Wait till you see. A bit of color never hurt anybody, and usually it helps. There!" She stepped back and viewed the results.

When finally I turned to the mirror I saw someone new; a slender woman with blue eyes made bluer by the reflection of the dress, by the darkened length of her lashes; a woman with a mass of golden hair, a few tendrils curling around her ears.

Memories made me weak; of mama sweeping down the curving stairs on her way to a ball; the ladies of Chapultepec drifting like bright butterflies, overflowing the palace rooms into the gardens. How I had watched, impatient for the time when I would be one of them. And suddenly I was, only the world had changed.

"Don't cry," Blanche warned. "You'll get black on your face. What you crying for anyhow when you look like that?"

I shook my head, tired of remembering. "Thank you," I whispered. "I don't deserve all this."

"Bah!" she said. "We fight the good fight, that's all." She tossed a blue bonnet at me. "I have a feeling in my bones about you. Try this bonnet, then we read the cards and see if I'm right."

"Shuffle," she ordered when we were seated at one of the gaming tables. She handed me the cards.

When I tried, it was a disaster, cards falling onto my lap and the floor.

She made a disgusted noise in her throat. "Watch me. Learn to use your fingers, to make the cards obey." In her hands the cards danced and flew. Finally she pushed them across the table.

"Shuffle for yourself. What is it you want to know? What do you wish with your heart? Then cut three piles."

"Is there a child?" I asked, doing what I was told. "Will I marry and have a happy life?"

She turned the piles face up and studied them before laying them out in rows.

I tried to read her face, but she wore the bland mask of the born gambler. When she raised her head, I caught a glimpse of what seemed like fear in her eyes, but the expression was gone as quickly as it had come, and I forgot it when she began to speak.

"Yes. I see a child. A boy child. And a husband." She

bent over the cards again. "I see many men. Many husbands. One of them clever with cards and a gun. No..." she stopped my question with a gesture, "let me finish. You'll travel to an empty land, so big it is, it's got no end. And many mountains. Fire, horses, violence. A long life, perhaps longer than you wish. Longer than the gambling man. Strange...very strange, this. And you so young. There! Let it be!." She swept the cards together, her hands trembling. "The child isn't the fat one's," she said. "Why didn't you tell me?"

Her knowledge was uncanny, like the gypsies who used to come to the house in Hungary. They traded horses, begged sometimes, and told fortunes. Once, when I was very young, I had slipped away to the field where the fortune teller had set up. She told me something similar, about travel and living a long time. About a man, a very special man whom I would love. Perhaps it was standard fortune teller fare, but something in Blanche's attitude told me that she had lifted the veil of privacy and looked inward with glittering eyes.

"I wasn't sure," I answered. "And the other man...he was my guardian, too. He took care of me. He was kind."

"Kind! Let me tell you, he was not kind. He made a baby, then left you. This is kindness? In this life trust nobody except yourself, and sometimes not that. Be sure what you want. You still want this baby?"

"Yes," I said.

She stood up abruptly. "Then I wish you luck tonight, cousin. Luck for however long it takes you. I'll leave you here. Me, I have an appointment with my own gentleman. So when you come back, you come quietly."

I wanted to ask more, but she swept out of the room and left me. While I waited impatiently for Silas, I tried to imagine the child growing in my body. All I could summon were recollections of my brothers and sisters in their cradles, their embroidered baptismal gowns, all looking alike - blue-eyed and yellow haired with the long, patrician nose of the Haroneys.

CHAPTER Five

It took Silas two weeks to propose, during which time I paced the floor, wracked my brains, and, taking Blanche's advice lowered the necklines of the gowns she lent me almost to the point of scandal.

Oddly enough, what initiated his offer wasn't my flirtatious ways nor even the sight of my flesh. It was a horse.

Over dinners, on walks through the newly created Botanical Gardens, Silas had coaxed much of my story out of me. He was fascinated by my knowledge of royalty, by my memories of life in Hungary, and most of all by my love of horses, passed on to me by my father and grandmother.

Could I, he asked, tell if a horse could run fast by looking at it.

"If that were possible, we'd all be rich," I said. "I can make a guess, but that's all."

"Come with me to the match tomorrow," he said. "Maybe you can give me a tip."

Dubiously, I agreed.

"I told you ~ that man will gamble on two fleas," Blanche grumbled. "He picked it up on the river."

"The river!" I was startled. Silas had said nothing about that part of his life, only telling me that, recovering from a war injury, he'd stayed behind with relatives when his parents moved West.

"Not long. Just long enough to get the itch," she said. "I guess he made out fine though. He got the one store from his uncle, and then bought another before you could turn around. Had to have a stash somewhere. Now..." she dug into a closet, "you take this parasol and keep in the shade. And don't let him bet more than he's got."

The race course was laid out in a straight line cut through a fallow field West of the river. It was actually two tracks with a barrier between to separate the running horses. The animals themselves were standing in a grove of trees, each with an attendant and a crowd of admirers.

"Come on," Silas said, taking my arm. "Let's go take a look."

"I don't guarantee a thing," I said.

It had been a long time since I'd been around good horses, and these were both fine specimens, somewhat smaller than those I'd been used to, but sleek and well-muscled with beautiful heads. One was an iron grey, the other a dark brown, almost black that responded to my chirp with a flashing, curious eye.

I spoke to him softly in the Magyar of my youth, the old words coming haltingly at first, then faster as he pricked his ears and nickered softly.

"What did you say?" Silas asked. "What language was that?"

"Horse language. He knows. Look at him. Look at those eyes. If you have to bet, bet on him. Only..." I laughed, "you're betting on me, too, and I might be wrong."

"I'll risk it." He placed his wager, then came and walked with me to the sidelines.

"We'll see the finish from here," he said. "It's a quarter mile from the start."

"That's all?" I was perplexed. The horses I knew weren't even warmed up at that distance.

"These are short horses. Quarter horses. Typically American. I guess you called them sprinters."

I was fascinated, never having heard of such a thing, and I was even more fascinated when the pair broke quickly and evenly and dashed toward us at what seemed incredible speed. At the finish, the dark horse led by a length.

Silas cheered. Then he turned and kissed me, hard. I felt the same jolt of electricity that I always felt when he touched me, and I kissed him back.

"We're a thousand dollars richer. How'd you like to spend it?"

A fortune! What I couldn't do with it! "I can't think," I said. "But it's yours, not mine. Put it in the bank for a rainy day."

"Let's get married and use it for our honeymoon. I'll take you on the river."

I didn't have to pretend shock. The suddenness of his proposal stunned me into silence. "Honeymoon!" I gasped when I recovered.

"We're two of a kind, Kate, and we're both alone. Marry

me. We'll have fun. I've had more fun these past two weeks with you than I can remember."

He meant it. A look at his face through my lowered lashes told me so. But I'd learned my lessons well. "I don't know what to say," I murmured.

"Say yes." He bent over, forcing me to look at him. "Say yes, Kate."

I had a qualm of conscience then. What I was doing was wrong, and yet Silas was right. We were two of a kind, and in the past weeks I'd come to recognize that. I was learning a new and happy life with him, always aware of the attraction that flared between us. Why was I hesitating?

I thought of my family, untouched by scandal, at least as far as I knew. But I had no family anymore. We were scattered like a handful of seed on the vastness of America. It was up to me to put down roots and grow. And who better to grow with than Silas with his brilliant eyes, his games of chance, the security of two fine stores?

I shrugged, forgiving myself for sins I couldn't help. Then I put out my hands. "Yes," I said. "Yes, yes, yes!"

Silas was right. Marriage was fun. Two weeks later we were headed for New Orleans, me with a trousseau of Blanche's castoffs and a head ringing with her advice.

"Mind you, play the virgin. Let him think he's first. That way, he'll never question the baby. They all want to take the credit anyhow. And... with a wave of a finger, "keep away from those cards or those river gamblers'll have all you've got."

Well, there was no harm in watching, and no way to keep Silas out of the gambling salons. Dressed in luxury, I accompanied him to the tables each night, laughing when he won, upset when he didn't which wasn't often.

"There are tricks," he said.

"Show me."

He did. He knew them all, and I learned fast. By the time we were back in St. Louis I could palm a card, mark the edge of another, deal as I wanted.

"Maybe we ought to sell the stores and go out West into the business," Silas said, watching me.

"No," I answered, "it isn't a good idea. I think...I think there are going to be three of us soon."

I watched comprehension dawn in his eyes. "You mean...Are you sure?"

"Almost. It...it must have happened right away. Are you glad?"

He grinned. "By God I am! We'll have to look for a house. Hire a girl to help out. When, do you think?"

We were living in Silas's quarters above one of the stores. We had three rooms and a porch where we sat on warm Fall nights watching the river. I loved those rooms and that high perch, fussed over all like a nesting bird, hung new curtains, swept the floors and put down a red Turkey carpet. I didn't want to leave.

"I'm not sure," I said. "But let's stay here awhile. I love it. It feels like home."

He got up and laid a hand on my hair. "Alright. But no more carrying things up those stairs. Or moving furniture. You hear?"

I turned and put my arms around his waist. "You're so good to me."

"Why not?" He stooped and picked me up in his arms. "Shall we celebrate?"

His intention was clear. Laughing, I kissed him in assent.

CHAPTER Six

Wars, revolutions, have far-reaching consequences. I knew those consequences first hand, and with Silas and later with Doc, I saw that the Civil War had left marks on every American, rich and poor.

Silas bore physical scars in addition to those in his mind. His parents had lost their home, and he, in turn was homeless, but he had discovered his own mettle, a discovery that led him, after the surrender, to a love of risk. As he saw it, life was short and full of danger. Best to live it to the fullest; a philosophy I understood very well. It wasn't so different from my own.

Inheriting his uncle's store put an end to his short time on the river but, as Blanche deduced, "He'd got the itch." He lived to win. Stealing me out of the convent was a form of vic-

tory. Enlarging his assets, by whatever means, was more difficult. But he'd made up his mind to recoup the war's losses, and
set out to do so.

He imagined a chain of stores selling bonnets, shawls,
ladies' finery, even jewels; a grand house in town; an even
grander one in the country. He swept me along in his enthusi-
asm.

There was money to be made in the aftermath of war.
Even I could see that. I advised him on fashions, surpassed his
imaginings. Together we planned an Empire and were happy in
it, although in my happiness I failed to see the pit opening at my
feet. I turned a blind eye on Silas's absences until Blanche,
breathless and fanning herself, climbed the stairs one afternoon
to tell me.

I took her into the parlor, and she looked around at my
efforts. "I can see your hand here, little cousin," she said, sink-
ing into a chair. "But those stairs! Soon enough you'll be moving, though."

"Moving?"

"Ah! I've let it out!" She gave me a mischievous glance
that told me she'd done just as she intended.

"Let out what?" I plunked down on the new horsehair
sofa, glad to be off my feet.

"If I tell you, you'll have to pretend to be surprised when
Silas does," she said. "That man of yours went out and won you
a house two nights ago. A fancy place, too, I might tell you."

"A house?" I asked, sounding like a parrot.

"At cards, child. He staked one of the stores and got
lucky. If he hadn't, you'd be moving anyway. Didn't I tell you
you'd have to watch him?"

I shook my head, digesting it all. So that was where he
was when he said he'd be working late! At the gaming tables.

Well, at least he'd won. I said as much to Blanche who raised one eyebrow.

"You're as bad as he is. A pair of fools. Keep your hands on some money for the bad times. Because they'll come, mark my words. Now..." she arranged her skirts, "now, let's talk woman talk. How's this baby coming, and how do you feel?"

We spent the rest of the afternoon in chatter. I'd missed her, the sharpness of her tongue, the wisdom she doled out in almost every sentence. And I was sorry when she rose to leave.

"I'll come see you soon," I promised. "I've been so busy settling in I haven't had time to get away."

"No you won't." She turned, one hand on the door. "You'll stay right here and make friends of your own. Think how it will look. Mrs. Melvin visiting a kept woman."

"I don't care, and you're my friend," I said.

"That's nice. You're a lady like I said. But don't worry about my feelings. Best worry about your own reputation."

The trouble was that most of the young wives whom I'd met through Silas were so dull. They had nothing to say and never noticed the lack, simply clung to their husbands' arms (men who, like Silas, had survived the war and were self-assured and quick), and agreed with everything anyone said.

From my point of view it seemed better to be a business woman as Blanche was, and never mind reputation. What was that anyhow but a method devised to keep young females from thinking for themselves.

"We're all kept if you think about it," I remarked.

She laughed. "Of course, child. But nobody talks about that. Now, I'm going back to my Mr. Stonebreak and you take care to be surprised about your new house. But if you ever need me, send a message. I'll come quick."

I'd caught a glimpse of Jonas Stonebreak one night when

I peered through Blanche's parlor door. He looked almost as bad as Otto, red-faced and with a bulging waist. Still, he kept the police away and paid Blanche well, and oddly she never complained or even talked about him.

"Take care," I said, hugging her. Then I watched as she descended the stairs to the yard below, looking like a graceful and exotic bird.

Of course I acted surprised, and was when I saw the house, a tall brick with wide, vine-shaded verandahs and a strip of lawn. Though it was winter, I knew how it would look in summer; cool, shadowed, the perfect place to sit with a baby, to plan the future with Silas. Oh, I had come up in the world! From murderess to chatelaine, and all because of my young and daring husband.

I threw my arms around him. "It's perfect! When can we move? We'll need furniture. And a servant. Shall we have a servant?"

"As many as you need." He spoke as if we were rich, as if money overflowed our pockets, and I believed him, the more fool I.

Captain Fisher's son was born in April and christened Michael Joseph, for Silas's father and mine. Looking at him, I saw a reflection of myself, a fair-haired child with blue eyes and the promise of a determined chin beneath what would become the arrogant Haroney nose.

So had we all looked, suckling at our mother's breast. What had happened to the others, left on Otto's farm? I'd made several attempts to reach Mina by letter, using the name, "Mrs. Silas Melvin," but had received no answer. Perhaps they were scattered again and I would never find them. The thought hurt. I clutched Michael close, so close that he began to cry, pushing against me with tiny fists.

"You're my family," I told him, looking down on his puckered face with a surge of love unlike any other. "Mine."

But my life has never followed a straight or peaceful path. What I loved was always taken from me, too soon for more than a glimpse of happiness.

I've tasted passion, love, pain and sorrow in large doses, and survived all of it, for what reason I don't know. But here I am, like a clay jar overflowing with memories, all of them as vivid as if they just happened.

In spite of the fact that Silas's stores made a fine profit, we never had enough money, and I knew why though I never nagged Silas about it. He was bitten with the gambling bug and couldn't control it. For awhile we had a string of horses that we raced and that I loved until they were sold to pay a debt; and once, for several months, we had to let the two maids go, not having any money to pay them.

While I didn't mind so much for myself, I worried about the future, about a proper school for Michael, a decent home for all of us. And in spite of Blanche's advice, I had only a few dollars saved in the bottom of one of my trunks.

But I needn't have worried. Fate, as always with me, took a hand.

I can see us all on that glaring August afternoon, a proper family group on the wisteria-shaded verandah; Michael and I on our way out for a walk, Silas home early pausing beside us.

Michael lets go of my hand. "Daddy!" he cries and holds up his arms begging to be hoisted on his father's shoulders.

Instead of lifting him high in the air, Silas pats the top of his golden head. "Later," he says. "Go with your mother now." To me, "I've got an awful headache. I came home to lie down before supper."

"Shall I stay with you?" He does look ill, white-faced with shadows under his eyes that weren't there in the morning.

"No. Take your walk. I passed a medicine show a few blocks down that Michael might like to see."

And so we went with Michael chattering beside me.

I don't remember when he fell silent. Whether it was during the Indian War dance, an exciting performance with chanting and the beat of a large, painted drum, or later, during the medicine man's spiel. But he was quiet on the way home, dragging his feet and at last demanding to be carried.

"A big boy like you!" I exclaimed, laughing. "Why, you could almost carry me."

Usually he responded to my teasing with giggles.

This time his face crumpled. "Please, Mama," he begged.

I saw he was flushed with fever and took him quickly into my arms, hurrying as best I could, the heat of his body burning through my clothes.

Except for a cold or two, Michael had never been ill, and the suddeness of this made me frantic. I tripped on the verandah steps, nearly dropping him, and when I called for Maria, the maid, my voice was shrill.

Together we got him upstairs and into bed where I sponged his body with cool water and sang to him, old songs, old lulabyes remembered from childhood. When he dropped into a restless sleep, I ran across the hall to Silas.

He, too was feverish, and vomiting into the basin. When I had sponged him and made him comfortable, I ran into the hall and called to Maria. There was no answer. Slowly I understood that she had run off and left me, terrified of the plague.

I was alone in this, as I always had been at times of crisis, and I spent the night moving between the sick rooms, doing what I could, losing all track of time. I prayed that night, over and over in my head. "Dear God, don't let them die," until the words turned meaningless, annoying, like the insistant buzzing of a fly.

My prayers were, as ever, meaningless. No one heard. Michael died in my arms the next afternoon, and Silas shortly after, so quickly I had no time to prepare myself.

Still I went back and forth between the rooms, unable to stop hoping. Surely the little one only slept! Surely Silas would open those fiery eyes at any moment and wipe the pain away!

But when night came, hot, humid, and smelling of death and decay, it brought reality ~ and panic ~ with it.

My mind wasn't working. Thoughts skittered across it like dried leaves. I ran out the door and through the dark streets like a mad woman, uncaring of threat or danger. I ran until I reached Blanche's house and with my hands curled into angry but useless fists, I beseiged her door.

CHAPTER Seven

There were few mourners at the cemetery; all those quick-witted young men, their over-dressed wives, those so-called "friends" were conspicuous by their absence.

Only Blanche stood with me, and the faithful Nancy, and the pompous McClain, Silas's lawyer, although his reasons for being there that brutally hot August afternoon were those of business, not friendship.

Once again I had lost all that I loved; my bright-eyed child, my reckless husband who had saved me, given me respectability, the warmth of love.

There seemed nothing left for me, certainly not life. I wished that I, too, were being smothered by shovels of earth. I wept, and my tears fell on the parched ground and were swallowed like rain.

"You come with me tonight," Blanche said when all was over and the priest, an elderly man in a cassock faded brown with age, had blessed me and gone.

"I want to go home," I said, realizing as I spoke that I had said these words before, and that home meant an empty house, echoing rooms.

She shook her head. "Not tonight. Tomorrow, maybe." She put a slim, surprisingly strong arm around my waist and led me toward the waiting carriage. I was too tired to argue, and went with her, thrusting my way through what seemed like fog.

"Mrs. Melvin." McClain's voice cut through my daze. "I'm sorry to intrude at such a time, believe me, but there's Mr. Melvin's will. If it wouldn't be too much trouble, could you come to my office for a few minutes? It won't take long."

Blanche answered for me. "We'll come. I'll wait with the carriage. Better so, eh?"

The lawyer nodded, replaced his hat on his bald head, and stepped into his own carriage. "Follow me," he said.

His news, of course, was bad. There were debts and more debts, and mortgages I'd known nothing about. What it amounted to was that I was penniless, not for the first time nor for the last, but being a pauper is never easy. It robs you of your wits, your dignity. It terrifies, gives nightmares, dreams of starvation, cold, a lingering death. I was a woman raised to a vanished life, unskilled, alone in a hostile world with only Blanche to keep the horror away.

She wasted no time. "Nancy will get what can be saved. Give her the key. You have money somewhere? Jewels?"

"Yes." At least I had those things that could be pawned, sold, traded for necessities.

"Where?"

I told her, and she dispatched Nancy in a rented hack. "Now," she said, settling herself in the seat and removing her large black hat and veil, "now, cousin, we go home."

Once there she went into the kitchen and returned with two tall glasses.

"Drink," she said. "This is cool and you'll feel better."

Whatever was in the glass made me long for sleep as she'd intended. Shortly I went to my room, lay down, and before I could submit to grief or worry, fell asleep.

I awoke once. It seemed like morning. Rain was falling on the roof, and in the kitchen Nancy was singing in her deep, rich voice that flowed through the house like the music of a cello.

"Amazing grace, abide with me...."

I closed my eyes and slept again.

When I awoke it was late afternoon and still raining. I pictured the graves, humps of mud slowly settling in the downpour. There was nothing I could do for Silas and Michael but mourn, quietly, deep in my heart. And even so, I was mourning not so much for them as for my self. It was a bitter thought, but the truth of it stopped me.

Who was I now? What name best suited me? How different was I than before? Over and over death had passed me by. For what reason? Not motherhood, for Michael was gone and I had no wish to bear another child to be taken from me.

I slipped out of bed, pulled off my nightgown, and stood looking at myself in the mirror, something I had never done. Women were discouraged from becoming familiar with their bodies, from doing anything more than bathe them hurriedly, often beneath a sheet or gown. Bodies were a source of wickedness. I knew that only too well, yet I was curious.

Who was hidden within that small frame, behind those

voluptuous breasts? Who was it who responded with delight to the caresses of men? Who mourned, murdered, fought unceasingly for life despite all odds? Would she show herself in the mirror?

Whoever she was, I pitied her at first. The shadows beneath long blue eyes, the downturned lips, the sag of narrow shoulders spoke clearly of sorrow. But as I watched, she smiled, and light shivered across her face and caught in her eyes. "Not dead yet," she seemed to be saying. "Badly hurt, but not broken."

I reached out my hands to clasp hers, and she did the same.

"Help me," I pleaded, and she nodded.

"Always."

She looked wanton, mischievous despite her fragile bones. I liked her, this illusion, if that's what she was. Actually, she seemed more like a mother, dredged up out of my own body. Not the mother who had born me, but the woman I would have chosen had I a choice in the matter.

"Always."

I turned my back, and she was gone, but the warmth remained. And the relief. I wasn't alone anymore.

Dressed, I wandered to the kitchen and found Blanche overseeing a steaming kettle.

"Hungry?" she asked.

"Yes." I couldn't remember my last meal. It must have been breakfast on the veranda with Silas. Never again would I have such a pleasure, never again see his eyes twinkling at me over the edge of his cup. I clenched my fists, fighting the pain. What was loved, familiar, a piece of self was gone and would never repeat.

Blanche set a plate before me. "Jambalaya. Good for

you," she said.

Seduced by the scents of spices and thick sauce, I took a bite, and then another. "Heaven! You should open a restaurant. You'd be famous up and down the river," I said when I'd emptied the plate.

"And get old before time," she retorted. "Bad legs and droopy bosom from feeding all those fat ones. No, cousin. I like what I do. And you..." she cocked her head. "What do you do now?"

"I don't know."

"Can you sew?"

"Lord, no." My fumbling attempts with a needle had long before brought lectures and thumbs pricked raw.

"Teach school?"

"Languages, maybe. But who'd pay for that? Maybe I could be a childrens' nurse. I'd like that, I think."

"Too soon," she said, making the decision for me. "Stay here awhile. Be my friend. I don't have one. Only Nancy and her conversation is..." she smiled wickedly, "dull!"

"I can't just let you support me!"

"Bah! You'll be my ~ what do they call it? My companion. Say yes! And maybe catch another man someday."

"I don't want another man."

"So you say now. But you will. You were born for men. Some of us are."

Was she right? Certainly I preferred the company of men over the prattle of women, and I had been a rough and tumble child and not the demure creature my mother had wished me. Certainly the things I had done left me outside the pale of convention, but what did that mean?

"Maybe," I said.

She took hesitation as assent. "Good. Your things are in

the front room. Nancy took care of it. No need to go back to that place."

"I want to say goodbye," I said. "Just one time."

"You already did." She drummed her fingers on the table. "You want to keep picking scabs off the wound, or you want to let it heal? You decide. Only you better decide right."

The image she conjured made me squirm, yet there was truth in it.

"Let go, cousin," she urged. "Let go, and see what life has laid by for you."

I gave in. "Alright. I'll stay here. But only for a little while. And thank you. For everything."

"Bah!" she said, getting to her feet with that rustle of silk. "We help each other. That's all. It's what women do. They got nobody else."

CHAPTER Eight

Although in the weeks that followed I sometimes woke thinking Michael was calling for me, although I ached to hold him more often than I admitted, and ached for the feel of Silas next to me, it lessened as Fall passed and Winter set in; an early winter, damp, cold, snowy, with a bite to it that made me glad of a place to live.

As Blanche promised, I became her companion, no longer visible in the gaming rooms, a hidden presence on those nights when Jonas Stonebreak came.

Several times on those nights I thought I heard Blanche cry out, and started down the hall to her room, but both times I was met by Nancy who shooed me away. "Leave it be. It ain't your business," she said grimly, and I obeyed, returning to the books I had begun reading: Dickens, Ouida, the novels of Zola that I'd discovered in Keith and Woods Bookstore.

It was a quiet life, and long before the end, I'd begun to chafe at idleness. It's not in me to do nothing, and never has been.

•

The knock on the door came when both Blanche and Nancy were busy in the gaming rooms, an imperious knock demanding attention, the rapping of a man not used to being kept waiting. I hurried down the hall to answer.

He stood for a moment, snow whirling around him making the cape he wore seem alive.

"Please come in," I said. "It's a fierce night."

He did, and gratefully I closed out the cold before turning to meet his eyes, cool as silver dollars and as unreadable.

"May I take your things?" I asked, and held out my hands for his hat and cloak.

He stared at me, a penetrating search that took in my face and my body beneath my clothes. No one had looked at me like that for a long time, and in spite of myself, I responded with a smile.

One corner of his mouth turned up as if in answer. Then he said, "You look like hell in black."

So much for my vanity! My anger erupted as surely as if he had lit a match to a fuse.

"How dare you! How dare you speak to me in such a way! I'm in mourning for my husband and child, and you know nothing about it." I'd backed down the hall as I spoke and stood, hands clenched into fists. I wanted to hit this man, scratch his face, assuage my wounded pride.

"Mourning is a waste of time," he said, unperturbed,

thrusting his hat at me. "Where are the card rooms?"

I jerked my head toward the sliding door. "In there."

He nodded as if I were no more than an insect, and passed by me.

I hissed at his retreating figure. "Who do you think you are?"

At the door he turned and smiled, the wicked grimace of a victorious tom cat. "Dr. John Holliday," he said and disappeared within.

"Who is that man?" I demanded of Nancy later. "That Dr. Holliday?"

She shrugged. "I dunno. But he sure had some luck tonight. Cleaned out the other gentlemen in no time."

"He's no gentleman," I said.

"Maybe not. But he sure can handle cards."

I thought he was probably crooked. There were plenty like him around. Men of vanished fortunes who turned to gambling to repair them. I hoped I'd never lay eyes on him again, and took care to stay in my rooms on those nights when the parlor was in use.

As the winter dragged on, I spent much of my time in my room, banished there almost every evening, locked away from the sounds of male talk and laughter, and from the frightening whimpers that, with more and more frequency, escaped from the bed where Blanche and Stonebreak played out their alliance.

One morning she failed to hide the bruises on her arms and around her throat, and I couldn't keep quiet.

"How can you stand it?" I shouted at her. "He hurts you, and you let him. You, with all your talk about being smart, being kind."

She adjusted the scarf more carefully around her slender neck. "We do what we have to, cousin. I told you that, also. He

70

owns this house. He owns me until I pay him back. That should be soon. Then maybe things change."

"I don't understand."

"I hope you never do," she answered. "But understand one thing. I take only so much. Then there is this." She pulled a derringer from a table drawer with the swiftness of familiarity.

"I hope you kill him," I said, feeling betrayed by her submission, unable to comprehend what seemed to me to be weakness.

"You have a lot to learn yet," she remarked, sounding bitter for the first time. " You're a white woman. I'm not white or black. I don't fit anywhere. Think about that, cousin. Think what you'd do if you were me and had no place to go except the bottom of that river out there."

I learned what she was trying to tell me two days later. Again I was in my room reading, or trying to, hearing instead angry voices and then the sound of fists battering bone, a chair knocked over in a struggle.

Blanche's scream was cut off suddenly, inexplicably, and I didn't wait but pulled open my door and ran down the hall, shoving Nancy aside in my haste. I was remembering Otto, smelling him, tasting the foul taste of his breath in my mouth.

Jonas Stonebreak was standing over Blanche, a crumpled Blanche, her beauty distorted by the grimace of death, by the wound in her throat made from Stonebreak's knife.

How could there be so much blood? It flowed onto the carpet and down into the sea-green silk of Blanche's dress. It filled my head, my eyes with a rage I couldn't control.

"Pig!" I screamed. "Murderer! Filthy, rotten son of a bitch! What did she do to deserve killing? I'll see you hanged."

He lunged at me then, his intentions clear, and I ran, put-

71

ting the sofa between us while I wrenched open the table drawer where the derringer was hidden. Then, with a calmness I never thought possible, I aimed at his face and pulled the trigger.

His head burst open like a melon, a spattering of flesh and bone that I can see even now, though I try to forget. I think I screamed, or Nancy did, coming to the door and finding slaughter.

Footsteps sounded in the hall, and terror took over. I threw down the pistol and ran to my room where I snatched up my cloak and, without stopping to fasten it, pushed up the window and climbed out into the night.

An icy wind blew off the river. I had forgotten my gloves and bonnet, and my warm boots. Gradually my hands and feet lost all feeling and, when I thought I had lost my pursuers, I stumbled onto a bench and sat, tucking them under me for warmth.

Blanche was back there lying in her own blood. Blanche who had taken me in, guided me, cared for me with something close to love. Where was the justice in that? Where the reason?

"No place to go but the bottom of the river," she'd said. I knew what she meant. This time my crime was obvious. This time I would be hanged for the murder of a prominent citizen, regardless of whether or not he deserved it. I was guilty. I could not plead otherwise.

The cold closed around me. Snow beat at my face, froze in my hair, began to cover me like a shroud as I huddled into myself seeking warmth. I got up then and stumbled. My feet weighted me like stones.

There were always bodies, nameless lumps of flesh found frozen in alleys, washed up on the banks of the river. Should I become one of them before they cracked my neck at the end of a rope? I stood, hesitant, unable to think or to will myself down to the banks.

"The bottom of the river." Who would miss me? Who mourn? No one.

Then I heard voices, and turning fled, still fighting for life, for dreams. I slipped once and fell, cutting my cheek on a curbstone. For a moment the blood was warm, and then it froze and I forgot it, heading into the wind, quickening my pace as I turned a corner onto a narrow street.

"Watch where you're going!" The man staggered as we collided, and I put out a hand to steady myself.

He caught it, keeping me on my feet, and peered down at me.

"Why it's the little widow!" he said. "What are you doing out this time of night?"

"Let me go!" I struggled to pull free, but his fingers were made of iron.

"Calm down, for God's sake. You've got blood all over your face. Are you hurt?"

I kicked him in the shins, wanting only release. I triggered his anger instead.

He pinned my arms to my sides and shook me till my teeth rattled. "If you were a man, I'd kill you," he said. "As it is, you'd better explain. And fast."

I thought quickly, not trusting him. "It's Blanche. She's dead. Knifed. I ran away."

His body tensed. I could feel it against me. "Who did it?"

"Jonas Stonebreak. He...they fought, and when she screamed I went in. It...it was too late." I began to cry, and wriggled in his grasp trying to wipe my face. "He's dead, too."

He swore, and his fingers tightened till I wanted to

scream. He said, "Stonebreak was a no good son of a bitch. I'm surprised he lasted this long." He shook me again. "Stop sniveling. Who killed him? Blanche? Whoever did, they ought to get a medal."

Could I depend on him? Something, a voice deep inside me said, Yes. I said, "I did."

"You? The little widow?" He peered at me again. Then he laughed, throwing his head back and showing a gleam of white teeth. "Are they after you?"

"Yes. I think so. I left without anything, and I'm cold."

He laughed again. " Come on. I'll hide you out till we know what's happening."

"Where?"

"What the hell difference does it make?" he said. "I won't turn you over to the law, if that's what you're thinking. The bastard had it coming."

"I just want to know where we're going."

"To my rooms." He started walking, pulling me with him.

The memory of our first meeting was still alive. "Don't think because I'm grateful I'll sleep with you," I told him.

"Christ," he said. "You ought to see yourself. You look like a drowned river rat. But I'll help you anyhow. At no charge."

Dear God how I hated him! But I was in his hands for better or worse. I cursed him in Hungarian. It sounded better that way.

"What was that?" he asked, slowing his pace.

I swallowed hard. "You wouldn't want to know."

He chuckled. "Don't bet on it. And what's your name? I can't keep calling you 'the widow'"

"Kate Elder," I said. I was back where I'd started.

Chapter Nine

"Am I going to have a scar?"

I was sitting on a chair in Doc's front room, and he was cleaning the cut on my face.

"I doubt it. But it beats hanging." His fingers, sure and light, moved across my cheek.

I leaned back and closed my eyes, allowing myself to relax for the first time in what seemed like days. "What kind of doctor are you?"

"A dentist," he said. "Sit still now. This might sting." But before he could do anything, he doubled over in a fit of coughing.

I sat up and looked at him. "Better take care of yourself. That's a bad cough."

He wiped his lips with his handkerchief, and I caught a glimpse of blood. "Too late," he said. "I've got a year, give or take a few months."

He had the classic symptoms; the flush over hollow cheeks, the feverish eyes, but in spite of disease he was handsome, fine-featured, with a hint of humor in the lines around his mouth.

"Are you sure?" I asked, feeling, for no reason, a sense of loss.

"Dead sure, if you'll pardon the bad joke."

"I'm sorry." And much to my surprise, I meant it.

"Don't waste your time." He approached me again with a bottle and a piece of gauze.

"Don't tell me what to feel," I snapped. "If I want to feel sorry, I will, and that's that."

He shrugged. "You talk too damn much. Sit still and be quiet."

Whatever he put on the cut, it stung, wiping out my compassion. "Don't you swear at me." My voice came out ragged from pain and nerves. "That's no way to talk to a lady."

He stepped back, eyeing his work for a moment. Then he said, "Ladies don't live in whore houses. And they don't go around killing people, either."

His words hit home, stinging more than the antiseptic. For years I'd gone around denying my upbringing, making light of it. Now, when I wanted it back, it eluded me. I buried my face in my hands.

"Oh, for Christ's sake," he said. "Nobody's perfect. Why should you be?" He replaced his medicines in his bag and wiped his hands. Then he turned around. "Stop sniveling."

I hated him again. "You don't know anything," I said. "you don't know what it's like to be alone, hungry, hunted for

76

doing what you had to. You're a man. And a damned arrogant one. So sure of yourself. So ready to walk all over me. Go away and leave me alone."

He chuckled, unperturbed. "You can leave any time," he said. "I live here."

That was true. I could take my chances on the streets, freeze to death, get hanged. It made no difference to him. That stung more than anything.

Why should his indifference hurt? Why should I have to prove my worth to him who'd insulted me more times than I could count?

I was past answering questions. Too much had happened too quickly. "I don't know what to do," I said. "I even thought about killing myself. Everything's too hard all of a sudden."

He unscrewed the cap off another bottle and poured liquid into a glass. Then he added water and handed it to me. "Drink this. Then go get some sleep. And don't worry about your virtue. I'm going out."

"What for?"

"None of your damned business." He pulled on his coat and adjusted his hat, bowing at me from the door.

"What's in the glass?"

"Christ, you're full of questions! Nothing that'll hurt. I don't poison people."

"Just with your words," I said. "That's all."

"That's enough. Now go to bed. I'll be back in a bit."

I did as he said, having nothing else to do. I thought of snooping in his kit, his rooms, but the potion was strong, and without taking off more than my shoes I lay down on the bed and fell asleep.

•

I stayed with Doc, hidden in his rooms, for more than a month, nearly going crazy from confinement.

"Be glad it's not the jail," He said when I complained. "You'd be climbing the bars."

The investigation over Blanche's and Stonebreak's deaths went on, not because of Blanche, but because of her lover's prominence. The police were, Doc reported, looking for me for questioning. The news made me shake.

"I can't!" I whispered. "I can't go there!"

"Of course not. I'll get you out of here when the heat's off and not before. So get used to your cell."

"I wish I had my clothes," I said. "And my books."

"Books!" He looked at me as if I were joking.

I stamped my foot. "Yes, books. I'm not stupid. But I am bored. Bored silly locked up in here and you gone most of the time."

"Are you inviting me to stay with you?"

Oh, he had nerve. And conceit, too, just because he was handsome and had nothing to lose. "Go away," I said. "I wouldn't invite you to my funeral."

"Will you come to mine?"

"I'll dance on your grave." I wondered why he provoked me so easily, and why I couldn't simply remain silent.

His mouth quirked in a one-sided smile. "I'm sure you'll have lots of company," he said.

"I'm sure I will."

He was still smiling. I couldn't stand it. How could he be so calm? How could all the mean things I said leave him unmoved?

"Oh, go to hell and leave me alone," I snapped, losing all patience. "I'll survive. Just go."

He did, closing the door gently, mockingly behind him.

I paced the floor, stirred the fire, went to the window and watched the traffic splashing through the sleet. I was as much a prisoner as if I were, indeed, in jail locked away from life. Tears burned in my eyes, and my head began to ache. I lay down on the bed and cried myself to sleep.

A thump on the bed woke me. Doc was standing at the foot grinning that malicious grin that always got to me. I sat straight up. "What are you doing?" I asked.

He pointed at the valise he'd dumped beside me. "Your things, Madame."

Inside were my dresses, toiletries, shoes, books, and my mother's garnets that I'd kept when I'd sold the other jewels Silas bought me.

Wordless for once, I stared at the contents. "How?" I finally managed to ask. "How?"

"The faithful Nancy." He sat down on the edge of the bed. "She's still at the house hoping it isn't true, that the old days will come back."

"What'll happen to her?"

He shrugged. "God knows. What happens to any of them? The system betrayed them all."

"Life did," I corrected him.

He sat in silence thinking thoughts I couldn't share. What was he seeing? What secrets lay in his past?

Before I could intrude, he broke the spell. "Get dressed," he commanded. "Supper's on the way."

We'd formed the habit of eating together at the small table in front of the fire. We'd eat and argue, and then Doc would leave for an evening's pleasure while I sat and stared at the flames before going to bed. It was a lonely life and alien to me. Even Doc's presence was preferable to such solitude.

"Are you going out tonight?" I asked.

"Not tonight. It's miserable as I learned on my errand of mercy." He grinned again. "I didn't want you wasting away for your worldly goods. And besides, you look god-awful in those rags, and I'm tired looking at you in them."

I threw a shoe at him. He ducked, and it bounced off the wall. "Such a nasty temper!" he said. "You really should learn to control it." Then he was gone. Only his mocking laughter stayed, echoing in my ears.

So I looked awful! I'd show him! What he needed was a dose of his own arrogance, a woman he couldn't reduce to mindlessness with his sharp tongue and slippery attitude.

I dressed carefully in green velvet trimmed in heavy lace and cut low over my bosom. I colored my cheeks, arranged my hair on the top of my head, fastened the garnets around my throat. Then I looked in the mirror.

What I saw was my mother, breathless before a ball. What I saw was that buried part of my self armed for battle.

"You're beautiful," she said. "So is he."

"Him!"

Her laughter chimed like distant bells. "Oh, Kate," she said. "What a fool you are."

"I've had enough of dying." I faced the mirror. "It's like I'm cursed."

"Then fight. I hate quitters."

She was gone. All I saw was myself dressed for battle, armed with a necklace the color of blood.

I opened the door and stood, awaiting approval. "The river rat is gone," I said, moving across the room, swaying my hips. "I hope you like the replacement."

His brows rose in astonishment as he took in my changed appearance. "I think it's time you told me just who you really are," he said.

"It's a long story."

He leaned back in his chair and crossed his legs on the fire fender. "It's a good night for stories," he said.

I told him, leaving out Otto. One murder was enough, and besides, he was looking at me in a way I recognized, a way that made me want to rush through all the sordid details. Shamelessly I romanticized my early life. It made the later part more awful. I left out the Captain, too, making of myself an orphan then a gambler's widow struggling to survive.

"You're either a damned good actress and a liar, or what you just told me happened," he observed when I'd finished.

I smiled across at him and leaned on the table showing my breasts. "I've lied when I had to, but this isn't one of the times," I said. I could feel my heart beating in response to his undisguised interest.

The world had shrunk to that small room lit by the dying fire that turned Doc's eyes into molten metal.

"Sometimes I don't know who I am or why I do things," I confessed. "I'm not who I was raised to be at all. Everything I learned turned out to be fairy tales."

"That's usually the case." There was bitter knowledge on his face.

"Why?"

"The world kicks us around. Wars happen. Look at Nancy. She's lost. Look at you. You lived through two revolutions. The Civil War ruined my life. Killed my mother. We can change with the world, or we can die. Dealer's choice."

"It isn't fair."

"Nobody said it would be. Kids believe. Then they find out it's bullshit."

"Where will it end?" I was tired of running and hiding. I wanted a home. Security. A family around me.

He got up and poked the fire. The shadows played along the hollows of his face making him remote, a pagan god careless of his power.

"In the grave," he said, smiling his bitter smile.

"I don't want you to die." I blurted out the words without thinking.

"Tough luck, Kate." He put down the poker and came to stand beside me. "But I'm not dead yet, am I?"

He caressed the fading scar on my cheek. That was enough. I stopped thinking and threw the past, the future to the flames. There was only the present, this shattered man and I, pieces of the selves we might have been.

It would always be that way with us, a fight, our passions forged in our bones. His for life, a staving off of the inevitable; mine the need to comprehend the enemy, death. Love was a fury raging against fate, and we were its victims.

I didn't understand it then. I'm not sure I do now - old, looking back, still full of wanting. What I know is that with Doc the rules were thrown away and the anguish of living vanished.

We lay beside the fire naked and vulnerable. His hands seemed to burn me, eating my flesh. I didn't care. I would be consumed, or he would. It made no difference. We were both doomed. Infinity was the moment. I opened my self and drew him in.

Chapter Ten

Years later I learned about the symptoms of tuberculosis. In my time with Doc, I simply suffered the consequences. To my shame, I often let my temper get the better of common sense, but I misunderstood his bouts of anger when his body betrayed him, and when he turned on me as scapegoat.

I loved him passionately, self-centeredly. And so I failed to see that his fury at himself was taken out on me with my good health a constant reminder of illness.

More and more in the month that followed, our love making ended in bouts of rage. We were each a match to the other's timber and couldn't help ourselves.

"You're an insatiable bitch!" he screamed at me one night after a fit of coughing had interrupted us. "You'll kill me before the rot does!"

I sat up in bed and screamed back, feeling like he'd stuck the knife he always carried between my breasts and into my heart.

"I'm trying to keep you alive!" I yelled. "I'm not insa - whatever you said. I don't even know what it means!"

Tears of frustration trickled down my face. He couldn't see! He trusted no one, certainly not a woman.

"It means you're eating me alive. You and your body and those goddamned hungry eyes of yours. It means I'm getting the hell out of here." He was throwing shirts, cravats, embroidered waist coats in mismatched piles onto the bed, the floor.

Just as wildly I began tossing them back into drawers. "You can't just leave. Where'll you go?"

"Away from here." He grabbed one end of a flowered vest. "Give me that! And for Christ's sake put on some clothes."

"No!" I tugged at the cloth until the seams gave way and I fell backwards onto the pillows where I lay still and smiled at him. If words didn't work, seduction might.

He put his hands around my throat. "Whore!" he said.

"I'm not," I choked. "I love you. That's all."

"That's what they all say."

He bent suddenly and kissed me, bruising my lips so that I squirmed, trying to get away. "No, by God. This time we'll finish what we started."

There was something of my own savagery in the way he took me, as if he were trying to blot out reality, as if in the whole world there were only the two of us on a tangled bed in the light of a dying fire.

When I woke in the morning the fire had turned to ashes, and I was alone.

"Doc?" The word bounced back from the empty rooms,

and I shivered at the sound, pulling the covers around me.

Doc had gone. I knew it before I found his note propped up on the dresser. He needed his freedom, he said. His peace to live and die without argument. The rooms we had shared were paid up until the end of the month, and he had asked a friend, Anson McGraw, to look after me, get me out of town. He left me five hundred dollars.

I threw his note and the money on the floor and stamped on them. What good was money without Doc? What good, anything? I felt ripped in half, part agony, part anger. I threw myself across the bed and wept until I had no more tears. Clutching Doc's pillow, I fell asleep.

A knock at the door awakened me. From the light that filtered in through a crack in the draperies, it seemed to be mid-afternoon, a bleak day that echoed my sorrow.

"Who is it? Who's there?" I couldn't think of anyone who would come at that hour, at least not anyone I'd want to see.

"Anson McGraw," came the answer in a deep, masculine voice.

And there I was, my face swollen, hair unbound, wrapped in a sheet torn from the bed. "I'm sorry," I said. "I can't see you now."

"Are you alright?" He sounded concerned.

"Yes...no...I don't know," I responded. "Can you come some other time?"

"In an hour." It was a statement.

"Fine," I said. "An hour."

I heard his footsteps on the stairs. They were firm, unhurried, the tread of a decisive man. I didn't want to meet him or anyone. I wanted to be alone with the ache in my breast. But I couldn't afford to be temperamental. Doc had said McGraw would help me leave town, which I had to do. And perhaps he could tell me where Doc had gone so I could follow. I wasn't about to be cast off so easily, left behind like some worn out shoe.

How dare he shove my love back at me? How dare he overlook the long, sweet hours? I'd find him if it took years. The world was not so big, after all. And I'd learn to hold my tongue if that's what was necessary to keep him. We belonged to one another. My bones knew it, cracking with longing, and my heart that seemed too swollen to be contained.

The mirror showed a haggard face with red-rimmed eyes still glazed from grief. I stirred the fire and added wood, watched until it burst into flame. When the room warmed, I washed, holding a cloth over my face a long time. Then I set to work with powder and rouge, painting a smile over the damage of tears and blessing Blanche for educating me so well, blessing my mama whose words came back to me...

"Never let a gentleman see you disheveled. A lady must always be fresh, well-groomed, and pleasant in her speech."

Well, as for the last part, what could she know of the life I'd been living? Still, perhaps there was truth in her words for Doc was gone because of my temper, my wild words.

Had I forgotten how to please? To act like a lady? I didn't know. That world was gone, and this was all I had. This and Anson McGraw who would be returning shortly.

I chose an afternoon dress of plum wool with a lace collar and cuffs, not my most flattering color, but the dress was well-cut and in it I certainly did not appear as a discarded plaything.

When the imperious knock came again, I was ready. I squared my shoulders and opened the door.

Anson McGraw had chestnut hair, broad shoulders, and a way of knowing what he wanted as soon as he saw it, be it horses, houses, land, or women.

Within five minutes he made me a proposition. Would I go with him to Wichita and act the part of his wife?

"Wichita!" I said. "Where's that?"

He gave me an astonished look out of bright hazel eyes. "Haven't you been reading the papers, Kate? It's the biggest cattle shipping town in Kansas. The end of the line for the railroad, for now, anyway. The place is booming. Almost one hundred thousand cattle shipped out last year. I won some town lots and a piece of grassland in a card game, and right now's the time to sell. Town property is sky high. Farmland, too. The Indians own most of it so it's selling at a premium."

"And...?"

"And I'm going to sell out and move on. There's money to be made everywhere the railroad goes all the way to California, and I'm going to make it. But I need a lady partner to help me. Make me look respectable. Entertain buyers."

"And you aren't respectable of course. Any more than I'm a lady."

"You'll do. I knew as soon as I saw you. Besides, Doc told me you'd do."

"Did Doc tell you I have to leave town?" I was thinking of possible blackmail.

Anson shook his head. "He said you wanted to. Didn't give a reason. Is there something I should know?"

I smiled sweetly. "Not really. Do you know where Doc went?"

"No." There was a finality in his voice that told me the subject of Doc was closed.

I hid my irritation with another smile and sat back in my chair. There are always a thousand ways to get information. "How do you know Doc?" I asked.

"We went to school together in Philadelphia."

"You're a dentist, too?" I was startled.

"I was. The war put an end to it."

"Why?"

"My home was burned. My family scattered. Nobody was interested in their teeth, let me tell you. Besides, too many ghosts walk around Antietam. So I left." He spread his well-manicured hands. "I discovered the dexterity necessary for dentistry served as well at the card table. Like our friend Holliday. Certainly there's more money in it. And fun."

He stared at his hands for a minute then said, "Well? Are you coming with me or not?"

"What's in it for me?" I asked. "Am I on salary?"

He looked shocked, the way most men do when they meet a woman with brains. "Spoken like a real lady," he said finally. "But you're right to ask. You'll get a ticket out of here. Some new clothes. And a percentage of what I make."

"What percentage?"

"Jesus!" he said. "What are you? A banker?"

"I'm a lone woman making my own way," I answered. "I can't afford to be simple-minded."

He got up out of his chair and came to where I sat. Bending down he took my chin in his hand. "That you definitely aren't," he said. "Five percent."

"Ten."

He showed a gleam of white teeth. "Didn't your mother ever tell you greed was unbecoming in a lady?"

"We never discussed money," I answered haughtily. "But that was then. This is now. Besides, you'll find damn few ladies around willing to help you."

That pleased him. He squeezed my chin harder. "By God, a woman after my own heart. Alright. Ten percent. But you'd better be worth it."

I concealed my pleasure. "Mr. McGraw," I said, "I'm worth fifty."

Chapter Eleven

A week later we boarded a train bound for Kansas, and I caught my first glimpse of the prairie country where I would spend the next five years of my life. I caught a glimpse and I fell instantly and shamelessly in love.

I wanted to scoop it in my arms, all of it. I wanted to listen to its song and sing my own music in return. I wanted to touch and taste and smell the wind that bent the grass and twisted the branches of the few, hardy trees.

The track led straight out into the heart of it all, and around us the land rose and fell, curved against the great blue sky like the body of a woman heavy with child. Grass covered her, and flowers. Birds and rabbits fled across and over her as our iron monster approached. And once I saw a buffalo herd, one of the last, Anson explained to me as I pressed my nose against the window to stare at the huge beasts.

"But they can't kill them all!" I cried, distressed. "They're magnificent!"

"Progress, Kate," he said. "That's what they call it. Kill the buffalo, starve the Indians, use the land for farming and cattle. It will happen. It is happening. And we're a part of it."

I thought about my parents as I often did, of their hope and excitement as they went to their destruction. "Progress!" I said, bitterly. "My parents died in the name of progress."

He reached over and took my hand. "Many do," he said. "But not us, Kate. Not us."

I remembered his words later.

Wichita was a cluster of wooden buildings on a great, flat plain, both cut in two by the Arkansas River.

"That's it?" I asked in disbelief. "That's all of it?"

"Are you going to sulk?" he asked, raising an eyebrow.

"Certainly not! I'm surprised, that's all. It doesn't look like any city I ever saw."

"St. Louis looked like this once," he said. "You have to imagine." He gave me his arm and helped me onto the station platform where the noise and stink hit me like a wall.

"What...what's that smell?" I hated sounding faint-hearted, but the stink was overpowering. I held my handkerchief to my nose and peered over the top of it.

"Cattle. Buffalo hides." He pointed to the stacks of hides, to the stock pens where what seemed to be a million long-horned cattle were bawling and clacking their horns.

They looked like a sea, a restless and mottled ocean of bodies contained in a too-small space. In spite of the stench, I was fascinated.

"Imagine bringing that many cows all the way here," I

91

said. "What a job!"

"It is." He chuckled. "You're imagining already. Now let's imagine ourselves out of here and into a hotel."

"And in a tub of hot water." I was stiff from the long trip and in need of a bath.

"Most definitely."

As he spoke we were accosted by a strange-looking man with one eye and a long, tobacco-stained beard. "You'll want to put up at the Occidental," he said. "We got Brussels carpets and soft beds. And the best food in town. Just the place for fine ladies and gents."

"Can you take us and our luggage?" Anson asked, deciding, somehow, to trust him.

"Yep." He spat a stream of tobacco juice that just missed my skirt.

"No more of that, please." I drew myself up, haughty as any grande dame.

Behind his filthy whiskers he grumbled what seemed to be an apology. Then he went off after the luggage.

"Interesting fellow," Anson remarked, twinkling at my reaction. "And don't over do the lady act. He's just trying to make out like the rest of us."

"The rest of us don't spit in the street."

"This is the frontier," he said. "They do any damn thing they please in the street."

I laughed. "Anything?"

He caught my meaning. "Just about. But they stay this side of the line in Delano."

From the seat of the wagon he pointed out the layout of the town. Railroad, stockyards, saloons and dance halls on one side, Douglas Avenue, Main Street and civilization on the other. "And fortunes made on both sides," he added. "When those trail drivers get paid off, they run hog wild. Spend all their money. Most of them don't know a poker chip from a cow chip."

It sounded like fun, and I said so.

He laughed. "It depends. But as for you - you stay away from there. It's no place for decent women."

I thought I'd go anyway, on my own when he was out, just to see what it was like. After all, I was hardly a decent woman anymore.

That I'd be working there myself in a short while never occured to me. If it had, I might not have left St. Louis. Well, it's my life. I did what I had to do and made it through the years; not without scars and not without regrets, but without apologies.

Chapter Twelve

Wichita was my introduction to the West, and I could-n't have had a better one. I kept falling in love. With the racket of horses and men in the streets, the constant banging of hammers and the rasping of saws as buildings went up almost overnight, and wooden sidewalks sprang out of the mud like mushrooms.

With the raucous abandon of the inhabitants of Delano whose piano and banjo music, laughter, shouting, and gunshots could be heard across the river night and day. With the arrival of those vast herds of Texas cattle that grazed beyond the town limits and kept me awake at night with their insistent bawling, as much as the wildness of the trail hands did.

With the prairie, again and again. The immensity of it,

and how it surrounded the bustling town as if it could retake it, cover it once more with long grasses and shimmering cottonwood trees.

Anson and I drove out one afternoon to see his land. We picnicked beside the river and drove back in moonlight that poured over us like liquid silver, lighting our path as well as any lantern. It was my first experience with such a moon. I was struck silent by the absolute clarity of the night.

"Say something," Anson ordered after we'd driven several miles.

"I can't. It's too beautiful."

"I'm glad you like it." He put his free arm around me and pulled me closer.

"How could I not like it?" I asked.

"It's not for everybody. It's a hard place. Especially if you start with nothing like most of them. Women go crazy out here. Men, too."

I cuddled against him gratefully. The night was cool. "But..." I searched for the words for what I was feeling..."but it's so big it makes me feel that way, too. Like I can do anything. Like there's no limit to what I could do. Do you understand?"

"Absolutely."

I could see him smiling, the moon etching lines on his face. Suddenly I was sleepy. From fresh air, the long journey, too much emotion given out over the past months. I put my head on his shoulder.

He turned and looked down at me with something like sorrow in his eyes.

"What?" I asked him, puzzled. "What's the matter?"

"Nothing. Go to sleep. I'll wake you when we get home."

"You look sad," I persisted. "Why?"

95

He shook his head. "Not sad. Just wondering why life gives us too little, too late."

"Grab what you can," I retorted. "Otherwise you're out in the cold looking in. Isn't that what you said about making money?"

He slapped the reins, and the horse quickened its pace. "I wasn't talking about money," he said. "But go to sleep and never mind me."

I thought, suddenly, that he was thinking about proposing, and debated over what I'd say if he did. I wasn't in love with him, but he was comfortable and fun to be with, and he'd been raised a gentleman. Besides, there were plenty of women who married without love. I, however, had never pictured myself as one of them.

He didn't propose, though, and I didn't pursue the conversation. Doc was still uppermost in my mind. He always was; always will be. We were one heart in two bodies, and that's never easy. Anson and I had simply struck a bargain - one in which, ultimately, neither of us gained a thing.

By the end of that week, Anson had sold his grazeland and, at dinner one night, sealed a deal with Bill Grieffenstein for his town lots.

Grieffenstein was the man who had been there before anyone even thought of a town named Wichita. He'd operated a trading post near the junction of the two rivers, and at this point was a successful businessman bent on expanding his town holdings.

I'd eaten so much I was ready to burst. The one-eyed runner hadn't lied when he'd boasted about the hotel dining room. We'd been served turtle soup, game birds, platters of roast meat and ham, hot relishes, more vegetables than I'd ever seen, and enough cakes, ices and puddings to faze anyone.

When the last dish was cleared away, Anson leaned back in his chair and took out his cigar case, offering it to Grieffenstein.

"Do you mind, Kate?" he asked.

"Not at all." I stifled a yawn that threatened to become a belch, something no lady did ~ ever ~ in public or in private if she could help it.

Silently I cursed my corset, vowing to toss it in the river as soon as possible. Awful things they were, cutting off breath and any hope of freedom in the name of some false notion of beauty.

"If you don't mind, I'll go upstairs," I said. "Please don't disturb yourselves."

Both men stood, and Grieffenstein took my hand. "Your husband is a lucky man," he said, bowing.

Over his head, Anson winked. "I may be late, Kate," he said. "Don't worry, and don't wait up." There was a gleam in his eye I should have recognized but didn't.

I went upstairs and immediately pulled off my dress and the offending corset. Then I crawled into bed and fell asleep.

When I woke in the morning, Anson hadn't returned. My first thought was that he'd conned me and absconded with the money Griffenstein had paid him, but his clothes were still hanging in the wardrobe and the few books he carried were stacked beside the bed. A pair of cuff links lay on the bureau beside his razor and hair brush.

Outside the town was in full swing. A beam of warm sunlight found its way through the crack in the curtains. It was that which had awakened me.

Something was wrong. I knew it. I dressed quickly, fumbling over buttons with shaking fingers and pulling my hair into a simple bun over which I jammed a bonnet.

Downstairs, I went straight to the clerk at the reception desk. "Have you seen Mr. McGraw this morning?"

He looked up over spectacles that had slipped down his nose. "Why no, ma'am, I haven't. But I just came on. If you want, I'll ask around."

"Please." Instinct was shouting in my head louder and louder. "And hurry!"

He left his place and disappeared, coming back a few minutes later with the one-eyed runner.

"Zach says he saw him last night," he informed me. "What time was that, Zach?"

"When I drove him crost the river," Zach said, giving me a piercing stare out of his good eye. "He was out to double his money, he said, though I told him he shouldn't go around carryin' it on him. 'Leave it with your missus,' I told him. But he just laughed. Now you're tellin' me he aint come home. Sounds like a job fer the cops."

I didn't want anything to do with the police. "There must be something we can do," I said, my voice trembling.

"I'll go with you," Zach offered. "Best not walk around alone."

"Alright." If Anson were somewhere hurt, I'd better find out, and the quicker the better. "Let's go."

That was how I met Wyatt Earp who was the city police. He was one of the handsomest men I'd ever seen, and with the coldest blue eyes, like river ice in January. Killer eyes. And a mass of red-gold hair that he kept tossing off his forehead like a high-strung horse.

When I finished explaining about Anson, he frowned, and the ice in his eyes cracked a bit so I could see there was a person underneath after all.

"Best come with me," he said, taking my arm.

"Where are we going?"

"I don't want to scare you, Mrs. McGraw, but they found a body in the river this morning. It could be your husband."

"Does he...does he have on a striped vest?" I asked, and then prayed that the answer would be "no."

Wyatt's hold on my arm tightened. "Yes, ma'am." He pulled me back and sat me on a chair like I was a doll.

"No papers? No money?" I had to know.

"Nothing. Whoever did it took everything."

"Are you...are they...sure he's dead?"

Wyatt nodded.

I'd known it all along in my bones, the way you know such things. Without warning I began to cry. "He was a good man," I said. "He didn't deserve killing. He didn't!"

"I'm sure of that." Wyatt hesitated. "Mrs. McGraw, I hate to ask this, but we need to identify the body. Once you do that, you can arrange for burial."

"I'm not Mrs. McGraw!" I blurted the truth, foolishly, sealing my fate.

He tossed his hair out of his eyes. "Is there a Mrs. McGraw? Is there any family?"

"No. Just me. We were...traveling together."

He rubbed his jaw and stared at me with those eyes that could see right through you. "What is your name, then?"

"Kate Elder."

He stood up, not nearly as solicitous of my feelings as he had been. "Well, Kate, let's go. You'll still have to arrange for the funeral if there's nobody else."

His attitude told me plainly what I could expect as a dead man's concubine, and I cursed myself for giving it all away in a fit of hysterics.

"Do you think you can find who did it?" I asked, refusing to be daunted.

He shook his head. "It's not like we caught them in the act, but I'll see if anybody heard or saw anything. My brother works up the street from where the body was found. He might know. Or Bessie."

"Bessie?"

"His wife."

"I'd be grateful, Mr. Earp," I said. "Anson didn't deserve to die. And maybe you'll recover some of the money. It was a great deal. He'd just sold two lots, and Zach says he went over to gamble."

"He might have lost it gambling," Wyatt said.

I smiled. "Anson hardly ever lost. He probably won and somebody saw and robbed him."

"Jim will know that easy enough. But whether we can find who killed him is tough. I'll take you to see him, then I'll go see Jim."

I was feeling giddy and reached for his arm. "Let's get it over with," I said, sick at the very thought but knowing I'd do what I had to do for Anson. He'd rescued me, cared for me, probably loved me. The least I could do was give him a decent funeral. As decent as I could. Without my ten percent I was very nearly broke.

Chapter Thirteen

It was the sorriest graveyard I ever saw; just a bare piece of ground on a little rise, with the wind rushing over the scattered graves, most not even marked.

Anson had few mourners and not even a priest to pray over him. The undertaker read a psalm while Zach and I stood under a grey and threatening sky listening to the pitiful words being swept away by the passing of the wind.

When the little ceremony was over, Zach drove me back to town and waited while I bundled Anson's clothes together.

I was broke and jobless in a town where a dead gambler's mistress had no rightful place. Zach was positive he could get a few dollars from the sale of Anson's clothing, and I was desperate. I'd paid for the funeral and our hotel stay out of the money

Doc had left me, but there wasn't much more and no way to replace it.

In my search for work I'd been ushered out of the bank, the grocery stores, and the homes of women who called themselves "decent;" a quick and bitter education.

Anson's words kept repeating in my head. "A hard country if you have nothing."

He'd spoken the truth. Charity didn't exist in those towns in the early days. It was every man for himself and no room for a woman, particularly a fallen one. Those lived, died, and were buried on the wrong side of the tracks, their very existence denied by everybody.

I stood on the sidewalk watching Zach guide his horse through the mud and felt like a rag picker reduced to selling a dead man's clothes. Next I'd start on my own ~ the fur piece, the fancy gowns, the hats blooming with ostrich feathers and cloth roses. A woman in my circumstances had no use for such clothing.

And then I had to find another place to stay. The Occidental was beyond my resources. I had no place to go and no money to get there if I had.

I fought back tears. Surely I hadn't come this far and through so much adversity simply to die and be buried out on the prairie! Surely something would happen to save me!

I turned to go back to packing and sorting, then saw Wyatt Earp riding toward me on a big bay horse, a fine animal for those parts, and in spite of my troubles I stopped to admire it.

"Kate," he said, reining up in front of me.

"Mr. Earp," I said, seeing a glimmer of hope. "Have you found out anything? About who killed Anson?"

He dismounted, looped his reins over the rail, and came

up on the sidewalk beside me. Lord, he was a looker! Six feet of fighting muscle ready to strike, and those damned blue eyes. I hardly came up to his shoulders, and tilted my head to see him better.

"Not a thing," he said. "Oh, he won at the card tables. I found half a dozen witnesses. But what happened after he left is anybody's guess. Is everything alright?"

I laughed bitterly. "If being broke and homeless is 'alright,' then yes, I'm fine."

To give him his due, he wanted to help. He couldn't resist a female in trouble, a trait that often got him into more hot water than he bargained for. "What's the matter?" he asked, bending down slightly.

"Matter? I just told you. I'm broke and nobody in town wants a fallen woman around. Do you know of any jobs I could do? I'm strong. I could even sweep floors."

He continued to search my face. Finally he said, "I may be sticking my foot in it, but you could go see Bessie."

"Your sister-in-law?"

He nodded.

"What can she do?"

"She runs a dance hall. She always needs help." He looked away as he spoke.

"If you mean a brothel, why don't you say so?" I asked, aware of the euphemisms of the time.

To give him credit, he was embarrassed. "Well...." he hesitated, at a loss for an answer.

Me, Mary Katharine Haroney, a soiled dove! Me! I felt like screaming, letting anger flood the street. How dare he suggest such a thing? Then some inner voice said with a hint of scorn, "What do you call what you've been doing with Anson?" It brought me up short and I stood thinking.

Wyatt found his voice. "Look, Kate," he said, "I didn't mean to insult you, but it's not a bad place. Bessie's honest, and it beats going hungry."

He was right of course. Being alive was better than being dead, no matter what, and he knew that well.

"This is horrible," I said, and he, having enough of female vapours, turned away and spoke over his shoulder.

"Let me know what you decide."

I'd already decided, but his attitude annoyed me. I'd go to Bessie on my own with no help from him. "I will," I said. "I will."

He stepped onto the bay, tipped his hat, and rode off.

"You son of a bitch," I said to his back and immediately felt better.

Ten minutes later I was on my way across the bridge. If no one wanted my brains, my heart, my decency, I'd sell them my body. It was as simple as that. Given the choice between living and dying of starvation, I always chose living and be damned to opinion. Opinion didn't put meals on the table. Work, any kind of work, did. Besides, with the optimism of my youth I figured I wouldn't always be homeless and on the edge fighting for survival.

Finding Bessie was easy. She ran the biggest whore house on the street, and when I told her Wyatt had sent me she hired me on the spot.

"A little class is good for business," was how she put it. She looked closely at me inspecting my freshly pressed suit, the hat with the blue feather. "This your first job?"

"Yes."

"Then there's a few things you'd better get straight. Sell them whiskey first. All they want. You drink tea. And no fight-ing with the other girls. They're a good bunch, but they get onery once in awhile. And keep yourself clean. Nothing turns a man off quicker, though some of these cowboys stink so bad they can't tell the difference. Think you can handle that?"

I didn't know, but I nodded. "What do I do?" I asked. "I mean, do I say something to them or what?"

She laughed, and her little brown eyes danced in her face. "Kid, you don't have to say anything. When they come off that trail or in from the buffalo hunt they're so horny that's all they can think about. Just get them to your room before they jump you in the bar."

"And then..." It sounded awful.

"Then think about something else. Shut your eyes and let them get it off. Get their money first. Three dollars a trick. I get a third."

I was worth two dollars. If there was money to be made in a house, it wasn't the girls who were making it. Bessie read my mind.

"You won't get more anyplace else," she said. "Besides, the food's good here, and you get a cut on the drinks. And with Wyatt on the force we don't get hauled into jail near as often as the rest."

They say your life flashes through your mind before death. In that instant I saw them all: Maximillian; his dark-eyed consort; my mother and father. I heard the sound of their voices, saw the riches of our table, the elegance of fine linen, silk gowns, jewels. I remembered Silas and Blanche. And I remembered Doc.

The pain rose in my throat, but I throttled it. This job would keep me alive until I could go out and find him. I never thought of suicide like so many of the girls. What kept me going was the hope of freedom. And Doc.

"How did you come here?" I asked Bessie.

"I saved my money. If you're smart, that's what you'll do. Most of 'em spend it on booze and drugs and end up with nothing. But I've got two kids to support."

"Here?" I hoped my shock didn't show.

She shook her head. "Back East. But I want them with me. Kids need a mother. A father, too. Theirs ran off, but I've got Jim now. He cusses like a polecat, but what the hell. He's a good man."

She crossed the room and opened a drawer, pulling out a sponge on the end of a string. "Use this with vinegar," she said. "If you get pregnant anyhow, I'll do what I can."

"Like what?"

"Like get rid of it. Pregnant girls don't appeal to the customers."

"I see." And I did, indeed, see. It was a harsh world. Sordid. Unembellished. Lacking in grace or caring. I threw back my shoulders. "What room is mine?"

Bessie was a business woman, but she was also kind hearted. She looked straight into my eyes. "It's a tough life, Kate. You can live and hope, or you can die. Me, I like living."

"Me, too," I whispered. "Me, too."

"Good. You'll do. It's in your face. Now come on and see your room."

It was a board shed tacked onto the main room. There was a bed, a chair, and some hooks on the wall behind a curtain where a small table held a wash basin. The tiny window was nailed shut.

"Keep it that way," Bessie advised. "This town has more flies than people."

When she'd gone I sat on the bed and stared at the dusty, splintered floor. I'd hit bottom. From here the only way to go was up.

CHAPTER Fourteen

Women were at a premium in cattle towns. Bessie's house and all the others did a booming business from noon until the next morning.

Old and young, bearded and smooth-shaven, clean and dirty, the men, the buffalo hunters, drovers, railroad workers, entrepreneurs, came to Delano. They drank, they gambled, they bought themselves a woman and used her, sometimes in such haste they didn't even take off their clothes.

Bessie's advice to "Think about something else," was useless to me. All I could do was shut my eyes and pray I didn't scream. Selling my services to a gentleman was one thing. Taking on the world was another.

"You look peaky, kid." Bessie looked at me over the

breakfast table. I'd been at work for two weeks.

"I'm alright." I kept my eyes on my coffee cup.

The other girls, Arlette and Fannie, were wolfing down eggs, grits, and fried steak with healthy appetites.

Arlette paused, her fork in the air. "The first month ~ it is the hardest. After that..." she gave a Gallic shrug and grinned, "they're like fleas. They come. You scratch. They go."

Everyone but Bessie joined in the laughter. She thought a minute then said, "There's not near as many this year as last. And if the damned politicians move the quarantine line West of here we may as well pack up and go for all the men we'll see around this place."

"Quarantine!" The word frightened me, bringing back memories of Silas and Michael.

She read my face. "Not people. Cattle. Some sickness the Texas cattle bring with them. It seems like they're immune but the Kansas cows aren't. There's been a lot of talk but nothing done so far."

"Where will you go?"

"Wherever Jim says. He's itchy-footed like all those Earps. There's not a one of 'em can stay put for long. Always looking to strike it rich some other place."

Like me. I'd been moving as long as I could remember. Unlike the Earps, however, all I really wanted to do was stay put in a home of my own. I sighed.

Bessie gave me a sharp look. "Go out and get some air. Like I said, you look peaky."

I wasn't sick, only in a kind of daze. So much had happened I couldn't take it all in. I was grieving, and what I wanted to do was to go to sleep shutting out the noise, the filth, the thrusting bodies, the necessity to feed and clothe and care for myself. I wanted peace. It was a long time coming.

I'd just stepped out onto the hot, dusty street intending to take Bessie's advice, when a pistol shot made me duck into a doorway.

A cowboy still under the influence from the night before, stumbled out of the Keno parlor where he'd obviously slept. He had a pistol and was bent on destruction, shooting at any target that took his fancy.

There was a gun law in Delano, but somehow he'd sneaked his weapon past the police. He fired a round, chipping a hitching rail and startling a horse, and stopped to reload. No one made a move toward him, though the doors and windows of all the houses and tents were filled with observers. Then Wyatt, driving a horse and light buggy, pulled up on the corner.

"Now you'll see something." Jim had come out and was standing beside me. "Christ! That kid's got no nerves." He was smiling behind his beard and watching his younger brother who was walking up the street toward the law breaker.

"Give me the gun, kid," he said. He held out his hand.

The cowboy hesitated. He was just a youngster in over his head, but dangerous nevertheless.

Wyatt stood his ground, one hand held out, the other resting on his own pistol. "Hurry up," he said. "I don't have all day."

Even from a distance I could see his eyes. They looked like chips of blue ice. I squirmed like I was impaled on them. "Go on, kid," I murmured. "Give it to him."

Jim chuckled. "Hell. If he don't, he's dead meat."

Evidently the kid thought so, too. He handed over his pistol without a word then stared at the dusty street.

"Get him out of here," Wyatt said over his shoulder. "A day in jail and a fine'll sober him up." He turned and walked back the way he'd come, the crowd parting to let him through.

109

Within minutes Main Street was back to its business. The brass band in the Alamo Beer Hall struck up a tune, and two girls from Ida May's house came out to drum up early customers.

So far I'd avoided making friends with the riff-raff that populated Delano, and I intended to keep on like that. Most of the girls were what my Mama would have called, "Common," or worse; they were lacking in manners, refinement, or any of the kindness I'd been brought up to expect. Brawls among them were the usual way of settling a grievance. Two girls had been jailed only a week before for a fight at the race track where, cheered on by a crowd of rowdies, they tore each other's clothes to shreds.

I wanted no part of any of it, and that morning I kept my eyes on the sidewalk and headed toward the river, hoping to get out of town unnoticed.

But Stella, the bolder of the two, caught sight of me. "Hey!" she yelled, her voice rising above the din of the street. "Hey, stuckup!"

I kept walking, going faster as she crossed the street.

Her heels clattered on the boards behind me. "Hey," she shouted again. "I'm talking to you with your big nose up in the air."

Still I went on, hoping for intervention that didn't come. She grabbed my shoulder, forcing me to stop and turn around.

At her touch the same fury that had driven me to kill two me came to life. "Get your hands off me you painted whore," I said, and the words cracked like pistol shots.

She went for me, fingers curled into claws, and I tottered backwards, unprepared for the suddenness of her attack.

How quickly the crowd gathered! From the corner of my eye I saw them come ~ the salesmen, the drovers, the men on horseback, the gamblers urging us on.

I deflected Stella with one arm and kicked her in the shins. Then I went for her throat, hearing as I did someone say, "Here's fifty says Big Nose Kate'll take her."

The name stung, more so because Stella had bestowed it. It lent fuel to my anger and gave me the strength to push her against the wall of a saloon.

What I would have done I don't know because at that moment the mob quieted and Wyatt dragged us apart and held us, spitting like cats, by the backs of our dresses.

"Calm down," he said, "or you'll go to jail like Annie and Emma. Who started this?"

Stella twisted, trying to free herself. "She called me a whore," she hissed through a missing front tooth. A pity I hadn't loosened it, but it had been gone a long time.

"Call a spade a spade," I hissed back and looked up into Wyatt's unreadable eyes. "She grabbed me. I was minding my own business. Ask anybody."

"That's true enough." A man at the edge of the crowd spoke up. "I saw it. Stella went after Big Nose Kate from behind."

Wyatt gave both of us a shake. "Alright, Kate," he said. "Go on about your business. And you..." he turned to the still wriggling Stella, "you go on back to Ida's. Any more trouble and you'll end up in jail with a fine to pay. Understand?"

She didn't answer, only wrenched herself loose and sauntered across the street swaying her hips and setting her hat straight as she went.

I did the same, thanking God my dress hadn't gotten ripped. Then I looked back at Wyatt wondering what he must think of me. "I'm sorry," I said. "I've never done such a thing in my life." God knew that was true! Brawling in the streets like

111

a hussy!

"Just don't do it again," he said. "You girls are more trouble than a herd of Texans."

To him I was a whore. It hurt. "I'm not like that," I told him, unable to meet his eyes for the shame of it.

He shrugged. "We do what we have to," he said. "Don't apologize." Then he turned on his heel and left.

Cottonwoods shaded the riverbank, and the coolness was welcome after the shimmer of midsummer heat. I unbuttoned my blouse at the neck and took off my bonnet, enjoying the breeze and the solitude.

Living at Bessie's was, in a way, like being back at the convent, though the nuns would have fainted at the comparison. We were a company of women with all the jealousies, complaints, and quarrels of a bunch of school girls forced together, unable to break free.

Now as I walked I listened to the quiet, and I heard the prairie singing its sweet music that tugged at my heart. The song of larks, the murmur of the river, low but humming between the banks, among the roots of cottonwoods and willows, the rustle of grass like the sound of silken skirts, all comforted yet filled me with a terrible longing.

I had made a shambles of my life and I could not go back and redo, only go forward hoping. For what? For love, and life, and decency. For laughter. Above all for that. I had not laughed in what seemed like years. There had been no reason for it.

Sighing, I sat, propping my back against a tree and looking upward through the pattering leaves to a hard, blue sky. From far away came the wonderful, steady, driving sound of a horse trotting, and I squinted down the trail that followed the river.

The horse came on ~ an iron grey with a beautiful head

~ and I recognized Wyatt handling the lines with great skill.

He pulled up beside me, and the grey dropped its head and began to graze.

"I thought I told you to stay out of trouble," he said, unsmiling.

Good looking or not, or maybe because of that, he was impossible!

"I'm not in trouble." I planted my feet firmly. "All I did was go for a walk on Bessie's orders."

"Then you both need your heads examined." He wound the reins around the whip socket and stepped down. "Out here is as dangerous as in town. It's crawling with snakes - rattlers and the two-legged kind."

"I have a gun." I patted the derringer, courtesy of Anson, that I carried in my pocket.

"And I suppose you know how to use it."

Little did he know! "Of course." I smiled sweetly. He was as deadly as a snake himself. Playing with him was asking for trouble. "My papa taught me when I was little." And he had. Without knowing to what use I'd put those lessons.

I decided to move the conversation to safer ground and walked over to the grey. "This is a fine horse," I said, stroking its muscled neck.

Wyatt crossed his arms and leaned against the side of the buggy. "And how do you know that?" His expression indicated that he thought me ridiculous.

I'd show him! I walked around the animal touching, looking. "Good shoulders. There's speed there. And in those hind legs. Driving power. Deep chested. And..." I twinkled, "hard mouthed."

He stared. "Now how can you tell that?"

"You had trouble pulling him in. He drops his jaw and

gets around the bit. You ought to change it. Give him something to think about." My fingers itched to take the reins and drive myself. "Can I drive?" I asked.

He laughed. "This isn't a livery stable hack. He'd eat you up," he said.

"I doubt it."

"Did your papa teach you to drive, too?" Again there was that tinge of arrogance in his voice.

He was detestable! "Yes," I said. "He did." And I scrambled up on the seat before he could stop me.

He grabbed my hands. "I told you no, and I meant no," he said. "I've got him entered in a race, and I want him in one piece."

"Then take me for a drive. Please?"

He nodded once. "Alright. But behave yourself and sit tight."

How that man could handle a horse! My respect for him grew as we headed across the prairie, the horse moving like a machine, never slowing, never breaking from that long, reaching trot.

When we finally circled and headed back to town I said, "You'll win. You're good."

One corner of his mouth twitched. "Thanks."

"Where'd you learn?"

He shrugged. "I've been around horses all my life. I like them. They like me. I was driving freight before I was twenty. And when my folks went to California I went along. I learned as I went."

"Now can I try?" I was determined.

"Oh, for God's sake, Kate. He'll pull your arms loose. You're the one said he's hard mouthed."

"But you'll be here to help."

He sighed. "Alright. But keep him to a walk."

He watched as I took the reins, slipping them through my fingers and across my palms, feeling along their length for the horse's mouth. He watched as I became five years old and fearless, though my papa's words rang in my ears. "Driving is more dangerous than riding, Katya. You aren't a part of your horse back here. You can't feel him except through your hands, so be alert always. Think with your fingers. Watch everything with those bright eyes."

It came back in a rush, all of it. The day, the graveled drive in front of the house, the chestnut pony, and the lesson in the language I thought I'd forgotten.

"Good horse," I called in Magyar. "Walk out now and don't disgrace me with this lout who calls himself your master." And the horse lifted his head, flicked back an ear and walked on proudly.

"What was that? What did you say?" Wyatt was staring at me as if he hadn't seen me before.

"Horse talk," I said. "I put a spell on him. Told him to win his race. Now be quiet and let me get the feel of him." I chuckled at how I was able to say that and make Wyatt obey just like the horse.

Then I tightened the lines and asked for more speed, and got it - that reaching trot that reduced the prairie to a golden blur.

"Kate! Bring him down! You promised!"

But I hadn't. He only assumed I had. Ahead of us Wichita huddled on a roll of the prairie, a cluster of shacks, tents, stockyards. It looked insubstantial, like a mirage that would vanish as we drove through.

"Damn it, Kate!" His long-fingered hands covered mine, took the reins, and pulled back into a walk.

"You didn't have to do that," I said. "I had him."

115

He let out a long breath. "Next time do what I tell you."

So there would be a next time. My heart gave a bump, and I put my hand to my throat to cover the fluttering pulse. He was domineering and cool to the point of iciness, but there was something in the way he looked, in the feel of his hands over mine that spoke of vulnerability. I smiled up at him. "I promise," I whispered. "Cross my heart."

CHAPTER Fifteen

Bessie was different from most madams. True to her word, she looked after her girls, fed us well, made sure we stayed healthy to the best of her ability. Unlike many, she refused to exercise psychological control over us. We had our freedom as long as we worked during business hours and stayed out of trouble.

When I got back she took a look at me and said, "You look better, kid. Now grab a bite and get ready for business."

I took a slice of dried apple pie and went to my room where I slipped out of my street clothes and into a loose satin wrapper. Then I rouged my cheeks, darkened my lashes, inserted the hateful vinegar-soaked sponge, and went out to the water barrel to fill the pitcher that would be empty before the night was half over.

While I was dipping from the barrel, I heard Jim's voice on the other side of the wall.

"You got a woman," he was saying. "You trying for a harem or something?"

And I swore it was Wyatt who answered. "This one's different."

Jim chuckled. "They're all the same naked."

Then the sound of their footsteps drowned the rest of the conversation.

I stood still in the dark. Was I the one under discussion? And what had Jim meant when he said, "You already got a woman?"

As far as I knew Wyatt was a loner. He slept on a cot in the jail and picked up a meal wherever he could, sometimes at the Keno Palace where he called Keno, sometimes in Bessie's kitchen. I'd never seen him with a woman.

I was so lost in thought I overfilled the pitcher and water sloshed on my red slippers. Well, I'd have to ask. If I got the chance. Maybe I'd even ask Wyatt, though those icy eyes didn't exactly give rise to questioning.

But we got busy that night and stayed busy, and the servicing of dozens of randy customers drove curiosity out of my head. As Arlette and Bessie had said, I became two people: on the outside Big Nose Kate, for the hated nickname stuck; on the inside Mary Katharine Haroney who had known the sweetness of real passion and whom I protected at all costs.

When Wyatt stopped by on his rounds that Thursday evening and asked if I'd like to accompany him on a final training run, I simply asked Bessie for time off and agreed to be ready the following day.

The others were more excited than I. They clustered

118

around me offering me their gloves, their bonnets, their precious scarves to wear while I was out.

"So handsome, that one. I'd do him for free," Arlette said, rolling her eyes. "I'd even do him like you do instead of playing his flute."

Arlette's specialty, in demand by many, was sex in the French manner, an act which held less appeal for me than the regular way.

"I don't 'do' him at all," I reminded her. "What he wants is somebody to help drive his horse."

She smiled wickedly. "Ah, oui, oui. What he wants, cherie, is to ride yours."

"Argue all you want," Bessie put in. "Just don't get in over your head with him. Not that I'm sticking my nose in your business," she added after I looked at her in irritation.

"It seems everybody around here has their nose in my business," I said.

Bessie shook her head till her curls danced. "All I meant was, he's not worth breaking your heart over."

Unconcerned about yet another heartbreak, I pinned on my hat. "Don't worry," I said over my shoulder. "I'll be fine."

"If I had a dime for every time I heard that one, I'd be rich," Bessie remarked.

"You've got a dollar for every trick I've turned this last month. You're rich enough as it is." I laughed, thinking of the money locked in my trunk. My grubstake steadily growing. My ticket out when I knew where I was headed.

Then Wyatt pulled up outside and I left the room, putting Bessie's concern out of my head.

He was driving a light carriage with room for only the two of us. He helped me in, then turned expertly and headed South out of town.

119

"Where are we going?"

"We'll follow the river for about ten miles. I want to work him hard today then rest him till Sunday. You've got good hands, and I took your advice and got a different bit. I want you to bring him back."

"Good hands," indeed! I wanted to say, "I told you so," but simply smiled.

We drove in three mile heats, resting in between each one. "It's the way the race will be," Wyatt explained. "Three two-mile heats, best two takes it. I want to go three miles today so he won't be looking for the finish during the race."

The grey hardly worked up a sweat. He was doing what he'd been born to do, and seemed to grow more powerful with every mile.

"Where'd you get him?" I asked when we'd pulled up beside a cottonwood. "You don't see horses like this too often."

"I won him in a card game." Wyatt's face was expressionless. I thought he was joking.

"You didn't!"

"I did. You don't think I could afford a horse like this on a policeman's salary, do you?"

"What luck," I said.

"Not luck. Jim taught me all I know about cards. I knew what I was doing."

I'd seen Jim at work out front at Bessie's. He was one of the best. "Why be a policeman at all? You could make a better living gambling."

He picked up the reins. "I do both," he said, matter of factly. "I'm just as good with a gun."

Ignorant as I was, I didn't know then how good.

We pulled up after the final heat and Wyatt helped me out then tied the horse loosely.

"Let him blow awhile. He's earned it," he said.

I was already headed toward the river, entranced by prairie billowing around me and the coolness of the water. I stopped to take a deep breath of the pure air, so unlike Wichita's stock yards and buffalo hides. I looked up at the sky, brilliant blue and ringed by thunderheads, and I remembered a game I'd played as a child where we'd spin in a circle as fast as we could until we were dizzy and fell into the grass, the world whirling around us. I held out my arms and began to dance.

Wyatt said, "Steady, Kate. You're as bad as the horse."

"You don't know what it's like to be out here. Free." I kept dancing even when my hat fell off and my hair blew loose from its knot. Even when Wyatt slipped his hand around my waist and led off in a waltz.

I opened my eyes and stared at him in astonishment. He was smiling, and his eyes had lost their usual frosty look. His hair blew across his forehead, and he tossed it off with that swift, habitual motion. No doubt of it. He was handsome. And he smelled clean, like new hay, like the grasses crushed under our feet. I threw Bessie's caution to the wind and moved closer, saying nothing, letting my body speak for me.

He picked me up and carried me into the dappled shade, and I held to him fiercely, listening to his heart beat under the blue cloth of his shirt, to the sound of his breathing, quick in my ear.

What did heartbreak have to do with this prairie music, with the first man since Anson who had looked at me as a woman, not simply as an object paid to receive lust? I ran my fingers through that lion's mane of red gold hair, and lifted my face to his. The rest followed swiftly, tinged with something like desperation, as if each of us had second sight and knew that this, too, would pass.

I thought he called out a name, an unfamiliar one, but I couldn't be sure. Later, lying side by side in the thick grass, my curiosity got the better of me.

"Who's Rilla?" I asked, tracing his cheekbone with one finger.

He looked startled. "Who told you about her?"

"You did. You called her a few minutes ago."

"God, Kate, I'm sorry. I didn't mean..."

"I know you didn't. I was just curious."

"Rilla was my wife. She's dead. She died having my son, and I wasn't even there. They're both buried back in Missouri."

"Now I'm sorry," I said. "For reminding you."

A corner of his mouth twisted in a bitter smile. "You didn't know. Besides, you remind me of her. You have that honey-colored hair."

And he, as a young man had buried his face in it, as he'd done with mine. Had called out her name. Rilla. There was so much sorrow in the world. Wyatt with his memories. Doc with his broken dreams and diseased lungs. Me with my loneliness. Was everyone like us? I wondered. Did everyone wander the earth looking for solace?

I reached out for him, and he came to me and, as I knew he would, ran his fingers through my hair.

The sun was far to the West. Around us the land bloomed like a huge flower in the long rays. I sat up. "Bessie won't like me being late."

"I'll take care of Bessie."

"Did you ever find out anything about who killed Anson?" I asked as I scrambled up on the buggy seat.

"No. And I'm sorry about that, too."

"You can't help it. I just remembered how he told me

122

once that this country eats people for breakfast. But it's so beautiful that's hard to understand."

He didn't answer for a minute. Then he said, "The ones who can't handle it get buried." His hand came down over mine. "Pull him in. He's eager to get home."

I wasn't. No matter how well we were treated, Bessie's place wasn't home.

We heard the shouts and shooting while we were still a mile out of town.

"Give me the reins!" Wyatt reached over.

I shrugged him off. "You better be ready to take care of whatever it is. Sit tight."

Off we went, arriving in the midst of one of Delano's favorite pastimes. Several of the girls were running a race dressed only in boots and ribbons. They were headed toward the river neck and neck amidst shouts of pleasure and the cracking of whips.

I pulled up. "What're you going to do?"

"Nothing. Unless a fight starts. A dollar says Lizzie wins."

I stared at him. "You're as bad as Jim. He'll bet on anything."

"I back my hunches."

"And I save my money. Such as it is."

"What for? Most of you girls spend it as fast as you get it."

If he tried, he couldn't have hurt or insulted me more.

I threw the reins at him and jumped out. "Go to hell," I yelled, not caring who heard me. "Go to hell and stay there!"

Once inside I tore off my hat and my clothes and washed myself in a fury. But I couldn't wash away the memory of Wyatt's face and the hunger in his eyes.

CHAPTER Sixteen

"**A**re you sure you won't come to the track?" Bessie stopped by my room for the tenth time.

"No thanks. I'll just keep an eye on things here," I said. "You have a good time and don't forget my bet." Regardless of how I felt about Wyatt, I knew his horse for a winner. Maybe I was one of those women who picked good horses but couldn't pick a man to save themselves. The thought was bitter.

"I will," she said. "I haven't had a day off in a year."

She bustled out, taking Arlette and Fannie with her and leaving me with Hurley the bartender to mind the store.

I did a laundry and hung it in the tiny back yard, praying a dust storm wouldn't blow up before the lace on my petticoat was dry. Then I wandered back inside.

Business was slow. It was a Sunday morning, and those who hadn't gone to hear the preacher set up in a tent in an empty lot had gone to the track. Flies buzzed. Heat waves danced at the open door.

"Pour me a whiskey," I said to Hurley who looked disapprovingly at me.

He had a voice like a rusty wheel and prize fighter's arms. "Now, Kate, you know you gals ain't supposed to drink this stuff."

I threw a coin on the bar. "There's my money. Now shut up and pour me one. And no water in it, mind you."

He did as he was told, then poured one for himself.

"Cheat," I said to him, grinning. Then I wandered to a table, sat down, shuffled the cards, and, without thinking, dealt myself five.

I was studying them ~ a pair of red queens, a pair of red kings, and the ten of clubs ~ when a figure in the door blotted out the sunlight.

"Come on in," I invited. "We're open."

Then I realized that the figure belonged to a woman, and that she had the reddest hair I'd ever seen. It sprang from her head like fire, and when she walked into the dim interior, she brought that fire along.

"Where's Bessie?" she asked without preamble.

Close up she wasn't beautiful. With that mane of hers she didn't need to be.

"At the track. I'm minding the store. Can I help you?"

She shook her head and her curls moved, flickered with a life of their own. "I'll wait."

"Suit yourself." I went back to the cards, wondering what Blanche would have made of them.

She walked around looking at the pictures above the bar,

at herself in the beveled glass mirror that was Bessie's pride and joy. Her heels clicked on the floor sharply, like a hammer. Finally she came and stood over me, so close I could smell her - sweat and dust, a long road travelled.

"Who are you?" she asked.

It was the wrong question. I laid the cards, face down, on the table. "Who are you?" I countered, looking into her eyes.

They were sad eyes, grey, with shadows in them. They made me uncomfortable.

"Celie Ann," she said. "They call me Mattie. I've come to work."

"Oh," I said, assuming she had worked for Bessie in the past and deciding to play hostess. "Would you like something to drink? A glass of water? Some lemonade while you're waiting?"

"I'll have what you're having." She gestured at the whiskey.

"I paid for this," I said. "It's Jim's good stuff."

She smiled. "Jim won't care. Not if it's me. Wyatt's my man."

How far away everything seemed! The flies, the heat, the brilliant rectangle of doorway; and the woman who called herself Mattie. I took a deep breath, steadying myself.

"Your man?" I hoped my voice didn't betray me.

"Yeah." She lifted the glass. "Cheers," she said and tossed off the contents like water. Then she held it out for a refill.

Hurley poured, grumbling. "There'll be hell to pay if you ain't who you say."

"Oh, I am alright. Mattie Earp come to the big city from that no good farm he stuck me on."

"Does he expect you?" I asked.

"Nope!" She plunked herself down across from me. "I thought I'd surprise him."

"You will." And I intended to be there to see the reunion. The wife named Rilla might be dead and buried, but this one was very much alive. All the hurt came back. Even the memory of our love making was tarnished by the appearance of this creature who said he was "her man." An awful term. Possessive. Denigrating. Almost as bad as my having been used.

My heart wasn't broken, but my pride had suffered a second great blow. I squirmed in my chair wanting to get away, to be by myself where it didn't matter if my feelings showed on my face.

"You don't look too happy to see me, either," Mattie said. "Guess he's been after you, too."

"That's none of your business."

"It is, too. Stuck with those old folks while he's down here chasing every skirt in the place." She had a dusting of freckles across her nose that darkened as she spoke.

"I don't ask if they're married when they come in here," I said. "That's not my business, either."

"Don't I know it!" Her mouth twisted. "I wasn't blaming you. It's him. He said he'd send for me. I waited and waited, and then I couldn't stand it!" She slammed her glass down so hard the contents slopped over.

She loved him. That was plain. A new emotion rose up and complicated the others. God knew I'd loved and been thwarted enough times.

"I'm sorry," I told her. "Really."

But Mattie was always prickly. It went with that hair and that stubborn jaw. "Don't waste your time," she said.

She stood and shook out her skirts. "I'm going for a

walk. See what the town has to offer."

"Plenty. Watch your step," I said. "If you don't, Wyatt might haul you into the jail." I managed a smile which stayed until my face started to ache, until Mattie had stepped back into the light and sauntered off down the sun-blasted street.

CHAPTER Seventeen

I heard them coming all the way across the bridge. They were shouting and laughing, and Jim was cussing the way only he could.

"That son of a bitch! That son of a bitch is faster'n hell! By Christ, Wyatt, you did yourself proud!"

The horse had won, as I knew it would. And the money I'd asked Bessie to bet would have tripled. Soon I'd be out of here, and Wyatt could have his woman, for all the good it would do him.

They came in all at once, a noisy, happy bunch. Bessie dropped a sack in my hands. "A hundred bucks, kid," she said, the plume on her hat wobbling. "You're rich."

"A hundred!"

"Yeah. He went off at ten to one, the damn fools. Think they'd never laid eyes on a real horse before."

"Maybe they never did."

"All you need is a pair of eyes," she said. "Same with people. You can tell by looking."

Well, I'd looked at Mattie and figured Wyatt had his hands full. I opened my mouth to announce her arrival.

Wyatt grabbed my waist. "Your spell worked. Took two heats in a row and set a record."

"I told you, didn't I?" I said.

"You did. And I sold him to a fellow from back East who wants to take him on the circuit. Made a bundle."

"You'll need it."

"Why?"

"Because your wife's here looking for you."

If I'd punched him in the stomach he couldn't have been more stunned. "Mattie?" he said finally. "Here?"

"Somewhere. She went out awhile ago to see what the town had to offer." I couldn't keep the bitterness out of my voice.

He turned on his heel and went out, leaving Jim staring after. "What was that about?" he asked me.

"His wife's looking for him."

Jim's reaction was the same as Wyatt's. "Mattie?"

"That's what she said."

"Oh, Christ," he muttered. "Now we'll never have any peace."

Having already seen Mattie, I believed him. I left him to put my winnings in my trunk. Nearly two hundred dollars. Nearly enough.

•

It seemed that with Mattie's arrival all hell broke loose. Close on her heels came the grasshoppers, billions of them. They blackened the sky, ate everything in sight, fouled the water, and our tempers, too. They appeared in our beds, on our plates, littered the streets with their brittle, ugly bodies, chewed through our clothes hung out to dry, and made life impossible.

The roads were clogged with farmers who had lost their crops and their homesteads to the invasion. Beaten, they hung their heads and slogged back to where they felt they'd always belonged, their wives and children plodding behind like dogs.

The rains held off. The heat worsened. The town stank like an open sewer, and out on the prairie the waiting herds drifted and bawled out of hunger, for the locusts had left them nothing to eat.

"Like in the Bible," Bessie said. "What do you think we done wrong?"

"Everything," I answered. "Every goddamned thing."

"Sure seems like it." She stopped to listen as Mattie's voice rose in a whine. "And if that girl don't stop complaining, I'm going to put her out, family or no family."

The question had been on my mind since Mattie had come to work and Wyatt had made himself scarce. "What's she doing working here if she wants Wyatt so bad?"

"Can't teach an old whore new tricks. No joke meant. She thinks she'll make him jealous."

"It won't work."

"Course not, but she don't know that. She loves him, and he took her out of a house in Fort Scott the first time."

I knew that girls often married and left the brothel behind, but for the life of me, I couldn't see Wyatt with Mattie. "Why?" I asked. "They're such a mismatch."

"Back then you couldn't tell him that. He was grieving,

131

and there was Mattie like a stray kitten with its claws tucked in. All big eyed and scrawny, and so damned hungry. They both were. So..." she raised her hands. "Now they're stuck with each other, and neither of 'em'll admit the mistake. Both bull headed."

I still felt a twinge of pity for Mattie, fighting with all that she had. It wasn't much, but she'd given her heart away and was set on getting it back.

Bessie eyed me across the table. "Guess he got to you, too. I warned you, didn't I?"

"My heart's not broken."

"Lucky for you. Keep it that way."

"Sure," I said. "Don't worry."

But the memory of that afternoon on the prairie couldn't be banished. I thought about it often. Sometimes while I was working I closed my eyes and turned the man into Wyatt, the miserable, closed-up room into a thousand miles of rolling country. Sometimes it even helped.

CHAPTER Eighteen

Abel Cochran had been at Bessie's three nights running, and every one of those nights he'd spent with me, talking mostly about himself but asking me questions as well. When he did come to my room, he was polite, quick, and passionless, which in its way was a relief. Nothing was as dreadful as faked passion. I knew the difference.

Abel was older than most of the Texas cowboys, a rancher who'd come North with his own herd for the adventure and to oversee the selling. He was lean, with greying hair, and an amazing smile made eye-catching by four gold front teeth that glittered even in Bessie's smoke-filled front room. And Abel was wealthy, owning a big spread somewhere in West Texas, a ranch so big it took three days to ride the boundary. At least that's what he told me, his eyes gleaming, his voice caressing not me but the vastness of his empire.

"It'd make your head spin to see it, little lady," he said, "and that's the truth."

"That one is wife hunting," Arlette said.

"Here?"

"Of course here. Where else could he have such a choice? You could be rich, if you play the right cards," she added. "And nevaire say where you come from."

This advice came after Cochran had purchased me for an entire evening, paying Bessie fifty dollars for the privilege. He was taking me to supper and to see a melodrama performed by a traveling group out of St. Louis. Everyone expected that, by the end of the evening, he would propose.

"He knows class when he sees it, kid. Same as me," Bessie said.

"We'll have a big party. Dance all night maybe," said Arlette.

Only Fannie and Mattie were diffident, Fannie because she was dull-witted, and Mattie probably because she'd imagined a life of riches for herself and Wyatt but was as far from her goal as she'd been at the start.

Her grey eyes lingered on my garnets, hungrily, I thought. Then she said, "What good's money stuck on a ranch where you can't spend it?"

They were all jumping the gun. I had no intentions of marrying Abel. But my share of fifty dollars would add to my grubstake. Besides, an evening on the town with a gentleman was an event to look forward to, and at the end of it we would at least be surrounded with the luxury of the Occidental ~ a soft bed, starched sheets, and plenty of soap and water.

"Wishful thinking," I told them. "He's leaving for Texas

in a few days."

"Hell," said Bessie. "He can always exchange his ticket. Or get you one."

As usual, they were correct in their predictions. Abel, never one to mince words, proposed over the supper table.

"I'm headed home day after tomorrow," he said. "And I'd be pleased if you'd come with me." He never took his eyes off me, simply made his speech and then waited for my answer.

"But..." I began.

"As my wife, of course." He leaned back in his chair. "I've told you about my place. It's big and it needs a woman in it to make it home. You're a real lady. And we do get along."

"Accept!" my mind urged.

"No!" countered my heart.

Despite the past three nights, we were strangers. Perhaps we always would be. Married, I'd be free of Bessie's, wealthy, respected, and probably lonelier than even Abel was.

"We do get along," he'd said, sounding like a pale imitation of Silas. But he wasn't Silas, and I wasn't the foolish young thing I'd been then. Living had turned me cynical. And for better or worse, Doc still had my heart.

"I don't know what to say." I used the tried and true words of all women caught short and stalling for time. "I just...I can't think."

He tried a different approach. "You'd like it, Kate. It's a fine life, and I have fine neighbors. Why, there's even a minister riding the circuit. And I'm near to Griffin. Lots of goings on there for the ladies. There's a hotel, stores, good doctors, even a dentist." He smiled and those gold teeth flashed at me.

In the midst of my dilemma I fastened on the one word that meant something to me. "A dentist!" I said.

Abel beamed. "Yep. Southerner come out for his lungs.

135

Fixed these teeth just before I left."

"Who?" I whispered. "Dear God, who?"

He looked at me puzzled, then understood. "Calls himself Holliday. Gambles mostly. But he'll fix teeth any time you need."

I think I said, "Doc." My heart did. Loud in my ears like the rushing of blood. I buried my face in my hands to hide my tears, and frightened Abel who jumped up and came to my side.

"Now don't cry, little lady. I didn't mean to upset you. I just thought we'd suit. I know we would."

I drew a deep breath and looked up. "You're very kind. And I'm honored. But...I just...."

"Say yes!" my head interrupted.

And again came the cry of my heart. "Doc!"

Recklessly I listened and suddenly saw the way. I smiled through my tears and uttered the fateful words. "Abel, I'm confused. I can't seem to think. Perhaps, if it's alright, I'll go with you to this place...this Griffin. We'll get to know each other on the way and maybe, when we get there, I'll know what I'm doing."

I held out my hands to him and waited, reading his thoughts as if his eyes were glass. He'd have me to himself for the duration, plenty of time to court me, to plead his case, to turn gratitude and confusion into what passed for love.

As usual he was direct. "I'd be honored to have you," he said. "How soon can you leave?"

CHAPTER Nineteen

We were four days out of Wichita headed South. I'd been jounced, jolted, strangled by dust, bitten by insects; drunk enough bitter coffee, eaten enough stew fit only for hogs to discourage anyone. Except I wasn't discouraged. I was having the time of my life.

Doc was waiting at the end of the trail. To get there I'd have stripped naked and run the distance and never mind the heat, the dust, the threat of Indians or the drama I'd left behind me.

No sooner had I announced to Bessie that I was leaving than my garnet necklace, the only thing of my mama's that I had left, disappeared. I searched my half-packed trunk, the pockets of my dresses, even the toes of my shoes.

"How could I have lost it?" I asked myself, standing in the midst of my belongings. I was sure I'd taken it off and put it in my small jewel case when I returned with Abel. Nearly in tears, I went to Bessie who helped me look.

"It isn't here, and that's a fact," she said finally, surveying the piles of clothing waiting to be folded and packed. "If I didn't know better, I'd say one of those girls got light-fingered."

I remembered how Mattie had looked the night before - envious, picturing herself in my finery. "I'll be right back," I said and went out and down the narrow corridor to Mattie's room.

Respectful of her privacy in spite of my suspicions, I knocked. When no one answered, I pushed open the door and went straight to the small chest against the wall and began searching the drawers.

There was pitifully little in any of them. A few pairs of much-repaired stockings, some plain petticoats, frayed and darned, a pile of ribbons and worn handkerchiefs, and a shawl rolled up in one corner of the third drawer. The poor creature had hardly a feather to fly with. No wonder she acted so spiteful at times! She'd come for her man and instead was reduced to poverty. Dear God, we were all so small, so helpless!

I was chastizing myself for my suspicions and was closing the drawer when the shawl rolled open revealing my necklace. I had it in my hands when she came in; no chance to give either of us a polite way out. Not with Mattie. Never with Mattie.

She was on the attack, guiltily but still fearsome, her red hair framing her face like a fire. "Who said you could come in here?"

I turned to meet her head on. "Nobody. I came for this." I held out the necklace.

"I found it! You must've dropped it out front. I was going to give it back when I saw you. You have no right coming in here and snooping. No right!" Her voice rose until I was sure they could hear her out on the street.

"Yes," I said. "Or I'd have missed it once I got to Texas." I wasn't going to be forced into a fight, but I wasn't going to let her off easy.

"I didn't steal it!"

"I didn't say you did."

"That's what you meant, Miss High and Mighty. Just because you caught yourself a rich man. Just because you're getting out of here!" She picked up a chair and threw it at me.

I ducked into the hall but she followed, tears of rage streaming down her cheeks. We were in the saloon when Bessie accosted us. "What the hell?" she yelled, loud enough to be heard.

I dangled the necklace for her to see, and Mattie, taking advantage, pushed me through the doors and out onto the street where the brawl continued until Wyatt stepped in and forcefully separated us.

"Get back inside," he said, his voice cold as a knife.

There was no arguing with him. He'd as soon slapped both of us unconscious from the sound of him. I did as I was told, but Mattie protested.

"She...."

"Shut up! Do what I tell you."

He pushed her in and came behind her. "As if there's not enough trouble in this town, my own family has to take up street fighting!" He looked like a young Apollo standing there, disgust, anger written in every muscle and bone.

Mattie seemed not to notice. She never did notice other's emotions, which led, ultimately, to her downfall. "She..."

139

she began again, only to be cut off.

"Get her out of here. She's disgusting." He jerked his head at Bessie who put an arm around Mattie's waist.

"I'm not! And you can't just get rid of me like that. You can't, you son of a bitch!" Her voice rose until it cracked. "Just shove me in a corner like I'm a nobody. Like you stuck me on that goddamned farm with your goddamned parents!"

Bessie yanked at her arms. "Come on, kid. Calm down. Nobody's getting rid of you."

Mattie burst into tears. "That's what you would say. You and all the rest of them." But she allowed herself to be led away.

Wyatt and I looked at each other, as adversaries not as the lovers we'd been. But when he spoke, his words surprised me.

"I heard you're leaving."

"Yes."

"Why?"

"You ought to be able to figure that one out."

He put his hands around my waist. "Don't go, Kate."

The whole scene was ridiculous. "What about your wife?" I asked. "You can't just ignore her and hope she disappears."

"Didn't you ever make a mistake?" He shook me as if to force an answer.

Foolish question! My whole life had been a mistake. But he needed to be told, and I told him, putting the memory of our love-making far behind me.

"Every day. But you have to face up to mistakes, not pretend they're not there. And that's what I'm doing. I'm leaving. There's a man I love, and I'm going to him. That may be another mistake, but by God, I'll do it and then worry." I sidestepped, freeing myself from his hands. "What happened with you and me is over. Done. No sense crying about what could have been. You have a wife. Another wife. Make it right with her."

"She's not my wife."

I laughed. Fearless he might be around men and horses, but he couldn't handle his problems with women. "The law says she is. You're a law man. You figure it out. Now I've got to get packed. I'm leaving on the stage tomorrow. And you can't stop me, so don't try."

"Kate..." he said, trying anyhow.

I hardened my heart. "Go comfort your wife," I said. "God knows she needs it. And you might start by buying her some decent underclothes."

I left him standing there ~ that young god, that stud horse, that evil star who would shine on the happiest and most wretched years of my life.

•

Abel leaned across the aisle and patted my knee. He'd opted to face backwards, giving me the seat opposite, another example of what was an ingrained politeness.

"You alright?"

"Yes."

"You look a mite pale. Not sick are you?"

"No," I said. In truth, I'd never felt better. "Where are we do you think?"

He glanced out. "Middle of Indian Territory, but no cause for alarm. MacKenzie wiped them out last winter at Palo Duro. Most of 'em are on the reservation or headed that way. Oh, there's still some renegades, bands that won't quit, but it's nowhere near like it was. My place is safe enough."

I followed his gaze out the window to the land so vast I

couldn't take it in. A golden land, rippling toward a horizon that was, probably, two days distant. Shamelessly I wanted it, coveted Abel's ranch and its far-flung boundaries. How did it feel, I wondered, to look out and out and know that all you saw was yours? Even the sky, its violent storms and tumultuous sunsets. Even the dawn that broke in sea waves of light.

For one moment, that lasted longer than any moment should, I was torn in half by my longing for possession of a piece of the country. For generations my family had lived close to the land, the seasons, the harvests of the sweet soil. This was in me, rooted deep like one of those desert trees that draw water from the bowels of earth.

For one moment I was tempted. I could reach out, take Abel's hand and say, "Yes. I will marry you. For your ranch, your cattle. Your rivers and sky." And I could turn my back on joining with the other part of my soul.

And then, looking, I thought that, given luck, in a country as vast as this one was,there would be another place, another time, and that Doc and I together could possess it. So the moment, the temptation passed, and I said to Abel, "What is this 'Palo Duro?' This 'hard wood'?"

He explained. Listening, I imagined it. A great rift in the level plain; a canyon a thousand feet deep, red-walled, magnificent, covered with the cedar trees that had given it its name. I closed my eyes and, in spite of the coach's bouncing, slept.

CHAPTER Twenty

A dead man was hanging from a tree outside the hotel when I came down for breakfast my first morning in Griffin.

The sight of the body, swaying gently, the face stiffened in a final snarl, stopped me in my tracks.

"Dear God!" I exclaimed, reaching for Abel's hand. "What...what's happening?"

He frowned at the grisly vision. "I should've warned you," he said. "Sometimes the vigilance committee takes the law into its own hands."

Aunt Hank, the Occidental Hotel's proprietress, laughed, a hearty sound that bounced off the ceiling. "A dead man for breakfast every morning!" she boomed. "That's Griffin's motto. But there's lots of good things happening, too. You'll get used to it all if you're here long enough!"

I didn't think I'd ever get used to it, and took my seat at he table so my back was to the swinging body and to the buzzards that were gathering overhead.

It would have suited me better to look out and get my bearings. All I'd seen the evening before was the bluff where the Fort was built, overlooking the town and the plains to the South, East and West, and the street called The Flat that ran along the banks of the Clear Fork; the street of shacks, tents, and hastily put together structures that was the heart and soul of all the vice in Griffin. It was in one of the gambling houses that I knew I'd find Doc if I could get away from Abel long enough to go look for him.

But the hanged man had ruined my appetite, for breakfast and for sight-seeing. I sipped coffee and watched Abel dig into steak, eggs, fried potatoes as if the body outside was no more to him than death from old age.

So I was the first to see Doc cross the small lobby and enter the dining room, his hat in his hand, his blond hair gleaming in the morning light.

My cup crashed into the saucer, spilling its contents onto the table and spattering my shirtwaist.

I sat staring while Abel jumped to his feet and Aunt Hank appeared waving a damp rag.

Doc was grinning wickedly as if he knew his presence had been the cause of my upset. I was sorry I hadn't thrown the cup, contents and all, in his face.

He ignored the look I shot him and sauntered over to us, unperturbed.

"Good morning, Abel," he said, still grinning. "Good morning, Kate. You're looking well in spite of the coffee on your...ah...your bodice."

144

"Bodice my foot!" I snapped, and then the humor of the scene caught me, and I laughed. "I'm very well, as you can see," I said.

It was Abel's turn to look surprised. "You know each other?" he asked.

"Dr. Holliday took care of my teeth in St. Louis," I lied.

"And her bite is worse than her bark by far," Doc said.

"But..." Abel began.

If I let them go on, I'd be trapped having to explain everything instead of extricating myself gracefully. "Won't you join us?" I interrupted.

And Abel said, as I knew he would, "Yes. Sit down, Holliday. Maybe you can take Kate's mind off our friend out there." He gestured over his shoulder at the hanged man.

"Frank Tyler," Doc said. "He got caught stealing back his own cattle from Larn who had stolen them from somebody else. Is that clear?"

Abel nodded. "I thought Larn would settle down after he married the Matthews girl and got elected sheriff."

"No chance. You cattle men ought to figure out a way to prove he's stealing everybody blind." Doc poured himself coffee from the pot and held it out to me. "Coffee, Kate?"

I shook my head. "Thank you, no. I think I'll go and change and then maybe look around the town." I was hoping Doc would go with me, but before he could volunteer, Abel frowned at me.

"Not on your own, Kate," he said.

And I'd considered marrying him! But no longer, not with Doc sitting across from me looking self-possessed and sleek as a cat. Abel might own half of Texas, but as his wife I would be expected to be above reproach. I'd be chaperoned, bossed, dependent on him for every desire, even that of taking a walk. With Doc you never knew, but that was the fun of it; that and the love making, like a swift flame that extinguished all propriety, all thought.

I said, "I'm sure I'll be fine," and started toward the door.

He called after me. "Kate! Remember who you are!" And he sounded as if we'd already exchanged vows, as if he owned me, as if I had to protect him instead of the other way around.

I kept hold of my temper, but decided to speak my mind. "I know who I am. Quite well. But you've just convinced me that we wouldn't suit at all as husband and wife. We're too different. I'm sorry, but I'm going for a walk and to look for employment."

I caught a glimpse of Doc's face. His eyebrows were raised in astonishment, and his eyes were gleaming.

"Don't look at me like that!" I said to him.

He stood and bowed, first to me, then to Abel. "I beg your pardon. It seems I'm intruding on a private discussion."

"Private be damned! You're the first to know I'm not marrying Abel."

"No," Doc said. "I never supposed you were."

Abel stood, too. "We'll talk about this alone," he said to me, coldly. "After you've got control of yourself."

I drew myself up and looked down my nose at him, copying my mother's patrician manner. "I have nothing else to say. I'm in complete control of myself, and I'm sorry if it appears otherwise."

Doc snorted, then brought his handkerchief to his lips to cover what I knew was laughter. I swept out of the room and headed for the stairs, hearing him close on my heels.

"Stop laughing!" I commanded without turning around. "For God's sake, it's bad enough without that!"

He caught up to me on the landing. "You conned him!" he exclaimed, still laughing. "You'd better tell me about it."

He'd understand if anyone would. Relief at finding him swept my indignation away and left me close to tears. "Oh, Doc," I said. "It's been awful."

"Don't cry, for Christ's sake. What's done is done. Where's your room?"

I handed him the key and pointed.

Once inside, I sat down heavily on the bed and let the tears come. "Don't tell me not to cry," I got out between sobs. "I've been through hell."

He sat down and took me in his arms. "It must have been to make you cry like this."

My body responded instantly. No matter what anyone says, the body never forgets. I looked up at him, but his face was the gambler's face. Unreadable.

"What happened, Kate?" he asked.

What would he think when I told him? When he heard, not only about Anson, but about the hundreds of others who had no names? Would he move away from me? Leave me on my own in another stinking boom town?

I couldn't risk it. I buried my face in his shoulder. "I can't talk about it. Please don't make me. Maybe someday I will, but not now."

He said, "Where's Anson?"

"Dead," I whispered into the black cloth of his coat. "Dead and robbed two weeks after we got to Wichita."

His arms tightened. "Ah," he said. "So I'm to rescue you again." Incredibly, I heard what sounded like gladness in his words.

But put that way, his presence seemed like charity. "I give as good as I get. You know that." I drew away and looked

147

at him once more. "You don't have to rescue me. But let me stay awhile. I missed you."

That wasn't the half of it, but to spill my heart out to him was always dangerous.

One eyebrow went up. He took my face in his hands. "Oddly enough," he said, "I missed you, too. I had nobody to fight with."

Fighting was the last thing on my mind. The warmth of his hands had seen to that. I met his kiss with my own, clinging to him like I was drowning, and I was, swept along on the current of that hunger born in my bones; a hunger for one man, and one man only. Doc Holliday.

I lay back on the pillow and said his name aloud. "Doc Holliday. Doc Holliday," like a magic charm, a love spell. Then I held out my arms and he came into them fiercely, working a magic of his own.

•

We were awakened by Abel pounding on the door.

"Kate!" he called. "We have to talk. Let me in!"

"Later!" I called back. "I'll come to you in half an hour." Then I turned to Doc. "What'll I say?"

He chuckled. "I've never known you to be at a loss for words before. But since you ask, just say you're sorry. And for God's sake leave me out of it."

"And I'll give him back my stage fare."

"You mean he actually paid your way? I don't believe it. I had to dun him for months for those gold teeth he's so proud of."

"He did," I said. "He...he really wanted to marry me."

"The more fool he."

The hour we'd spent splintered like glass. I flew at him.

148

"I'm the fool! I thought... I thought..." I couldn't get the words out past the lump in my throat.

He caught my wrists and pulled me against him. He was laughing again, that all-knowing laugh that drove me wild. "Kate, Kate," he said, close to my ear, "you'll have to learn to get used to my teasing you. Stop taking everything I say personally."

Somewhere in my tangled past, I'd made a vow that, if I ever got Doc back, I'd try to behave better. But I hadn't realized how hard it would be to do, or how vulnerable I always felt around him.

He had the power. All I had was love.

CHAPTER Twenty-one

That whole day had about it the quality of a farce, of a melodrama such as I'd seen played out on a stage but never in real life.

Now I can laugh about it, a little, but then I was involved and dealing with real feelings of real people. It was hard to face Abel and take the blame on myself, even though that was where it lay. I had, indeed, conned him, and the fact was shameful.

Hurt though he was, he remained the gentleman, refusing my offer of repayment and making an offer of his own.

"It's a tough town, Kate," he said. "Tougher than Wichita. I'm sorry you've changed your mind. Sorry if I seemed to be demanding too much. But if you need me or change your mind again, I'm just North of Larn's place. You can't miss me."

Smiling, I shook my head. I'd never change my mind. Then I kissed his cheek. Little did I know I'd be riding to him in the dead of night with the so-called "law" on my heels before a year had passed. But all that was in the future. In the present was Doc and the life I'd thought had gone forever.

We spent the rest of the day looking over the town that had risen out of the soil of the river bottoms like an evil mushroom, attracting every outlaw, every desperado, every two-bit gunman and gambler in what seemed like the world.

The Western Cattle Trail had come into its own the year before, following the Westward progress of the railroad in Kansas, and sometimes it seemed that all the cattle in Texas were moving up that Trail, crossing the Clear Fork of the Brazos to the West of town and stopping to rest and graze before pushing North toward the Red River, Indian Territory, and the railhead.

They left a trail that was miles wide, cut a swath across a thousand miles of grassland, and the sight of them, the sound of their bawling, always roused a kind of pride in me, as if they were mine or the country was, as if I owned the whole vast scene simply by looking and watching as I often did from the back of a rented horse.

Further to the West lay a country of canyons and escarpments, the Llano Estacado, the "Staked Plains," treeless, nearly waterless, empty, the home of buffalo and of the buffalo hunters whose trade ended at the freight depot in Griffin; hides stacked high awaiting shipment and drawing flies and stinking as they had in Wichita.

And, just like Wichita, Griffin lured in both the good and bad, the desperate and the hopeful.

I got a good look at both as Doc and I walked down the

151

infamous street along the river that afternoon. Stores, hotels, saloons, dance halls, gambling establishments stood side by side, and behind them the one room cribs where solitary women pursued their trade, selling their bodies, the only thing of value that they had, to anyone.

I looked at them, at their faces which were all too often vacant of any expression except desperation, and I shuddered at the thought that I could have become one of them in time ~ scrawny, unwashed, and without hope of anything but death.

Of course they died, and no one mourned or even noticed. They died of disease, of starvation, or when the light of the spirit fluttered and finally went out. They were the un-named victims of time and place, and I wept for them, unseen by any-one.

Doc tugged at my arm, bringing me back from horrors he'd never hear about from me with any luck. "Here's Shaughnessy's Bee Hive. Where I am when I'm not drilling teeth."

We'd stopped in front of an adobe building that had a painted sign hanging over the door. The picture was of a beehive covered in what seemed to be honeysuckle, and beneath that a poem that read:

> In this hive we are all alive,
> Good whiskey makes us funny.
> If you are dry step in and try
> The flavor of our honey.

"Goodness!" I said. "Whoever painted that?"

Doc shrugged. "Some artist passing through on his way to paint the wonders of the West. Sooner or later they all get here. You'll see."

"This whole town is a beehive," I commented, looking around at the bustling street.

"It is," Doc agreed. "What's better, half of these yokels never even held a deck of cards."

"So you're flush?"

He laughed. "Ah, Kate. Always thinking about money. It's one of the things I like best about you. That and your temper."

I stamped my foot in irritation. "Do you have to think badly of me all the time?" I asked. "I was thinking about setting up a game of my own."

He steered me toward the door, one hand firm on my arm. "Sweetheart, I have more than enough for both of us. Now's your chance to play housewife. Furnish a nest. Besides, Lottie wouldn't like the competition."

"Who's Lottie?"

"You'll see."

We stepped inside and it took a minute to adjust my eyes to the dimness. When I could see, I focused on a beautiful woman, a woman more out of place on the frontier than I was. A woman whose heavy hair, held in a web of gold lace, was that red-gold color seen in paintings, and whose eyes were black and bottomless.

"Well, Doc," she said, and her voice was deep, husky, like honey from a dark hive, "it looks like you've been busy."

"An old friend," he answered. "Kate Elder, this is Lottie Deno."

"How do you do?" We both spoke at once and then broke off smiling, embarrassed and assessing one another as we did so.

This was a lady fallen on hard times and making do, of that I had no doubt. This was another with a long history; like myself.

"I hope we can be friends, too," I said, and indeed I

hoped so. Since Blanche I'd been lonely for female laughter and conversation. Bessie and her girls had been well enough, but I'd shared no confidences with any of them.

Lottie wasn't easily won, however. "Who can tell?" she answered, smiling again to take the bite out of her words. Then she turned and called over her shoulder. "John? Come out. There's someone you should meet."

The heavy curtains separating the front room from those in the back that were clearly set aside for gambling, parted, and a barrel-chested man with hair as red as Lottie's came out.

"You're here early," he said to Doc, and then looked at me with the belligerent stare of the born brawler.

Lottie said, "This is Kate Elder. A friend of Doc's."

"A pleasure," he said, looking as if it was anything but.

Was Lottie his mistress? It seemed so, but they were an unlikely combination, she the queen bee who drew men off the street simply for the pleasure of looking at her, and Shaughnessy providing the muscle to keep them from doing anything more.

He and Doc moved over to the bar and poured drinks.

"Would you like something?" Lottie asked me in that husky drawl.

I would have loved a whiskey. The excitement of the day, the strain of the past few weeks, were taking their toll, but instinct warned me off. This woman was straight as an arrow.

"Water," I said, "If you have any that's drinkable."

She laughed. "Have a ginger beer. That or tea is what I usually have. Why they call that 'The Clear Fork,' is beyond me. It's been muddy since I came, and the gyp water out of the wells can upset you if you're not used to it."

"Then ginger beer, by all means," I said.

She toasted me with her glass. "To your stay in Griffin," she said. "How long have you known Doc?"

"He and I met in St. Louis," I said, evading a direct answer. "And you? Did you come here with John?"

Our eyes met and locked in a kind of duel, and for a moment we were both silent. At last Lottie laughed.

"I don't have a past. Only the present, and with any luck, a future. And the same goes for you I think. Agreed?"

Relieved, I nodded.

"Good," she said. "Where are you staying?"

"The Occidental. But Doc said something about looking for a house to rent."

"And I know just the one."

We drew our chairs closer and were deep in plans when Doc came back to us.

"Oh, Doc!" I was so happy my words tumbled out in a rush. "Lottie knows where there's a house. Near hers. She says it's perfect. Can we go see it before anybody else gets it?"

"I leave it in your hands," he said. He flexed his own long fingers. "As for me ~ I'll go to work and earn the cash to pay for it."

The house had two rooms and was built of local stone. Behind it was a space for a small garden, and beyond that the river rushed and chuckled beneath pecan trees that were bending down under the weight of the fall crop. Lottie's house was beyond, across a bend in the river.

"It's nice enough," she said, "except when the river's flooded. Then I wade or get a rowboat."

I was filled with happiness. Doc's health seemed improved, and we were together. I set about furnishing the house, braiding rugs, heaping the bed with quilts and blankets in case the winter was cold.

Almost daily I beat a path to Conrad and Rath's huge store, elbowing my way through the crowd of drovers, buffalo hunters, soldiers from the fort, ranchers and farmers and their wives, who not only purchased everything they needed from the store, but banked there as well. None of the so-called "good" women spoke to me, but I couldn't have cared less. I had all I'd ever wanted.

Doc was impressed by my efforts, but shook his head over the number of purchases. "What'll you do if we have to leave town fast?" he asked.

"Leave?" I was shocked. I was already rooted as deeply as the pecan trees. "Why? Where would we go?"

He shrugged. "I left Dallas in a hurry. With one bag and the clothes I was wearing. It could happen again."

"Why?" I repeated. "What did you do?"

"Shot a man who deserved it."

"Oh," I said, thinking that made murderers of us both.

He'd been watching me for my reaction, and laughed. "Tough as nails aren't you?" he said. "Behind those blue eyes of yours."

"I didn't have a choice."

"No," he said. "Neither did I. We haven't been very lucky."

"We are now. We're here. In our own place."

He sighed and coughed a little. "But for how long?"

"As long as our luck holds." I crossed my fingers behind my back and wished it would hold for a long time.

CHAPTER Twenty-two

The first crack in my happiness came a few weeks later. I'd gone to Conrad and Rath's to buy some thread as I was sewing curtains for all the windows.

I'd just stepped outside when I heard the sound of the stage coming in, the jingle of the traces, the thud of hooves, and I waited to see it turn the corner, the horses making their final effort before behind unharnessed and put up at Haverty's livery. It was always exciting to watch, and sometimes the passengers, themselves, were interesting.

The day was chilly. I remember it well. I had a flowered wool shawl that I pulled around me, and I stood back by the door out of the wind.

A woman got out first, dressed in green plaid with a little cape, and she looked half frozen as she stood, rubbing her hands together.

I stared at her curiously for a moment before I recognized her. "Mattie!" I exclaimed, and then was silent seeing Wyatt behind her, a leaner, deeply tanned Wyatt, moving like a lion on the scent.

Mattie looked up at the sound of her name, and seeing me broke into a smile. "Kate!" she called. "Of all people!"

It seemed she'd forgotten the circumstances of our parting. She came toward me like I was a long-lost friend, as, perhaps, in some strange way I was.

"What on earth are you doing here?" I asked, avoiding what threatened to be a hug.

"Wyatt's got business." She called over her shoulder. "Look who I found, honey. It's Kate."

I winced at the endearment as our eyes met over her head, his cold and piercing. He hadn't forgotten, even if Mattie had, nor had he forgiven me. I'd turned my back on him like few women ever did, and it stung that pride of his, that place in him that always had to win, regardless.

He said, "Kate," and it sounded as cold as his eyes.

Suddenly I shivered with a premonition of danger. In an instinctive gesture of self-protection, I wrapped my shawl more closely around me and walked across the wide porch to the street.

"How long are you staying?" I asked, hoping they were only passing through.

"Till I get a lead," he said.

"On who?"

"That's my business."

"If it's law business, forget asking Larn or Selman. They walk both sides of the line. Go ask around on the Flat," I said.

And be careful. You won't know who his friends are."

A hint of a smile crossed his face. "Thanks for the tip."

"Any time."

I left them and walked home, trying to get around the thought that if Wyatt or Mattie met Doc, they'd spill the beans about me; in innocence, of course, but most of the world's evils happen because of innocence.

For the first time since my arrival, I wasn't eager for the sound of Doc coming home. I built up the fire in the stove, put on a pot of coffee to warm, and sat down to figure out what I'd say when my past was thrown up in my face.

Doc came in a little while later. He'd been pulling teeth that afternoon, as he sometimes did, coming home for supper and then going to the Bee Hive.

I was getting ready to say I'd go with him that night, when he said, "Some fellow's coming here to see me. Earp from Wichita. Did you know him?"

Coming to the house! It was worse than I thought! I said, "He worked on Anson's murder, but he didn't find anything. I don't think he tried too hard."

Doc finished washing up and went to the shelf over the sink to pour a drink. "Well," he said, "he's after Dave Rudabaugh. Dave stuck up a train, and the railroad's plenty mad. Hired Earp to find him. Shaughnessy sent him to me."

"Who's Rudabaugh?"

"He was here a few weeks ago. Big man. Noisy. You may have seen him, but keep out of this. If it gets out I fingered him, we could be leaving here faster than you think. That's why Earp's coming here. We won't be seen together."

That made sense, but I was still worried. "Is Mattie coming?"

"Who's Mattie?"

159

"His wife."

"If she does, keep her busy. She doesn't have to know about it, either."

"God help me," I said.

"You don't like her?"

I laughed. "No, and neither will you. And Wyatt's stuck with her."

He took a sip of whiskey, coughed, and took a second swallow. "You sound like you knew them pretty well."

"I wish I hadn't. I wouldn't have if Anson had lived."

He coughed again and gave me a look. "Would you have stayed with him if he had?"

"I don't know," I said. "Life takes such funny turns, and I didn't know where you were."

"I wish I'd known."

"I wish you had, too." I meant every word. How different it could have been!

•

Doc and Wyatt; Wyatt and Doc. Two men, each part of the other's destiny, each a part of mine.

Doc opened the door, and they stood assessing one another, blue eyes boring into blue eyes, hands clasped in greeting. It was an historic meeting, a coming together of two fighting men who made their mark on the American West, and I was there, but paid no attention. I was too caught up in my own small problems.

Had I known then the power that Wyatt would exert over Doc, I'd have done anything to prevent it. But I probably wouldn't have succeeded. People are as they are, leading, following, believing what they need to believe, living as they must.

And Fate steps in when we least expect it, dealing the

160

cards we have to play.

Mattie came in behind Wyatt and stood, uncertain of her welcome, looking around at the front room which was both kitchen and parlor.

"My goodness!" she said. "It's different from what I expected, but then the girls all thought you'd marry Abel. At least Arlette and I did. All that money! But Bessie said she bet you had an ace up your sleeve, and I guess she was right. She sent her regards if I saw you. Arlette and Fanny did, too."

I led her to a chair near the stove and hoped Doc hadn't been paying attention. Then I kept her talking about trivialities as best I could while the two men, their faces lit by lamplight, sat at the table deep in discussion.

I remember how they looked then, like two birds of prey, both with strong bones and sharp eyes, both shaped by the life they led. They had serious faces, as if they'd come to terms with themselves and could handle whatever came, and my heart turned over with love and pride as I watched Doc.

Wyatt rose to leave in a short while. He'd gotten what he came for, and socializing never came easy to him.

"I'm off in the morning," he said, speaking to me for the first time. "Look out for Mattie for me."

"I'm going with you," she said.

"Not on horseback. I'll let you know where I am. Meantime, stay put and behave yourself."

Mattie's lower lip pushed out in a pout. When she looked like that it was enough to drive a person crazy.

I said, "We'll be fine. Don't worry." And I gave her a poke in the ribs.

When they had gone up the path, the moonlight showing the way, Doc closed the door. "Good man," he said.

I mumbled a reply and knew, when one corner of his

161

mouth curled up, that I was in for it.

"Who were all those females she was talking about? Arlette? Christ, what a name! And who's Bessie?"

"Wyatt's sister-in-law."

"What is she, a madam or something?"

No sense lying. I was caught and would face it out and be done with it. "Yes," I said. "And I don't want to talk about it."

His eyebrow mimicked the lift of his lip. "Why, Kate," he said. "You? A not-so-frail denizen? Good God!"

"How do you think I managed?" I said wearily. "Nobody respectable would give me a job. If Bessie hadn't, I'd have died on the street, and if you don't like it you can go to hell."

He laughed, but I heard, or thought I did, a hard edge to his laughter. But all he said was, "I don't give a damn. You did what you had to like the rest of us."

And maybe he meant what he said. Maybe it meant nothing to him. Maybe it was only my shame that made me think things changed from that time on; that our passion seemed tinged with regret, and that he kept himself a little apart as if trust came hard between a man and a woman who had sold herself to survive.

CHAPTER Twenty-three

The winter came in with a Blue Norther that froze a crust on the river and slowed the traffic on the Flat. The air was heavy with smoke from stoves and woodfires, and Doc took to coughing at night and sleeping sitting up by the stove, laced with my home made remedy of tea, honey, and brandy.

Mattie paced the floor of her room in the hotel for two weeks and then, when no word came from Wyatt, went to Molly McCabe's Palace of Pleasure and hired on.

"That girl!" I complained to Lottie. "I was supposed to see she didn't get into trouble, and now look. What'll Wyatt say?"

Lottie looked at the world straight on. "Nothing. He'll probably be glad she's earning money. Lord knows she's not the

163

only whore with a husband."

That was true. Many of the girls had husbands, absent or otherwise, but I couldn't see how they could go from work to their own man and feel good about it, especially in Mattie's case.

"It's not your way," Lottie said. "Or mine, either, but it's the way it is."

Doc said, "Stop fussing. She's not your problem. She's a woman grown," and went out, wrapping a scarf around his throat.

But I did fuss. I'd always felt sorry for Mattie without being able to do anything about it, like she was a younger sister, headstrong and foolish. It was a pattern that repeated over many years; me trying and failing, and Mattie going bull headed towards destruction.

About a month later, Molly McCabe's burned to the ground in the middle of the night, rousing the whole town and frightening us all.

Fire was a constant danger to those hastily built towns of board shacks and canvas tents. All that was needed to wipe out everything was a spark and a steady wind. Fortunately, that night was calm, and a bucket brigade and a band of men with shovels prevented total disaster.

All the girls escaped from Molly's unharmed and dressed in whatever came to hand, which caused much amusement later when the danger was over. But the scene lodged in my mind and stayed there like a bad dream; the screaming, the flames, the swarming people with buckets, blankets, hoes, even pots and pans, beating at the fire with terror on their faces.

"Now what?" I asked Mattie the next morning. She'd slept in our front room after her escape. All she had left was the fancy dress she'd been wearing, and it was torn and singed at the hem.

She stuck out her chin. "I'm tired of waiting around this town," she said. "I'm going back to Bessie's. She wrote and said she and Jim were moving on to Dodge."

"What if Wyatt comes here?"

She laughed her brittle laugh. "Oh, he won't. He's still hoping to get rid of me. And those Earps stick together like glue. He'll go back to Jim and Bessie, and there I'll be."

"Flat on your back," I thought, but didn't say. What a homecoming! Well, good riddance. I lent her clothes, and Doc gave her money, and we saw her off on the stage.

"You were right," he said after it pulled out. "She's nothing but trouble."

I was feeling relieved and silly. "Like me?"

"You're a different kind of trouble," he said, grinning. "Let's go home."

165

CHAPTER Twenty-four

With the coming of Spring I grew restless. The trees leafed out, the river turned red like all the rivers in that country, and overflowed its banks, and wildflowers covered the prairie as far as the eye could see with a rainbow of purple, yellow, and blue.

I woke every morning to the song of the mockingbird, and the bugle sounding reveille at the Fort, a sweet mingling of music that drifted through the open window and lured me up and out.

I started a garden, digging in the moist earth with hands that had been famished for the feel of growing things. And I went almost nightly to the Bee Hive with Doc, sometimes joining him, sometimes sitting in with Lottie at her table. The two

166

of us together were quite popular, even though we won more often than not.

Doc had been right. A lot of the men hadn't ever seen a deck of cards, but were foolish enough to want to try their luck. Most of them lost cheerfully and, after being cleaned out either gave up gambling altogether or learned the rules and came back for a rematch. Sometimes, in the case of young cowboys or kids straight off the farm, Lottie gave them back enough money to get home and a bit of advice. "Stay away from the tables, kid," she'd say. "You haven't got the knack." Then she'd sigh and say, "It probably won't do any good, but most of them don't have much, and how are they going to face their mothers?"

With Spring, the herds started coming again, cattle by the thousands resting up outside of town and cowboys coming in for supplies and a last spree before reaching Dodge.

The one thing that best helped my spring fever was renting a horse from Pete Haverty and riding out to explore. Sometimes Doc went along. At other times Nando, the half-breed orphan kid who worked for Pete and rode his big paint horse in races, went with me, and we'd run our own races on the straight aways, yelling like wild Indians and laughing at the feel of the wind in our faces.

I won Pete Haverty's respect the day of the big match race between his paint and a scraggle-tail grey a fellow drove in and boasted about.

Pete's horse had never been beaten; not at a quarter mile, not in two, but looking at the grey I got the feeling Pete had been conned. Sure the animal was crooked-legged and thin, but he was long in the body, and moved like he'd been oiled in the joints. "A long horse for a long race," went the old saying, and instinct told me this was the horse that would put the paint out to pasture.

167

"Don't do it, Pete," I said. "He's a sleeper."

"Ah, Kate," Haverty answered, "use yer eyes, darlin'. Sure and me paint'll make ten of him."

"Don't say I didn't warn you." I went and put ten dollars on the grey at odds of 50 to 1.

When the race was over, and the grey, moving like a machine had crossed the finish line so far ahead of the paint it seemed like a joke, I collected my five hundred dollars and shook a finger at Haverty. "Next time listen," I said, laughing to take the sting out of his loss.

"Next time!" He was red in the face and spluttering. "Sure and there won't be a next time! I'm sellin' that poor excuse of a beast to whoever wants him."

"I do," I said, surprising myself. "Here's two hundred dollars. It's all he's worth."

All Pete's horse trading instincts came out with my offer. "What would ye do with a horse like that? Sure and he's too much for a woman, and worth at least five hundred besides."

"Fine," I said. "You keep him. You won't find anybody here who wants him now. Rent him out. Use him up before time. Let him get stolen. I don't care." I started to walk away.

Before I'd gone ten feet he called me. "Ah, Kate, don't be hasty. Maybe ye can hold him if you try. Two fifty and he's yers."

"Done!" I said, and we shook on it.

Doc said, "Have you lost your mind?"

"Call it an investment," I said, stowing my winnings in the foot of a stocking where I kept all my money. Then I went down to the river bank to cut the greenest, tenderest new grass I could find.

I named him Gidran, after the horse that had been brought to Hungary to start a new line, and soon he was eating

168

out of my hand and nickering at my approach. An investment, indeed, but also a friendship, the like of which isn't possible between people.

•

With the warm weather, Doc's cough subsided. He'd gained weight, I hoped due to my cooking and the fact that we kept more decent hours than gamblers usually did.

When we rode out together we'd take a picnic and find a spot by the river where the horses could graze and we could eat, nap, and make slow love unseen under the trees.

"Little gypsy," he called me. "Little Hun."

"It's what you deserve," I told him. "Like unto like." I was happy again.

He taught me target shooting during those days, using rocks, bottles, anything we could find as a target.

"Get them with the first shot," he advised. "You might not get a second chance. And aim for the gut. It's the biggest spot."

I said, "I shot Stonebreak in the face."

"Beginner's luck." He tossed me his .45. "Now do what I tell you and don't argue."

He practiced pulling the knife he carried in a scabbard between his shoulders. "You never know," he said. "When they come at you, you'd better be ready or else you're dead meat."

"I thought you didn't care," I said. "About dying, I mean."

"I don't, but I'm not going to go shot in the gut and holding my stomach in my hands."

It was a frightful picture. I shuddered. "Don't," I pleaded. "Please don't."

"I have no intentions of it," he said and drew a bead on

the target and blew it away, smiling a particularly cruel smile. "And you were going to dance on my grave."

"That was then," I said. "This is now."

"Ah, but who can tell what will happen to us?"

"Whatever happens, I won't be dancing at your funeral. And this conversation is too morbid. I hate it. Let's ride!"

I jumped on Gidran and took off at a lope, knowing Doc couldn't catch me. So we rode further than usual, almost into a rustling and branding operation in a hollow beyond the bluff.

Even from a distance we recognized Larn and Selman, and Doc swore loudly as we wheeled our horses around and headed back.

"It's a cinch they knew you on that goddamned horse of yours," he said when we pulled up a few miles later. "You're an easy mark on him, and now so am I. Don't ride out alone anymore. Larn's a dead shot, and he's killed more than he'll admit to. And Selman, well you know about him."

Everybody in Griffin knew about Selman. How he'd left his family on the farm and moved in with Hurricane Minnie; how he spent his time cheating at cards, rustling, brawling, and involved in every evil operation around when he wasn't being deputized by Larn or working as cattle inspector.

"What'll he do?" I wasn't really worried.

"Christ knows. Just be careful. I wouldn't put it past either of them to try shooting us in the back after what we just saw. It's happened before."

For awhile I remembered Doc's warning, but life went on as it had, and although the Flat and the countryside were as violent as ever, and the vigilance committee, known locally as "the tin hat brigade," hanged several victims from the hanging tree, nothing intruded on the routine of our lives.

Nothing until one evening in May at the Bee Hive.

I saw the whole thing happen, but there was nothing I could do to stop events from spinning out into disaster.

Ed Bailey was a long-time resident of the Flat. He had a large number of friends and acquaintances, both good and bad, and an inflated opinion of himself. There was nothing unusual in his sitting down to play poker at Doc's table that evening. He often had, though he was a poor loser, and that night it seemed he was just looking for trouble, pushing his luck, sneaking looks at the deadwood when he could, and not even trying to be subtle about it.

Doc ignored him the first few times, but then his temper started to rise. Looking at the discards is as good as seeing into everyone's hands, and Bailey was looking and, naturally, winning big.

"Play poker, Ed," Doc said in that quiet voice of his that warned of trouble on the way. He told Ed twice, as I remember, and then he blew.

"Goddamnit! I told you to quit and I meant it!" Doc threw his cards on the table and stood, and Bailey stood, too, going for his pistol as he did.

But Doc was quicker. He hadn't spent all those hours practicing for nothing. His knife was stuck into Bailey's big gut the instant the pistol went off and richocheted off the table.

And it all happened so fast that no one had time to think or act before it was done and Bailey was on the floor screaming, blood spurting out from between his fingers.

"You all saw that?" Doc looked around at the others, a queer light in his eyes like he'd beat out dying still another time and was laughing about it.

It was a clear case of self-defense. Nobody said otherwise. Some of the men carted Ed away, and John Larn marched Doc off to the back room of the hotel that was used as a jail.

171

"Until we get it on the books and have a hearing," he explained, but I had a bad feeling like Doc was caught in a steel trap and me helpless to get him out.

I ran into his arms, and he held me tight for a minute. Then he said, "It's alright, Kate. Go on home. They can't hang me for defending myself."

But he was worried. I could feel it in his body, see it in his face, the skin taut over his cheekbones. I whispered in his ear, "I'll get you out if I have to, Doc. Somehow."

He chuckled. "I'm betting on you, Sweetheart. Now go on home, and come see me in the morning. And," he added in a low voice, "Make sure you lock the door tonight."

Then he went off, peaceably, while in my mind all I could see was the hanging tree and the buzzards that circled it, darkening the ground with their huge wings.

CHAPTER Twenty-five

The next morning I was up before reveille. I washed and dressed carefully and did my hair in a severe chignon, hoping that my respectable appearance would help Doc's cause. Then, knowing how clean Doc was about his person, and how he hated dirty linen and unwashed bodies, I packed him a change of clothes and headed off to the jail.

Selman was sitting on a chair outside the locked room looking bored and like he'd rather be someplace else. He smiled as he watched me come down the hall, an unpleasant expression that made the hair rise on the back of my neck.

Doc's warning came back in a rush, but it was too late. He was caught, and if I wasn't careful I might be, too. I forced an answering smile. "I'd like to see Doc," I said.

Selman stood and looked down at me, a calculated motion. "No visitors," he said.

"Why not?"

"You might have a weapon on you. I know you girls."

The little toad! He was equating me with the riff-raff, with the like of Hurricane Minnie who was in jail herself more often than not, and probably servicing him while she was there.

"You can search me," was all I said.

"I could." He motioned with his head to a small side room.

We went in and he searched my purse from which I'd removed my derringer, and the basket of Doc's clothes. Then he turned to me with a smirk and ran his hands over my body. Finally, he lifted my skirt and felt upwards along my leg.

When he reached my knee, I'd put up with enough. I flexed it and caught him on the chin. "That's high enough," I said. "Any further and I'll have to charge you."

"I could lock you up for assaulting an officer," he said, rubbing his jaw.

"It won't be the first time. Can I see Doc now?"

"I told you. No visitors."

If I'd been armed, I'd have shot him, but I was thinking fast.

"Where's Larn?" I managed to say.

A wicked grin split Selman's face. "Out. Bailey's crowd is making a lot of trouble over this. If he croaks, your friend'll swing."

The knot in my chest was growing bigger. "But it was self-defense. Everybody saw it."

"Sure," he said. "And Bailey's got good friends. Doc doesn't."

It was a nightmare. I wanted to scream, to batter on the

door that separated me from Doc. The situation called for action, but I was helpless, unarmed, face to face with one who wouldn't hesitate to throw me into jail as well. And one of us had to stay free. I had to spring Doc, and I hadn't the faintest notion how.

I took a deep breath. "Alright," I said. "I'll go. But give him his clean clothes and tell him I'll be back. Will you do that much?"

He opened the door and bowed, mocking me. "I might. But he won't need that stuff where he's going."

I whirled and ran past him down the hall to the street where I leaned against the railing to steady myself. I had to do something. But what?

Earlier there had been a mist rising from the river. Now nearly gone, it hovered in the tops of the trees and wove around the roofs of the cribs and shacks like pale smoke making the town seem fragile, unsubstantial, a figment of imagination that would disappear if I shut my eyes.

Instead I opened them wide as a plan came to me. Dear God! Was I smart enough, courageous enough to carry it out? I squared my shoulders. Of course. I was Mary Katharine Haroney, descended from a long line of fighting men and women. I was Kate Elder, and the man I loved was in danger. I'd succeed, or I'd go to the hanging tree with him and be damned to them!

My first stop was Haverty's, and I was in luck. Only Nando was there, and he was my friend and admirer. I'd paid him well for taking good care of Gidran, and besides, I'd gained his respect by beating him in our impromptu races.

On this morning I gave him a gold coin and explained what I needed. He looked at me with hope in his dark eyes.

"I'll go with you, *Senora*," he said. "Cook, take care of

horses, no?"

"No," I told him firmly. "You will stay here and keep out of trouble. And may God bless you."

"And you," he said, his shoulders slumping. "And *Senor* Doc. *Vaya con Dios.*"

Leaving him I reconnoitered the alley behind the hotel. It was narrow and littered with filth from the kitchen and from a row of sheds that must have served as stables or chicken roosts, but which now stood abandoned.

Carefully I looked around. No one was in sight. I slipped over to the window of the room where Doc was being held. It was closed and shuttered, but I managed to peep in through a crack. Doc was alone, sitting with his head in his hands. My heart turned over. He looked the picture of despair.

I tapped on the glass, once, twice, and he lifted his head and slowly looked around before coming to the window.

"Tonight!" I called through the glass, knowing how voices carried through those thin walls, but taking the chance.

Our eyes met and held in complete understanding. "Be careful," he mouthed back before retreating to his chair.

Oh, I'd be careful. But I was fighting mad and thinking clearly. The way I saw it now, Selman, Larn, the whole crew of Bailey's supporters didn't have a chance against a woman with her mind made up.

Without stopping, I ran the mile to Lottie's, where I pounded on the door until she answered, still rubbing sleep from her eyes.

"What's happened?" she asked when I stumbled inside. "They haven't swung Doc already?"

"Not yet. But they're going to."

"That's what I heard. If Bailey's friends don't get him, the vigilantes will. To make an example."

I laughed, and it didn't sound like me, coming out hard, dry, and knowing. "Just to get rid of him, you mean. Larn wants him to swing. He knows too much, and so do I. But they're not going to get him. Or me, either. I'm busting him out. Tonight."

Lottie didn't blink. All she said was, "How?"

When I told her, she whistled. "God! That's the wildest thing I ever heard. How can I help?"

I told her, and she listened, memorizing each order. When I finished, I said, "Yes. And could you send on a trunk for us when the heat's died down?"

"Where're you headed?"

"Dodge," I said.

Her eyebrows rose above her black eyes. "Dodge!" she said, making it sound like I'd said "hell." "But that's four hundred miles and still crawling with Indians."

"Better scalped than swinging," I said grimly, and meant it.

•

The May twilight lingered, and I cursed it, impatient to be off. I was dressed like a man in a pair of Doc's pants cut down to fit, an old shirt, a dark jacket, and a black felt hat that Lottie had pinched somewhere.

Around my waist, under my clothes, I had tied my money and my mother's jewels; my derringer and knife were deep in one pocket, and I had a pistol strapped to my waist. In the other pocket, safely wrapped, was a jug of kerosene.

Under the trees the shadows deepened. A few stars burst through into the darkening sky. It was time!

I took a deep breath and one last look around the little stone house where I'd been, so briefly, happy. God willing, we'd find another! Then I locked the door, hid the key for Lottie to find, and set out on foot for town.

The Flat was in full swing. Girls beckoned from open doors of cribs and saloons, and the night people thronged the street choosing their place of pleasure. A brass band boomed in one of the dance halls, and from Concepcion's house down by the river came the sound of a guitar and a few mournful words of a song. "And if my love leaves me....what will I do?"

I shivered. A bad omen? I couldn't afford superstition. What I was about to do was for Doc and me, for our lives that intertwined like roots under the ground. He'd saved me once. Now it was my turn. Hastily I crossed myself, just in case. Then I slipped down the alley behind the hotel and made for the shed across from Doc's room.

The door opened easily, and I went inside, but I was no sooner there than I was startled by the presence of another. I listened, trying not to breathe.

"Who's there?" I asked finally, and waited, all my muscles straining, ready to run.

Suddenly a horse snorted and stomped, and I let out my breath with a sigh. "Who put you in here?" I asked it, reaching out for it in the dark. It was munching on some old straw and was tied to the manger ~ a loose knot that I undid quickly, by feel.

Cautiously I led it to the door and looked out. The alley was still deserted, probably always was, but I wasn't taking chances. "Come on old boy," I whispered, and led the beast slowly away, sticking close to his neck and out of sight of anyone who happened to be looking out of the hotel.

There was a hitching rail at the end of the alley, and I tied him to it hoping he'd have sense enough to haul back and break free if necessary. Then I ran back to the shed, poured the jug of kerosene into the straw-filled manger, and struck a match.

The flame leaped up and swiftly became a roar. I ran out into the alley and shouted at the top of my lungs. "Fire! Fire!"

The fire at Molly McCabe's had nothing on this one. As I moved, the row of sheds went up like the dry kindling they were, and within seconds Selman and a deputy came pelting out to join the bucket brigade.

Two down; one to go. I dashed across the narrow street, pistol in my hand. Then I cracked open the door to the room. Larn was looking out the window at the rapidly spreading inferno.

"Don't move, you son of a bitch," I said, stepping inside.

He whirled, dropping his hand to his pistol, then thinking better of it.

"Don't try it. I'll drop you where you are," I said.

"She means it, John," Doc said. "Never argue with a woman behind a loaded forty-five."

Without hesitation, he crossed the room and took Larn's pistol. Then, his grin splitting his face, he looked at me. "It's your show. What'll I do with him?"

I'd liked to have shot the rustling, murderous bastard, but didn't want another killing on my conscience.

"Whatever you think. But do it fast. The whole town's going."

"Okay," Doc said. "Walk toward that door, John. Slowly."

Larn had no sooner turned than Doc struck him over the head with his pistol barrel. I looked at the body on the floor and wished it was Selman, wished I could kick him hard in the teeth. But the light of the fire was flickering over the walls, and smoke filled the room.

"Let's move," I said to him. "Now we're even."

Only the heat followed us, and that hideous, dancing light, as we hurried out of town toward Lottie's.

"Sweet Jesus," Doc panted, "you don't do anything by halves, do you?"

"Not where you're concerned."

We passed our house and crossed the bridge. True to his word, Nando had tied Gidran and a big black in the brush behind Lottie's. Each carried a saddle bag and a blanket roll.

We mounted swiftly, Doc following my lead as I headed West. "Now where?" he called in my ear.

"Dodge!" I called back, and the wind caught my words and took them, like a prayer.

"Shit!" Doc exclaimed, and then his laughter exploded, a wild, devil-take-all sound that exactly matched what I was feeling.

I'd set the whole damned town afire! My exhilaration was as powerful as passion. I clamped down on Gidran, gave him his head, and laughed as loudly as Doc all the way to the crossing of the Clear Fork and the Great Western Cattle Trail. We were on our way!

CHAPTER Twenty-six

The banks of the Clear Fork were deep in mud, and both horses spooked as they sank to their knees and struggled to find solid footing. Recklessly I slapped Gidran with the reins and urged him into the swift, dark water.

"You want to kill us both?" Doc yelled as his horse followed, plunging wildly.

I couldn't spare breath to answer. The river was deep, and Gidran had begun to swim. I slipped off, holding to one stirrup and trying to avoid his powerful hooves while keeping my own head above water.

We struck the opposite bank with a lurch, and Gidran scrambled up, pulling me with him like a sack of grain. My hair had come loose and hung over my face like river weed, and half

181

the silt in the territory seemed to be inside my clothes.

Looking at me, Doc laughed again. "Still a river rat!" he snorted. "By Christ, Kate, I'm beginning to think the role suits you."

Why was he always laughing? Why did he find humor in the most impossible situations? Sometimes, like now, he baffled me completely.

I stamped my foot, and water sloshed over the top of my boot. "Stop it!" I shouted. "Stop laughing at me. This isn't funny."

"What isn't?"

His refusal to listen overwhelmed me, and the chill that suddenly crept upwards from my toes; the endlessness of the land, the immensity of what I'd done combined into hysteria. I burst into tears and refused to be comforted, even when he took me in his arms. The wildness, the energy that had possessed me only minutes before had gone. I saw myself as no bigger than an ant in a world filled with danger, and with only a crazy man by my side.

"Whoa, Kate. Easy." Doc pressed my head to his shoulder. "Don't cry. It's over. Done. You showed them all. Now be easy."

His voice lulled me, and I leaned against him gathering strength. "Why can't you stay the same?" I asked and heard my voice wind out into the night like the cry of a bird. "Why can't you be nice all the time?"

"Nobody's nice all the time. And if I was, you, my dear, wouldn't be interested." He gave me a shake. "Now, since you've planned all this, where do we go from here?"

"I would be interested. I love you." There! It had slipped out, and after I'd promised myself.

"You pick the strangest times." Doc's teeth gleamed in

182

the moonlight. "Would you like to make love now?"

"Don't make fun!" I turned away and checked Gidran's girth. "No, I don't want to. We've got to get out of here." Automatically I checked for the bag of provisions that had been tied to the saddle. It wasn't there! But it had to be! I checked the river bank and saw only mud.

"What?" Doc was beside me.

"We've lost our food, such as it was. Now we've got nothing. It must have fallen in the river."

I was thinking fast. Off to the West a herd of cattle was bedded down for the night. Once in awhile, when the wind was right, I could hear bits of the songs the night riders were using to keep the animals calm.

"They'll head out tomorrow," I said, gesturing toward the camp. "And they'll cover any tracks we leave. But now we've got to go to Abel's. He's just North of here, and he'll help us."

"He's practically in Larn's backyard!"

"That's why. Larn won't look there. He'll check the Fort Davis road first. Then the road to Weatherford." I laughed suddenly. "After he gets the fire out."

"And if he woke up in time to save himself."

I hoped he hadn't. I hoped he'd died, curled up on the floor like a leaf. "He'd have hanged you," I said. "I don't give a damn if he died." I swung up on Gidran.

Doc stood looking at me, a strange expression on his face.

"Now what's the matter?" I asked.

"I never had a woman who looked like a street urchin say she loved me." That quirky eyebrow of his lifted in amusement. "I'll be goddamned but you amaze me."

"You'll be damned if you don't mount up and ride out of here, too," I reminded him. "And never mind your women."

183

"Always the last word." He wheeled the black and beat me to the start, and we thundered North under a moon like a chunk of silver in the dome of the Texas sky.

•

Abel was at first astonsihed to see us, especially me looking the way I did, and then displeased.

Of course he took us in and gave us a bed for the night, but in the morning he had plenty to say, starting with Doc.

"See here, Holliday, you can't drag this little lady all over Texas just because you're in a scrape. Best go on and leave her here. I'll see she's taken care of."

Doc looked like he was about to pull a joke. "Ask her who's dragging who around," he said. "This wasn't my idea."

"I'm going with Doc, and that's that," I interrupted. "Anyway, they're after me, too."

Abel pulled at his chin. "I can put you on a stage out of here, and nobody will know who you are."

"I'm going with Doc."

He knew when he was beaten, and took another tack. "At least leave that paint horse with me. I'll trade you. Every Indian in the Territory'll be after him. And you."

I hadn't thought of that, but the idea of leaving Gidran hurt. "I can't," I said. "He loves me."

"He won't love you when some Commanche's got hold of him. Be sensible."

"Never!" Doc said. "When is a woman sensible?"

Abel frowned at him. "Keep out of this. You got her into this mess. I'm trying to get her out."

From where I sat they looked like two dogs snarling over

a bone. And I was the bone. "Stop being ridiculous," I told them. "I'm leaving with Doc, and I'm taking Gidran, and I'll kill anybody who lays a hand on him or me."

"She will, too." Doc was enjoying himself with typical male vanity. I'd chosen him over one of the biggest ranchers in Texas, and he was gently rubbing it in.

Abel slammed a fist on the table. "You're both crazy!" he said. "Don't say I didn't try to stop you when you're out there on foot or staked to a tree."

I laid a hand over his. "I'm grateful," I said. "You're a good man. A kind one. But I have to do what I have to do. You understand?"

He shook his head. "I don't. I think you're both damn fools. But I'll give you an extra horse. He can carry your supplies. And..." he looked angrily at me, "when the Indians get hold of that paint critter, you can ride him yourself if you're still in one piece."

"Thank you," I answered, and meant it.

"Just get where you're going safe," he said and went out.

"Good man," Doc commented. "I misjudged him. Let's go give him a hand."

We followed him out through the yard to the corral. The night was fading. In the East a strip of red lay like a fire across the edge of the prairie. For a moment I thought my fire had run out of control, and then, as I watched, the sky broke into pieces of gold as the sun hammered its way up and broke through into day.

"Look!" I gasped.

"You'll see a few more before we're through," Doc said, but he, too, stopped and watched, letting the light fall on his face as if he welcomed the warmth of another day.

"We're going to make it." My words sounded like a

prayer.

He took my hand. "With you along, I don't doubt it."

The rare praise warmed me. I stood by his side feeling like we were two parts of a whole, like I had, in truth, been created out of his body, out of a piece of rib, and that the mystical joining would remain forever.

CHAPTER Twenty-seven

We made twenty-five miles that day, more than that the next, stopping only for brief periods to rest the horses and ourselves. We were sunburned and sweaty, and we ached from long hours at a lope, but we were gloriously happy.

We were free, and we had only ourselves to rely on. There was an even greater freedom in that, as if we were the only two people in the world, Adam and Eve in the garden that was the Texas prairie. And garden it was.

Bluebonnets covered acres of ground with that heart-rending color so much like the sky. It seemed that everything we looked at was blooming, growing, filled with a vitality that mirrored our own dawning sense of life.

The larks sang from morning till night, and flew up from

under our horse's hooves like small flutes, and the long-tailed flycatchers swooped and buzzed, dazzling us with their grace.

Fawns were being born in the thickets, the hidden places, and more than once we rode past one lying still and wide-eyed awaiting its mother.

I began to feel that there wasn't anything I couldn't do; that I could grow until I filled the space that surrounded me. I loved, and even my heart seemed to expand, taking everything inside - the prairie, the sky, Doc's happy presence at my side - with a hugeness I'd never known was possible.

At night, tired as our bodies were, our spirits sang. We made love, casting our clothes recklessly aside, laughing, imprinting the marks of our loving into the ground. For all I know those hollows are there still, a testimony to passion, as the marks of the great trails linger on the grassland to be seen and marveled at.

If we could choose a time and a place to die, I would have chosen that time, much as, then, I grasped hungrily at living. For on the long trail to Dodge our love was at its height, and our youth, our fire.

If I could, I'd have my bones scattered there, in Texas, with the long wind blowing over, and the larks singing hymns; with my flesh and Doc's feeding the ripple of bluebonnets and grassses into infinity.

But this is hindsight and useless. And I would not really have traded the rest of my long life, heartbreaking though some of it has been, to have died on the trek to Dodge.

•

We crossed the Red River into Indian Territory in the middle of a blinding rainstorm. Already soaked through, the river lapping over our boots made no difference in our misery.

188

"Let's stop somewhere," I said as we crossed the wide flood plain, winding our way around scrub willows and long dead trees deposited by earlier high water.

"Where would you suggest? Are there any hotels nearby?" Doc's irony was lost in a fit of coughing, and the sound of it stabbed me to the core.

I'd gotten us into this without a thought beyond escaping Griffin. Now there was no way to go except North to Dodge. If we could make it. Doc's face was milk white under his sunburn, and chills wracked my own healthy body. We had to find shelter, and soon.

I didn't waste breath apologizing but urged Gidran on, peering through half-closed eyes for any spot that would keep us fairly dry.

Indian Territory didn't seem any different from Texas. The prairie spread out around us, sodden in the rain, a grey flannel sky pulled down over it like a shawl.

When we spotted a substantial grove of trees we headed for it without speaking, and even the horses picked up the pace, wanting a place where they could turn their tails to the wind.

"Maybe we'll find some wood that's dry," I said, thinking, longingly, about a fire.

"Ah, yes. And perhaps a good cognac," came the shattering response.

"Will you stop? Do you always have to be making fun?"

He smirked at me from beneath the sodden brim of his hat. "Where's your sense of humor?"

"I don't have one!" I snapped. "And if you had any sense, you wouldn't be laughing. We could both get pneumonia and die out here."

"Just remember, Sweetheart, this little jaunt wasn't my idea."

That was the last thing in the world I needed to be reminded of. I kept riding, refusing to look at him.

"Cheer up," he said. "Thanks to you, we're both still alive. And I'd rather feed the buzzards than dance at the end of a rope any day."

The thought of losing him broke my determination. I slipped off Gidran and buried my face in his mane. We weren't much better off than we'd been in Griffin as far as I could see.

Doc took a new approach. He ignored me, unsaddling his horse and busying himself searching for the driest place to set up camp. His coldness was worse than his humor. I wanted loving arms, warmth, appreciation and got none of them. I began to hate him, and the hate warmed me, spurred me into action.

I unsaddled Gidran and tied him to a dead log, then dragged blankets, saddles and the bag of provisions over to the boulder where Doc was rigging a futile shelter out of branches and a piece of canvas.

I didn't speak, and after awhile he looked at me. "What now?" he asked.

"Nothing."

He laughed. "Your face is as black as the inside of a nun's habit."

"What would you know about that?"

He laughed again. "More than you think. I had a cousin who took the veil as they call it."

Curiosity got the better of me. "Why?"

"The usual reason. A broken heart."

"And did you get under her skirts?"

"No," he said, scowling. "More's the pity. She was a pretty thing. A real lady."

He was despicable, but I was too tired to argue. "Don't

tell me anymore. I don't want to hear," I said.

That eyebrow that so often betrayed him lifted. "Jealous?" he asked softly.

Was I? Yes, but I'd die rather than admit it. "Certainly not. I'm cold, tired, and hungry. That's all."

"Liar," he said and, without giving me a chance to answer, turned and spread out our bed rolls on top of more branches. When he finished he said, "Come on, Kate. I'll warm you. Think how romantic it will sound when you tell your grandchildren how we kept each other alive in Indian Territory."

I burst into tears at the thought of children, my baby buried, me homeless, with no husband, only this man who I loved and hated, was bound to for no reason I could name except the voice of my heart.

For once, wisely, he was silent, simply coming to where I stood and drawing me close. We spent the night in each other's arms drawing warmth and breath from one another, sustaining our lives as if we were the only humans left on earth.

Chapter Twenty-eight

I was home again, in Hungary. Sunlight was slipping through the curtains to warm my face, and the delicious smell of food cooking was luring me awake.

Breakfast! I sat up blinking, dazed. No, this wasn't Hungary, but the mouth-watering scent of food was definitely real.

"Doc!" I called, timidly at first, then louder. "Doc!"

He appeared out of the bushes, his hair wet and slicked back. "I was just washing up, if you can call it that. There's a creek down there."

"What's that smell?"

"That's the good news. There's a camp and a chuckwagon not half a mile from here. Don't know how we missed it last night."

"This country fools you," I said. "You think you can see for miles, but you can't. Besides, there was so much thunder we couldn't have heard a stampede. Let's go beg breakfast."

He held up his hand. "Not so fast. We can't just ride in an tell the truth."

"Why not? We're out of Larn's territory."

"If he's after us, it won't make any difference where he finds us. We're dead meat."

I hadn't thought about that, but I was ravenous and ready to take a chance. Three days of living on jerked beef and stale corn cakes were enough to make me reckless.

"You be you," I said," and I'll pretend I'm a boy. Your kid brother."

"You'll have to keep your mouth shut then. I know how hard that will be."

I ignored him. "For whatever they're cooking over there, I'll play dumb."

He settled his hat. "Alright. You're my younger brother, and you're deaf and dumb. Tie up your hair, don't take off your hat, and don't open your mouth no matter what. And leave that spotted critter here. We'll ride the other two."

I practiced silence all the way to the chuckwagon. Doc was right. It wasn't easy. I wanted to exclaim; over the size of the herd now plainly visible; over the sky, washed clean by the rain; over the pangs of hunger that nearly doubled me up in the saddle.

The cook came out to greet us, a big man, full-bearded, with a .45 strapped to his waist.

"Not taking chances, is he?" Doc murmured.

I didn't answer, simply pulled up and sat, hoping nobody could hear the growling in my stomach.

"Howdy," Redbeard said, looking from one to the other of us. "Where ye headed?"

"Dodge, I reckon." Doc smiled and swung off his horse.

Redbeard looked sceptical. "Huh!" he said. "You're travelin mighty light."

"Got burned out. You probably didn't hear. Griffin caught fire a few nights ago. There's nothing left for me there. We lost everything. I'm a dentist, and my brother's poorly. Poor kid's a dummy. I thought maybe we could pay you for some of that stew."

Redbeard bored holes straight through me. For a moment I was afraid that he'd seen me in town, or even played cards at Doc's table, but then he shook his head. "Folks like you got no business out here. Get down and come eat."

I sat where I was.

"Kind of slow-witted, is he?" Redbeard asked.

Doc sighed. "Yes, and it's a worry. I'm all he's got."

He looked at me with that wicked light I knew so well, and it was all I could do not to laugh. He had me at his mercy, and he knew it.

"I'll get you for that," I whispered as he gestured for me to dismount.

"I can hardly wait," he whispered back.

Redbeard dished up stew, biscuits, and coffee so thick and so black it went down like molasses, but we ate it all and didn't refuse seconds.

"I wish you'd let me pay," Doc said when he'd finished. "Maybe you have a tooth that needs attention?"

"Naw." Redbeard shook his head. Then he took another long look at Doc. "I didn't catch your name."

"Dr. John Henry. And my brother's Cady."

"Kid like that oughtn't to be running around out here,"

194

he said. "You ought to find him a place in town."

Doc sighed again. "I tried that. But he ran away and followed me. He's just not happy without me. And I promised our mother I'd look after him. Before she died," he added.

He was in his element. If I let him, he'd stand all day making up lies and having the time of his life. Our mother, indeed!

I got up and nodded my thanks at Redbeard, rubbing my stomach and grinning like a fool. Doc wasn't the only one who could play the game.

"Guess we'd best get going," he said. "We sure thank you. And if we get to Dodge we'll take care of your teeth or any of your boys for free."

Redbeard snorted. "Most of 'em's lost their teeth bustin' broncs or fist fighting. But I'll sure tell 'em. You take care now."

When we were out of sight we both burst out laughing.

"Our mother!" I said between gasps.

"God bless her! How did I do?"

"You were disgusting."

"Come on, Kate. It was a fine performance. Almost as good as yours."

"Almost. Except you had all the lines."

He chuckled. "For once. But you played the dummy like you were born to it."

I couldn't really be angry with him. We were well-fed, free as the wind, happy in our foolishness. It had been a long time since I'd played games or had no responsibilities. The thought sobered me, and he sensed my change of mood.

"What now?"

I told him.

"Life's hard," he said. "We both know that. Take your

195

pleasure when it comes because it might not come again."

I wanted to take my pleasure there and then, but Gidran was nickering at us, and the trail North called, the rain-wet grasses silver in the sunlight. We packed our things and rode on.

And on. Into a country of breaks and gullies, cliffs and creeks and cedar trees twisted by the never-ending wind.

"Is the whole country like this?" I asked as we pulled up on a ridge and looked out over the landscape that changed colors even as we watched.

"All the way to the Rockies, I guess."

"Have you seen them? The mountains?"

He shook his head. "No. But I'd like to. I've been thinking." He shifted in his saddle. "How about going on to Denver from Dodge? I've seen enough goddamned cattle towns for awhile. And the air out there is supposed to be good for the lungs."

He wanted me to go with him! My heart leaped. I'd been afraid to think about what would happen after Dodge.

"That sounds wonderful." My voice caught in my throat.

Of course he noticed. He noticed everything, it was part of his nature, part of the gambler's life. "Did you think I'd abandon you? Leave you on your own again to go back to servicing drovers?"

"I wasn't sure," I said. I'd been living moment by moment, not wanting to test the future.

"Hell, Kate! You've become a habit. Besides, who knows when you'll have to get me out of jail?"

"Let's hope that never happens again," I said. "Let's just be happy. It's not impossible, is it?"

The smile left his face. "I don't know," he said darkly. "I'm not sure I know what happiness is. Can you understand that?"

Was he making light of our time together? Telling me he hadn't been as happy as I? Were we strangers in spite of our intimacy?

"I've been happy," I said. "I'm happy now. Here. With you in the middle of this amazing place. Can't you see?" I struck the pommel of the saddle with my fist. "Can't you be satisfied?"

He lifted his reins and moved forward, speaking over his shoulder. "I don't have a future. Or a past. Where's the happiness in that?"

"So go on and die then," I said, angry at last. "Without having lived. But I'm going with you. That way at least one of us will be happy."

"You?"

"Me."

"Selfish bitch," he said and put his horse into a lope.

I followed. I might lose him to death, but I'd be damned if I'd lose him while he lived.

Chapter Twenty-nine

The next afternoon we ran into the Comanches.

We'd swung off the trail to the East to avoid a herd of longhorns that spread out for miles.

"Maybe we can beg another meal," I said, eyeing the dust cloud on the horizon.

"Don't push your luck." Doc touched his heels to the black and we moved away. But luck, it seemed, came with us.

The moving cattle had stirred up animals, driving them off their normal range. Rabbits, antelope, deer were everywhere, displaced, frightened by this new enemy, this stream of cattle, horses, men.

Doc dropped a fine buck before we'd ridden five miles.

"Now what?" I asked.

"Now we hang him, skin him, gut him and have ourselves a banquet."

It was easier looking at a dead man than at the deer, even with its eyes clouding over. "You do it," I said, turning away. "I'll do the cooking."

He laughed. "At last a chink in your armour. If you're going to puke, do it over there." He pointed to a grove of hackberries.

"Don't be disgusting. It's just...he's so beautiful."

He laid a hand on the horns. "He is at that. And we're hungry. Don't tell me you're too squeamish to eat?"

"Just get rid of those eyes," I answered and turned away only to come face to face with four Indians, two men and two women, one of them carrying an infant.

At my exclamation, Doc looked up. "Christ! There goes dinner!" He jerked out his pistol.

The silent group didn't move. A sorry sight they were, their clothes in rags, their feet bare, their faces and bodies filthy and gaunt from lack of food.

"Don't!" I warned. "They're half dead. There's no fight in them."

"The hell. They're Indians."

"Shoot them or that poor baby, and I'll kill you," I told him, and meant it, for I read the pleading in the mother's eyes.

"Hungry?" I asked her in Spanish, though the answer was plain.

She stared at me a long time. Then she nodded. Once.

"We won't hurt you," I said. "We're hungry, too. You must share with us."

The two men, one so old his skin looked like the sole of my boot, the other younger, obviously the baby's father, conferred. When they'd finished, they turned to me and spoke. I

199

translated for Doc.

"They're on the way to Fort Sill. They're behind the others because of the baby and the old woman. Put the gun away. You won't need it."

"You mean you believe this bullshit? They're renegades. They'll have our hair before tomorrow, and your precious horse, too."

But I'd seen too many like them to be swayed by Doc's suspicions. I'd been an immigrant, an outcast, and, too, I remembered the Walachian gypsies of my childhood, spurned, turned away, hated and feared.

Just then the baby began to cry, a thin, desperate wailing.

"Dear God, Doc," I said. "Let them eat. They don't even have weapons. If they did, they'd have shot something."

The crying penetrated even his suspicions. "Alright. But tell them no funny business. One move and I'll blow them to powder."

I left his words unspoken.

Quickly they went to work, skinning the deer, gathering grass, sticks, cow chips for the fire. They were quiet and efficient, and I watched them learning from their ease. When I brought out our coffee pot and our small stores of sugar and salt, they, in turn, watched me, murmuring with delight.

Still the child cried until I couldn't bear it. "Feed him first!" I demanded of the mother.

She gave me a scornful glance and shook her head. "Nada," she muttered, gesturing at her flat bosom. "Nothing."

Doc fished in his pocket and came up with a clean handkerchief. "Here." He tossed it at me. "Make the kid a sugar tit and get some liquid in him."

I stared in amazement, not because he'd managed to find a clean piece of cloth, but because he knew about sugar tits.

"Where'd you learn that?"

"Every brat in the South was raised with one, Sweetheart. During the war that was sometimes all they had. I doubt this kid will make it, but we can try."

The Indians ate the liver raw after offering it and being hastily refused. Then Tall Grass Blowing, the young woman, speared steaks on sticks and hung them over the fire.

Among the few belongings carried in the old woman's sack, she found a battered pot and began making a gruel for the baby who was sucking his sugar water weakly but steadily.

We ate, finally, like savages, using our fingers and teeth, tearing at the venison until we were full and then passing around the tin cup filled with coffee and sugar. The old ones smacked their lips, and their eyes shone. The young man, Wolf Ear, gave his share to his wife.

Doc didn't miss the gesture. "I'll be damned. A gentleman."

"Yes," I retorted. "And if you had any sense you'd stop worrying about your scalp. These people are licked."

"I know. It's not the first time I've seen faces like that. They were everywhere you looked after the war. I hoped I'd never see another. Or another kid dying of starvation."

Across the fire, the old people stretched out and went to sleep, looking like pitiable heaps of dirty rags. Tall Grass Blowing was feeding the child gruel and small pieces of meat, dipping her fingers into the pot and letting him suck, chewing the meat herself before offering it.

The low light of the flames lit her face, touched her eyes and the high bones of her cheeks. With her body curved around the child, she looked like a Madonna, a strange one, perhaps, in her ragged dress with her dark hair, but the notion remained.

"It's the Flight Into Egypt," I said. "Only sad because it's the end of something, not the beginning. Why are we doing this to them?"

Doc poked up the fire and watched the sparks rise like small stars. "It's not the first time. People have been fighting and conquering since Paradise. We had Caesar, we had Charlemagne and Napoleon. The Revolution, the Civil War. Somebody wins, somebody loses. You're looking at the losers right now. That's the way it is."

He was right. In Hungary since Arpad there had been wars. I was no stranger to the latest of them. Irrelevantly I said, "I'm no loser."

He looked at me annoyed. "Why do you always have to relate everything to yourself? It must be a female trait. Now get some sleep. Me, I'm keeping watch. One loser has his eyes on our horses."

Wolf Ear was sitting beyond the fire watching us, watching Gidran whose bold markings shone in the dark.

"Wake me when you're tired," I said. "I'll kill the son of a bitch if he puts a hand on that horse."

"An interesting confrontation." Doc settled himself, pulling his hat brim down to cover his eyes which would, I knew, remain open missing nothing.

He woke me after midnight. The fire had burned to coals; everyone, even the horses, slept.

The moon had passed its zenith and rode low in the West, making paths of light and mysterious shadows, but still so bright I could see for miles. The silence was the silence of the Great Plains, a dark, velvety thing upon which the smallest sound displayed itself like a precious jewel. The far off hunting of coyotes; cricket chirp, wind licking grass. It was hypnotic, that huge nothingness; you stretched your ears listening, waiting, holding your breath until you became part of it, until even your heart beat disturbed.

Sitting there, part of earth and silence, I forgot my sorrows, my journeys, my hopes and fears. I simply let them go and lifted my face to the moon.

First light comes early in June. The moon sets in the West, and the Eastern horizon lifts into brightness, into color; grey like a dove's wing, then yellow, crimson, apricot, a swirl of gypsy skirts, until the sun bursts through, bearing the sky on its shoulders.

How often I've watched the miracle, never tiring of it, always in awe! But that morning my excitement was shattered as, at the first approach of dawn, Gidran snorted a warning and I knew before I looked that Wolf Ear was near. I stumbled to my feet, not bothering to wake Doc.

"That's my horse," I said, coming to stand beside him, ready to do battle.

Wolf Ear looked at me out of his unreadable black eyes.

"His heart is my heart," I told him. "If you touch him, I'll kill you." I didn't blink or look away but stood firm, my hand on my pistol.

"You?" he said, and there was ridicule in the sound.

"Me. And you won't be the first."

He took a step toward Gidran in defiance, and I pulled the .45 and leveled it, thinking as I did. We had three horses, Gidran, the black Doc had been riding, and the tough little mustang Abel had given us. The black was tiring. We'd ridden hard, and he was used to grain and a stable yard. Traveling slowly, he'd make it to Fort Sill.

"Take the black," I said to Wolf Ear. "Get your wife and child to a white doctor."

"Pah!" He spat at my feet, a great gob of saliva. "What does the white doctor know?"

"Do you want your son to die?" I countered. "Do you?"

"Better die than live in white men's houses."

He meant it, and I understood. More than he knew, I understood, but I couldn't give up. The image of the woman and child, the grief so near to the surface, stayed with me.

"It's a terrible thing to lose a child," I said, speaking slowly, tearing words out of that place I had locked away. "I know this. Help your son to live. Let him make his own choice. Teach him to watch the sun rise, to listen to the night. These things do not die. These things belong to no one, and to us all."

He listened in amazement. Then the fight went out of him, and he relaxed. "It is the truth," he said at last. "How do you know this?"

"I just do."

He turned and went back to the fire where Tall Grass Blowing was cooking more meat.

"Quite a speech." Doc came up behind me.

"You don't speak Spanish," I retorted. "How would you know?"

"I speak enough to get by. Not like you. So you've given the thieving bastard my horse?"

"He's tired out. His hooves are worn down. Gidran and the mustang will do for us."

"They'll probably eat him," he said. "You realize that?"

I hadn't. Nor did I want to. "Shut up," I said. "Just shut up and let's get some food ourselves."

We watched them leave, growing smaller and smaller until at last they blended in with the prairie grasses and became one with the earth.

Then we split up our gear, our few supplies and what venison we could carry, and headed North again, I with the treasure Tall Grass Blowing had given me; a beaded medicine pouch containing a red bird's feather, a lump of blue turquoise, glass beads, some hair tied and braided with a sweet-scented grass. It was a priceless gift, "Good Medicine." I carried it with me for many years until that cold morning in Glenwood Springs when I tucked it into Doc's breast pocket and silently wished him "Godspeed."

Chapter Thirty

We rode into Camp Supply in the late afternoon. Originally a military supply base for the Indian fighting army, it had become, with the defeat of the Comanches and Southern Cheyennes, a road station and general store, a stopping place for freighters, mail coaches, homesteaders, buffalo hunters, everyone and anyone courageous enough to brave the West Texas plains and the Llano Estacado.

Coming in as we did from the solitude of open country, the place appeared to be a noisy bee hive of activity.

"Why, it's a city," I exclaimed. "Out here."

"Just about." Doc rubbed his jaw with one hand. "Maybe I can get rid of these damned whiskers."

"And maybe I can get a bath and some clothes."

"If not, we'll find a cake of soap and use the creek. Let's go," he said.

Our wishes, simple as they were, weren't easily granted. People, activity, did not guarantee the social graces on the frontier. Yes, I got a cake of soap and Doc dug up a razor somewhere, but the meal we managed to get was salted beef and hard beans, mostly inedible, and the sleeping arrangements horrified me.

I said, "Doc, I'm sleeping out on the prairie. There's fleas in that room, and there'll be at least thirty men in there tonight."

"So I observed." He scratched at himself. "Not much of a choice, is there?"

"None."

"One thing we can do. We can get on the stage in the morning and be in Dodge in twenty hours. Or so they say."

The meaning of his words sank in. Our Odyssey was over. Our days of freedom ended. Civilization, of a kind, was a day's journey away.

"Why can't we just go on by ourselves?" I asked.

"Because, little gypsy, I'm tired of this. I'd like a good cigar and a glass of whiskey. And a decent bed to love you in."

How could I answer that? I said, "Oh," though regret still stabbed at me. "What about Gidran? What'll I do with him?"

"That's your problem. You didn't imagine we'd take him to Denver, did you?"

I hadn't thought. He was mine, and I loved him. As I'd told Wolf Ear, "His heart was, indeed, my heart."

So much for dreams. They don't last. "I could turn him loose," I said.

"Sell him. We can use the money," came the reply.

207

I remember looking down at my feet in their man's boots and seeing that the leather was nearly worn through, that one sole was flapping. God alone knew what the rest of me looked like. I hadn't seen a mirror in weeks or even thought about it. What we'd had was a grand adventure, the kind few people ever have. But it was over. It was time to return to normal, if my life had ever been normal. It was time to move on. I understood that. Moving on was all I'd ever done.

"I'll meet you back here in an hour," I said and left without looking back.

It was easy to find a buyer for both horses. They were young, tough, and, despite the long ride, in prime shape. He was a young, wide-eyed Englishman out to make his fortune, and he was fascinated by Gidran's bold markings.

"I'll treat him well," he promised, noticing how I held the warm muzzle between my hands in farewell. "Don't worry."

I took the money and ran, feeling like a Judas. I'd sold my friend for a handful of coins.

•

Dodge! That first sight of the last of the cowtowns has stayed with me for over sixty years. I still don't know why a good wind didn't blow it away, that huddle of boards and canvas, that mirage squatting on the prairie on a rise above the river. In its nakedness it made even Wichita look good, and Griffin with its hills and trees seemed a paradise.

Doc took one look out of the coach window and said, "Denver, here we come."

We stayed long enough to have our baths, retrieve my trunk that, by some miracle, was waiting in Reynold's stage office, and get a good sample of the food and wine offered by the Dodge House. Then we headed West toward Denver, the

Queen City of the Plains, across the damndest, dryest, most endless piece of country I ever saw, a piece of land that, though we
couldn't tell, was rising slowly, steadily toward the mountains.

It was all yellow and blue ~ prairie, dust, and sky ~ and,
at the horizon, so faint I thought I was imagining it, a line of
purple, dark like the petals of an iris, and changeable, so I kept
blinking, hoping, running ahead in my mind and urging the
laboring team faster.

Doc said, "Calm down, for Christ's sake. You'll be too
worn out to enjoy anything."

But I couldn't. I was as excited as a child waiting for my
first true glimpse of the Rocky Mountains, that stone barrier
between East and West, that mysterious place of cliffs, canyons,
gold dust, the deepest snow, the swiftest rivers. How was I to
know that the saddest years of my life would be spent there, in
the purple hills where the river ran deep and as cold as my heart?

By 1876 Denver had existed for almost twenty years.
Situated at the foot of the mountains where the South Platte and
Cherry Creek meet, it was the hub of a great wheel. From
Denver you could go on to Fort Laramie and the route to
California and Oregon, to Cheyenne and the gold strikes at
Deadwood and the Black Hills, to the gold camps in the interi-
or of the Rockies, or South to Trinidad, Raton, the mountains of
New Mexico where the high plains began.

At first it was gold fever that helped settle the twin sites
of Auraria and Denver. Then came the immigrant wagon trains,
the opportunists, the con men, the gamblers, the business men
and bankers, women, children, actors, actresses, foreigners out
to "see the elephant," as the phrase went. At last came the railroads that linked the country and spelled the end of the frontier
as it had been for such a short, dazzling time.

When Doc and I arrived, the city had spread out, been

rebuilt out of bricks because of fire, and contained more saloons, dance halls, and gambling houses than any place I've been in.

The saloons, in addition to being watering holes, functioned as hospitals, churches, concert halls, theaters, libraries and amusement parks.

Within a week I'd witnessed a wedding in the Missouri House, attended a concert in Ed Chase's Palace, and seen the freak show while sipping lemonade in the Denver Gardens.

Doc had a table at Chase's and was winning steadily, and throwing his winnings around like they were in endless supply. He bought me a bonnet with a pleated lining and wide lavender ribbons that tied under my chin; a close-fitting jacket of the same shade worn over a dress of dove grey satin; a brooch set with pearls and amythests. From somewhere he purchased a bottle of French perfume, and I used it lavishly.

We bought shoes and boots, an embroidered waistcoat for Doc, a parasol for me. Too late; my complexion already showed the results of too much sun in spite of applications of buttermilk.

We played. And we played well, like children let out of school. Doc's luck held and so did his health. He seemed to have benefited from our flight across Texas. He, too, was tanned, with more than a hint of muscle.

We were a handsome pair! I checked in every mirror I passed; Doc, every inch the gentleman, and me in the trappings of a lady.

And then one night Doc came into our room in a hurry. "Get packed. We're leaving." He was already putting his things into a carpet bag.

"What for?" I was in my nightgown, ready for bed.

"I cut up a two-bit, crooked shit at the table. If you don't want to bust me out of jail again, get dressed. Or you can stay. Make up your mind. I'm leaving."

I'd already made up my mind. "Give me ten minutes," I said.

The sun was showing over the edge of the plains as we caught the stage going North to Cheyenne.

Chapter Thirty-one

"Gold in the Black Hills!" That was all people were talking about in Cheyenne; that and the slaughter of Custer and the Seventh Cavalry at the Little Bighorn a few months before.

A person was taking his life in his hands making the trip from Cheyenne to Deadwood in the autumn of '76. The Sioux and Cheyennes were raiding everywhere. Outlaw gangs held up coaches and freight wagons almost daily, and the weather any time from October on could leave passengers stranded.

But we did it, Doc and I and thousands of others. We were young. Foolish. Sure we were invinceable after what we'd been through. Doc who'd never expected to live to see the Rockies, and I because I still felt we belonged together.

We registered in hotels as Dr. and Mrs. Holliday. Doc's

doing. Legal or not, we were as good as married.

It was two hundred and sixty miles from Cheyenne to Deadwood, the hardest miles I've ever traveled, and the loveliest. Around us the High Plains shimmered in the autumn light. The slanting sun cast long shadows, intensified the gold of the drying grass, the dark green of the pines, and made of the sky a turquoise like the one I carried in my medicine pouch.

Along the rivers ~ the North Platte, the Niobrara, the Cheyenne ~ along Lodge Pole, Hat, and Old Woman Creeks ~ the yellow cottonwoods danced, and the sound the leaves made, like the rustle of skirts, the patter of tiny feet, caught at me, lifted me up into that peculiar happiness I've always felt in the open with the wind rushing past and life pouring excitement, like wine, all around.

Yes, our Concord coach pulled by a six-horse hitch and driven by a young man with magic in his fingers, got bogged down more than once so that we had to get out, push, pull, walk in mud up to our knees. Yes, the road houses were hell holes more often than not. But what did it matter!

Doc and I were together and on our way to more adventure. And it suited me. The days of parlors and propriety were long gone and buried. I was a new person. I was Kate. Haroney, Elder, Melvin; Big Nose Kate; Mrs. Doc Holliday, and I liked who I'd become. I bowed to no one, said what I liked, urged on by Doc who was as wild as I.

Mightily pleased with myself, I stepped out of the coach in Deadwood and came face to face with Wyatt.

"What are you doing here?" I demanded, hardly courteous, but I didn't feel I owed him any courtesy.

He looked at me coldly. "Business," he said. "You, too, I guess."

Obviously he thought I'd arrived to work. I pointed to

213

where Doc was watching our trunk being unloaded. "I'm with Doc," I said, then turned away before he could say anything more.

Of course we were bound to run into him again. Deadwood was one main street running through a canyon, a dismal place as I shortly found out.

There weren't enough rooms or houses to hold the gold-seekers who were rushing in. By some magic, Doc managed to find us a room in what was called, for lack of a better name, a "boarding house." It consisted of a kitchen with a long table where breakfast and dinner were served, and three unheated rooms tacked on behind, each equipped with a bed, a nightstand, and a pitcher and wash basin. Nails pounded into the splintered walls sufficed for a closet, and the ill-fitting door that opened out onto the yard let the freezing air in. By December the water in the pitcher was frozen solid at bed time, and we slept in our coats under the blankets. That boarding house made Bessie's place in Wichita look like a palace, and I said so, often and loudly.

"The money's rolling in," Doc said as I complained. "Just shut up and enjoy it."

"How? There's no place to spend it. No place to go. There's not even any food to buy since the blizzard."

The town was snowed in. There had been no movement in or out for three weeks, and supplies were low.

"We've been in worse places."

"Yes," I said, "but we never froze to death. I swear, I'm going to the desert when we get out of here. If we do."

"Wyatt and Morg are due in with a load of timber," he reminded me. "We won't freeze, Sweetheart. Come here and I'll warm you."

"My foot!"

He laughed. "It wasn't your foot I was thinking about."

"That's all you think about. You could be on your deathbed and think it." I pulled my shawl close around me.

"You'd like that, I assume." His eyes had turned to ice the way they did when trouble was coming.

Usually I placated him, but I was miserable; cold, hungry, closed in by weather and the walls of the canyon. "Go to hell," I said.

He put on his hat. "No. Only up the street where the women are friendlier."

"You wouldn't!"

"Try me." He meant it.

As usual when my temper got the better of me, I said the wrong thing. "I won't be here when you get back."

He shrugged. "Suit yourself." He left, slamming the door.

Now I'd done it! I wrestled with my pride for a long minute. Pride lost. I yanked open the door, but it was already dark out and bitterly cold, and Doc had disappeared leaving only footprints in the deep snow.

Chapter Thirty-two

I was on my way up the Gulch. A light snow was falling, and the air was so cold it froze my breath in my throat. Despite the weather, or maybe because of it, the saloons and dance halls were doing a raucous business. Music, laughter, shouts echoed over the street, and the dim light from kerosene lamps cast eerie shadows over the snow.

What I was doing there, I didn't know. I could hardly barge into the houses and demand to be told Doc's whereabouts. Perhaps if I lingered outside, I'd catch a glimpse of him or of Morgan Earp who'd become his shadow when he wasn't in the hills with Wyatt.

I was so busy straining my eyes in the dark that I tripped and fell to my knees before discovering that what had thrown me was a body, really a heap of dirty rags, and that the person within was cussing a blue streak. And the curses were directed at me.

"Watch your tongue!" I said hotly. "Better see to yourself instead of lying in the street tripping people."

"I'll be damned," came a voice slurred with booze. "A female."

"Yes, a female. Now get up and go home. If you have one."

"Don't," said the voice. "No home. Nobody." Followed by a sob.

It was the crying that alerted me. I bent over realizing that the sodden creature was a woman. Worse, it was that woman everybody talked about, Calamity Jane.

She was grinning at me, her teeth bared and brown even in the shadows. "Go home yourself, honey," she said. "Little critter like you'll freeze to death."

"So will you. Get up." I put my hands under her arms and heaved, and she rose up growling like a she-bear. "What the hell! Get your paws offa me!"

I said, "I'm taking you home."

"Told you. Don't have one. Don't need one, neither." Then she shivered from head to foot.

I'd been out on a cold night in the snow, homeless, lost, considering suicide. I knew how she felt, and it touched me. I thought for a minute.

Thanks to Wyatt's decision to cut and haul timber rather than gamble as Doc was doing, he and Morg had a house of their own, and Morg's woman, Lou, as well as being beautiful was both capable and practical. I'd have welcomed her as a friend if I hadn't been worried about running into Wyatt each time I went to call. It wasn't his innuendos that bothered me so much as the

217

notion that I, out of loneliness and a misplaced need for love, had given myself to him. And it had meant no more to him than if I'd been Fanny or Arlette, or even Mattie.

In this instance, however, I knew I could count on Lou for help, so I squelched my feelings and gave Calamity a good poke in the ribs saying again, "Come on."

Upright, she towered over me. "Bitch," she said. "I told you once, didn't I?"

"You did. But I don't want you on my conscience. We're going to see a friend."

"Oooh! A friend! A friend! A tea party, is it? With ladies and all?"

"I'm no lady. I've been in your shoes a couple of times, so shut up and come along."

Surprisingly, she did, grumbling to herself and bumping into things but following me on my march up the canyon.

Lou came to the door wrapped in a shawl and holding a lamp. Her hair shone golden in the feeble light, and her eyes were huge. "Kate! What on earth!"

I told her. Together we looked at Calamity who had collapsed at my feet. Lou's nostrils wrinkled.

"Yes. She smells like a pole cat," I agreed, "but we can't just leave her out in this weather."

"Can we get her in the shed? It's out of the wind, and there's straw for a bed."

Together we dragged the cursing creature around to the back.

"I'll get a blanket. And some coffee for her. And for you, too," Lou said. "What were you doing out on a night like this anyhow?"

Over coffee, huddled beside the stove, I told her. "Now I don't know what to do," I ended, and stared into the black liquid as if I could read the future there.

"For heaven's sake!" she exclaimed. "Go on back home. The man loves you. It's plain to see."

"He does?" How I'd missed this kind of talk! How comforting to be able to air my feelings to a woman like this one!

"Of course he does." She took my hands between her small ones. "You just both let your mouths run away with you, that's all. It happens. Even Morg and I fight once in awhile."

That was certainly what I'd done. Maybe she was right. I stood up. "You really think...?"

"Yes. I do. Come over tomorrow and let me know how you made out. By then Calamity should have slept it off. Maybe," she laughed, "maybe we can talk her into a bath."

"I doubt it. Not till Spring," I said and left, cheered.

Doc loved me. Lou had said so, and she wasn't one to make idle pronouncements. He loved me! I nearly ran home, skidding over the ice, my heart slamming against my ribs.

There was a light on in our room. He was back! He was waiting for me. "Thank God," I murmured to myself. Now I could apologize, be forgiven, be taken into his arms.

I'd just got the door open when I heard laughter, heard a girl's high-pitched voice ~ I can hear it still and taste the bitter rage - "Oh. That's nice."

All the tenderness, all the loving expectation was blotted out. I wasn't thinking, just moving, attacking like an animal defending its nest. I pulled the knife I always carried in my garter and went at the two of them screaming.

She was a puny little thing, no more than fifteen, and the sight of her thin face stopped me before I'd done more than grab her shoulder.

"Get the hell out of here!" I yelled. "Get out! Get out! Don't come back or I'll kill you."

219

Then I turned on Doc who was on his feet, up for anything. "You! Robbing babies of their virtue! I ought to cut you like a horse." I went for him, but he caught my wrist.

"Don't do it," he hissed. "Don't dare, or I'll have you locked up. Put away."

"That's right. Make it my fault."

"Isn't it?"

"No!" I twisted in his grasp. "I didn't bring that tart to our bed."

"You just kicked me out of it."

"I didn't."

He got the knife away from me and threw me down. "If you ever threaten me again, it's the end," he said, his words coming at me like icicles. "If you ever dare me again, it's the end. You're lucky you're a woman. I'd have killed any man, as you know." He tossed the knife into the corner. "You should see yourself," he said. "You're enough to make me sick."

I lay there hating him. Hating and hating, wanting to scratch out his eyes, maim him, make him less than perfect whatever way I could. I lay there, and our eyes locked and held, and the fury turned to passion, and the passion to a physical battle, each of us with murder in our hearts.

There was no love in our joining that night, but it brought a truce of sorts. I felt that our love was dying, the cracks festering into open wounds that might eventually destroy us.

Chapter Thirty-three

Dead shot that he was, Wyatt came home with a deer and a brace of game birds in addition to his timber.

"Come for Christmas dinner," Lou said. She hadn't a notion of how things were with Doc and me.

We were cautious around each other, and silent. One wrong word could push us over the edge, and I didn't want that to happen.

It was at that dinner that I heard the first mention of Dodge. Wyatt was set on going there. He was signed up to ride shotgun on one of the first stages out of Deadwood in the Spring.

"Then I'm headed South," he said. "I'm going back to Dodge. It's booming. Bessie and Jim are going."

"And Mattie?" I couldn't resist introducing her name.
He gave a curt nod. "Mattie, too."

"It didn't look like much when we were there," Doc said.

Wyatt leaned back in his chair. "You know what these towns are like. They go up overnight. Deadwood was nearly empty six months ago, and look at it now. By summer every cowboy in Texas will either be in Dodge or on the way."

"And we all know how they gamble." Doc had a gleam in his eye.

It looked like we were headed for Dodge, and I was in agreement. The cold, the gloom was catching hold of me more every day. I'd started to wonder about us, the life we led, always on the move either running away or afraid of having to run, stowed away for the winter like a couple of pack rats in a shack not fit even for animals.

I'd wonder, and then I'd push the thoughts away. Being with Doc was better than working the circuit in the company of whores. A lot better. Still I fretted, but kept quiet. There didn't seem to be a way to speak about my worries, and Doc wasn't giving me any opportunity.

So the winter passed, and with the Spring thaw thousands more poured into the little canyon; men, women, children, Chinamen with pigtails, the good and the evil, the whores and horse thieves.

Wyatt went out with the second haul, and Morg and Lou left shortly after. We stayed on a month or two, living in the Earp's house while Doc cleaned out the novices at the table. His winnings were mostly in the form of nuggets and gold dust.

"How are we going to get this out of here?" I asked. "They're sticking up the stage almost every day."

"Sew it in your skirt."

"How will I walk?"

"You'll manage."

I did, but I wasn't happy about it. I waddled. And the stories that came back to town about stage holdups were terrifying. Some women were searched by the outlaws, their garments ripped off.

"I'm counting on you," Doc said. "You and your knife."

I didn't answer. My knife was a sore subject.

We were about thirty miles north of Hat Creek where the road narrows into a ravine when the outlaws struck. There were four of them, masked, riding good horses. They got the chests of gold, then ordered us out. I made an ungraceful exit and stood waiting to be told what to do.

Oddly, I wasn't scared. Those road gangs hardly ever shot passengers, just took what they had.

Our passengers tossed down their wallets, their pouches of gold dust. Then it was my turn.

"I don't have anything," I said. "You can look in my purse." Inside I'd tucked a few coins to deter further searching.

The fellow looked, pulled out the money, and threw my purse angrily on the ground. "Hell!" he said. "You got more than that!" and came toward me.

The fourth rider, who hadn't dismounted but sat to one side with a .45 trained on us said, "Leave her alone."

"What for? She's probably got it on her."

"I said leave her. Get her boyfriend's fancy watch and chain, and let's go."

I stared at the rider. There was something familiar about him, about his hoarse voice, his peculiar eyes above the mask. It was Calamity! I knew I wasn't mistaken. I took a step forward.

"Stand still!" she commanded. "Or I'll blow that bird's nest hat on your head to feathers."

223

So I stood, watching them until they topped the ridge and stopped for a moment. I'd swear that she waved, a quick, subtle gesture. Then they were gone.

"Luck," Doc said.

"Maybe."

"What do you mean?"

"I mean that was Calamity, and she owed me." I'd never told him about the events of that dreadful night or about the following day when Lou and I cleaned her up, fed her, and saw her on her way.

"I owe you," she said before she left. "Sorry I cussed you out."

"You don't owe me a thing."

"Humph!" She cleared her throat, spat, and tramped down the hill, moving more like a man than a woman with long, easy strides.

"Jesus!" Doc said. "You get yourself into more scrapes."

"I felt sorry for her. She actually cried."

"Shit," he said. "Drunks usually do."

But it hadn't been like that. Road agent or not, mule-skinner or not, she'd struck a soft spot in me, and she knew it, remembered, and thanked me the only way she could.

Doc and I left Deadwood quite a bit richer because of her.

PART Two

Chapter Thirty-four

Dodge City, June, 1878

My dear Mina:
To have found my family at last! I couldn't believe it when I found Alexander in Denver. He looked so much like papa standing there in the hotel lobby. Ordinarily I wouldn't have spoken to someone I didn't know, but he turned and looked at me out of the Haroney blue eyes, and it was as if our reunion was meant!

I said, "You remind me so much of my father," and from there we discovered the truth of it. Oh, Mina, I've wondered over the years about all of you, and written. But the letters were returned, and I couldn't imagine what had happened to you, where you had gone.

I was afraid Otto was dead. What a relief to learn that I'm not his murderer! That I only left a scar he'll carry all his life! And deservedly. But I always believed him dead and have lived in terror of being arrested, even hung.

Alexander says that you have married, and Rosa, too. So much to say! So many years wasted, lost to us all!

I will be here in Dodge for some time as my husband, a gentleman from a fine family in Georgia, is a dentist and there is much work for him here. My teeth, fortunately, are fine. My health is fine, and my heart is full knowing you are well and happy and that we will certainly see each other again.

Write to me here. I love you.

       Your sister,
       Mary

Letters are wonderful things. You can muddle the truth and no one will be the wiser. I couldn't admit my past to my family. How could they understand? They were unaware of the choices one is forced to make when it comes to living or dying. I would have shocked them with the truth, even Alexander. Especially Alexander, who was every inch a proper and conventional husband and father, and who, when I found him, was on his way to a homestead in the West of Colorado, preparing a home for his wife and family.

Doc went along with my charade with that gleam in his eye I so loved, saying, "If you want to play the good wife, I'll go along. Christ knows I'd be doing the same thing for my family if I had one."

"And I didn't kill Otto," I said on the verge of tears of relief.

"Who in hell is Otto? Another lover on your string? You're full of surprises, aren't you?"

I'd forgotten that I never told Doc about that horrible time. Liars should have long memories, but in this case I'd done my best never to remember. I swallowed hard and explained.

Murder, however, never bothered Doc. "You should have killed him, the bastard. Raping a little girl. Any other corpses out of your past that I should know about?"

"No," I said, thinking about the little whore in Deadwood. That hadn't been rape. She, after all was no innocent, and some girls started at thirteen and were used up at twenty. The things I knew! The horrors I'd seen! Family or not, my relatives would never hear of such things from me.

So we entertained Alexander and saw him on his way, then came to Dodge which was wilder, even, than Griffin, and where we found Wyatt in charge of the whole town, cock of the walk, the Assistant City Marshal.

Doc set up his dental office in the Dodge house and life was going smoothly until the war between the Denver and Rio Grande and the Santa Fe Railroads began in Colorado.

The Santa Fe people sent a railroad car to Dodge and hired every man who could tote a gun ~ Doc, Bat Masterson, and J. J. Webb owner of the Lady Gay Saloon among them - and off they went to shoot it out over the right of way through the Royal Gorge.

When I learned Doc's plans, as he was packing his bag, I was furious.

"Why do you have to go? Webb's a no good, so he doesn't matter, but what if you get killed? And over a railroad, for God's sake!"

"If I die, I die. It'll happen someday anyhow. Besides," he grinned at me, "I've left you all my worldly possessions in my will. You'll be a rich widow. Or something."

"I don't want that. I want you." I put my arms around

him and held on. "I don't see why you have to go running off to fight."

"I love to fight." He kissed me. "Now behave yourself till I get back. Or is that asking too much?"

"I'll behave," I promised, and I did.

Short of going to work for Bessie or in a dance hall, there was little else to do. I wrote letters to my family and haunted the post office waiting for answers. I cleaned the little house we'd rented, and sewed curtains, and braided rugs and fended off patients saying Doc would be back soon.

Once or twice I called on Bessie, the only woman I knew in town. She was glad to see me and served drinks in her room where we gossiped like matrons.

Mattie was there, too, and the bitter lines in her face shocked me and sent me to the nearest mirror to see if I, too, were growing old and hard. But my eyes looked back at me blue and, yes, happily, and I thanked God for one thing. Doc wasn't Wyatt; could never be. And I wasn't Mattie. Not by a long shot.

"Wyatt's got himself a woman in town," Bessie whispered. "Name's Lily something-or-other. A real looker. Now he's come up in the world, he sure don't need Mattie."

"Pity," I said.

"Pity! Hell fire, I'm in the middle. All she does is mope and whine at me, and what can I do about it?"

"Nothing."

"That's right. I'd like to get out of this town. Out of this business. Just me and Jim and my kids. Go someplace quiet for a change, you know?"

"I do," I said, "but where?"

"How would I know where? All I've seen is cow towns and crazies, and I'm sure sick of those."

We all were, I think, even Doc, who came back from the

229

battle of the Royal Gorge and the chill of the high Rockies feverish and coughing, and with his pay-off money in his pocket.

"Where would you like to go, Sweetheart?" He was laid up and wanted dreams to play with.

"Las Vegas," I said. "They have hot mineral springs that are supposed to be good for the lungs."

His eyes burned like coals. "I'm no goddamned invalid!"

"Of course not." I was learning how to deal with his temper, his bouts of denial and frustration. "But they might help your cough. The dust around here certainly won't."

"Shit," he said. "I've already lived past my time."

"And I'm here to see you double that time. Why don't we leave when the rush is over?"

"I'll think about it. Right now Wyatt needs me around."

Wyatt! Always Wyatt, turning up like a bad penny, his family in tow to remind me of that part of my life I wanted to forget.

"He can damn well get along without you. He's a big boy, and you're not his keeper."

Doc's angry response was lost in a fit of coughing. I knew by the way he folded his handkerchief that he was spitting blood and hiding the evidence, and I was more determined than ever to get him out of there.

But fate, as always, sat down and played a winning hand.

Chapter Thirty-five

Dodge City, September, 1878

My dear Mina:
    My husband is a hero! You probably don't know about Western towns like Dodge, but they grew up only as drop-off spots for thousands of Texas cattle.
    In the spring and summer the cows are rounded up and driven hundreds of miles to be loaded onto railroad cars and shipped for food.
    Drovers - cowboys as we call them - come, too, and when they get to town they go wild. They haven't had a good meal, or a bath, or caught sight of anything civilized for months, so you can imagine.
    Our friend Wyatt Earp is the city marshal, and it's his job

to keep the peace and see that the cowboys behave themselves. They don't, always. Sometimes they get drunk and mean and go on a rampage.

One day last week several of them came at Wyatt, and their intention was plain. They were going to shoot him in cold blood, some say because of an old grudge, but the reason isn't clear. Anyway, they would have killed him except for my husband, whom everyone calls "Doc."

He heard the shouting and the threats and got a pistol and frightened them off, shooting one of the men in the shoulder and saving Wyatt's life without doubt.

Now, don't be worried about me. This doesn't happen very often, and we are quite safe. I just wanted to boast a bit about Doc. He is brave. And handsome. And very good to me. You should see my clothes and jewelry! Nearly as fine as Mama's was.

It was good to hear about Rosa's baby. She hasn't written, but I imagine she will when she's feeling better. And yes, I may come for a visit soon. The way the railroads are growing, we'll be able to go anywhere at all in comfort, not like the stage coaches in the old days.

Oh, Mina, it is so good to know you are there, and that I'm not really alone in the world.

With much love,
Your sister, Mary.

What I didn't tell Mina was that the Indians under Dull Knife were raiding within a few miles of town, and that we were terrified, sleeping with rifles and pistols loaded and cocked, making plans to defend Dodge and its citizens, even if it came to killing the women to prevent their capture.

On top of this hysteria came Doc's quick thinking and

quicker action that saved Wyatt's life and formed that peculiar bond that exists between partners in battle. I understood indebtedness, but I couldn't approve. It was as if Wyatt and Doc (and I because I was there) became a family, only I was on the edge of that family, privvy to nothing, shunted aside while they followed their male pursuits, left to nurse my annoyance into a fine rage. And I was always afraid that one day Wyatt would disclose the truth about our afternoon on the prairie. Then I'd have to admit the fact that I'd not only worked for Bessie but that, for a few hours, I'd loved Doc's best friend.

What would he think of me? Would he laugh? Dismiss me as a piece of trash who gave myself to every man in the name of love? Would they compare notes in an effort to best one another?

I ground my teeth in frustration, a habit I couldn't seem to stop, even in my sleep. Doc would wake me. "Cut it out," he'd say. "You'll ruin those nice teeth of yours."

But I couldn't stop. I felt I'd lost a friend, a lover, a fellow-adventurer, and not to any person I could complain about. Being men, they'd not understand. They were simply doing what men do - attending to business, gambling, talking, planning their next move, the profitable future ~ secure in the fact that one would defend the other. How could I complain about that without seeming like a scold?

I couldn't, so I made my own plans.

•

"You're making up my mind for me. As usual," Doc said.

I was careful about answering. "Nearly everybody says Las Vegas is filling up with the railroad coming in. Besides," I added, "I've been hearing about the hot springs. They might

233

help you. Dodge certainly isn't." I didn't say that Wyatt seemed firmly settled in Dodge and hadn't mentioned leaving.

Doc's next words surprised me. "What've we got to lose? This town's getting to me. How soon can you be ready?"

"Tomorrow morning. I'll pack for you, too."

He gave me a sideways look. "Why such a hurry?"

"Why not? We've left other places in a hurry."

"For good reasons. I suspect you have something up your sleeve. Better come clean."

"There's nothing. All I want is to get you well."

And he certainly wouldn't, gadding around with Wyatt and his others cronies until the early hours.

He reached for his hat. "I'll be back in awhile."

"Not too late," I said, and regretted my words as soon as I said them.

"When I need a nursemaid, I'll find one that suits me," he said coldly.

The door slammed, and I was alone. Just as well. It was easier to pack without him.

Chapter Thirty-six

Las Vegas is tucked against the foothills of the Sangre de Cristo Mountains of New Mexico. Mountains of the Blood of Christ, and well-named, for at times they burn red as fire, as blood, even in the winter snow; they burn until the color turns into sound, like music, like the low reverberations of an organ, and for relief you turn away, look to the East across the roll of the high plains, and they are mysterious and sweet, lavender, blue, and pale gold and filled with the singing of larks.

Las Vegas was the first town reached on the Santa Fe Trail after the long and dangerous journey from Missouri; a town of adobe houses and a Spanish-speaking population, mostly farmers and sheep herders who kept to the old ways even with the coming of a new and different culture. They were, for the most part, illiterate, religious, and superstitious, and they looked upon the arrival of the English-speaking traders and settlers with a mixture of humor and suspicion, bartering with them while at the same time keeping to themselves.

Six miles out of town lay Gallinas Canyon and the hot springs that had been used for centuries. The Indians knew of them, and the Spanish. The native curanderas made use of the mud for poultices, and by the time Doc and I arrived, a hotel and a small center had been built for the treatment of tuberculosis, rheumatism, and anything else the proprietors could think of.

The regimen was severe. Doc bathed in the hot springs and then was wrapped in a damp sheet and left lying on a rude bed in an unheated room, at the end of which time he was massaged, rubbed dry, and sent home.

Whether it was the clean, dry air of Las Vegas, the sweet and never-ending wind that came across the plains or down from the mountains, or the treatment, which he took three times a week, we hadn't been in town six months before Doc's health improved. He slept through the nights. His cough disappeared, and the blood stains that had so frightened me with it. And he gained weight, perhaps due to my cooking, for once again I was in my element.

We rented an adobe house, one of several standing in a long row along a dusty street. A portal shaded the front. Inside were two rooms; a kitchen with a fireplace and huge hearth, and next to it a small bedroom, heated by the same fireplace. The floors were packed earth stained red. Water was carried from the well and stored in ollas, those clay water jars so suited to the Southwest.

Each day a water-carrier came with his burro, and the wood cutter, his patient beast burdened with firewood, pinon from the mountains that burned hot, slowly, and with a scent like incense.

The old ways enchanted me, and I was fortunate, for I could speak the language. The neighbor women, shy at first, eventually accepted me. They taught me to cook ~ those fiery dishes beloved by the New Mexicans, not unlike some of the food of Hungary; stews rich with mutton or pork and chile; empanadas stuffed with sweetened pumpkins or with wild berries; concoctions of squash, corn, and peppers, and the ever-present bean.

"I should've bought into a restaurant instead of the saloon." Doc pushed his chair away from the table. "Or maybe you'd like to open a lunch counter down at the new depot. This stuff is hot enough to sell barrels of booze. If anyone lives long enough."

The saloon was still a sore spot with me. I'd hated J.J. Webb, formerly of Dodge's Gay Lady, since the day he announced loudly, and with more than a hint of malice, that he'd heard I'd been called Big Nose Kate. "Not a bad moniker," he said, his nasty little eyes gleaming with malice.

Doc, for some reason, had gone along with the joke. "It doesn't suit her face, just her character," he said.

I turned on my heels and went out, not trusting myself. I walked quickly up the street and past the plaza where the body of a man who'd shot a woman the night before still hung from the windmill in the center of the square. As I went I realized how much I had changed. The sight of a dead man, gruesome as it was, no longer bothered me. I'd simply seen too much.

Doc caught up with me as I started up the hill. "Don't be mad, Sweetheart. J.J. was just joking. So was I."

"I wish it was him hanging there," I said. "Him and you, too." And I left him standing in the street with a scowl on his face.

237

Now I looked at him. "Webb's trash," I said. "I told you. He'll get you in bad trouble some day."

"It's too bad you feel like that." Doc put his elbows on the table. "I was going to ask if you'd like to come and deal for us."

"What for? So you can bill me as Big Nose Kate and drag in the tourists?"

"Oh, Christ! Get off the subject. Nobody calls you that. What we need is a drawing card. Monte Verde is stealing our customers with her fancy clothes and jewelry. We thought we could use you as a drawing card."

I remembered Monte Verde from Deadwood where she'd set up a gambling house in a huge tent and slept in a decked out, fancy coach. She was beautiful. And cold as ice.

"That bitch!" I said. "She looks at me like I'm not there."

"She looks at all women that way. Why worry?"

"I don't. I just don't like her. But I'll come deal. It's boring sitting here alone all night. Only I want the usual cut."

"God, what a greedy thing you are!"

"Habit," I said. "I'm just used to looking out for myself."

He put his hands on my face and drew me toward him across the table. "You have me to do that, you know. Don't doubt it, Kate."

"I don't." My trouble was, I didn't know how long he'd last.

•

We stayed in Las Vegas more than a year. The climate suited Doc, and the excitement. The saloon turned a handsome profit, and the Dodge Boys, his old cronies, had come to town, all except Wyatt and he wasn't far behind though I didn't know it and couldn't have stopped him if I had.

"Bad company," my mama would have called those men and their fancy women, and she would have been right, but for the most part it was a fun company, lively, noisy, unpredictable, everyone planning to strike it rich by whatever means they could. Some actually did; then went on a spree and had to start from scratch.

But not me. Steadily I stashed my earnings away, knowing in my bones that hard times would come again. And I didn't protest when Doc bought me a pair of diamond ear-rings and a bracelet from the jeweler, Bill Leonard, who had a tiny shop next to the saloon, and where, in the dimness of his back room, he kept a small fortune in a safe.

"Where did he get all that stuff?" I wondered.

"Probably robbing stage coaches," Doc said. "Or conning rich dowagers."

"You mean he stole it?"

"I wouldn't be surprised. But who cares? It's not our problem."

"I knew there was a reason I didn't like him." I hadn't, either. It was a gut response, a goose on my grave, but I'd suppressed it because diamonds were as good as money. Every woman knew that. Or should have.

"Why feel anything about him one way or the other?" Doc asked.

"That's the way I am."

"Fire and ice. Diamonds suit you."

The ear-rings sparkled and swung against my skin with a cold solidarity. "Go to hell," I said, but I wasn't angry. "And thank you. They're beautiful."

The rift that had opened between us in Deadwood had

healed over. We were a pair again, partners, respected in what I called to myself, the "demi-monde" of New Mexico Territory.

"Come to bed," Doc said, "and stop admiring yourself. Let me do that for you."

He was lying on the bed watching as I preened before the little tin-framed mirror, and he wanted me with that desire that was, with him, always so close to desperation.

I turned, stepped out of my dress, then my petticoat and stockings, prolonging the moment, fanning the hunger I knew was there. When I went into his arms I was still wearing the earrings.

Chapter Thirty-seven

"**D**oc! There's a circus come to town!"

Everyone, men, women, shrieking children had run into the street to see the two huge Concord coaches drawn by prancing four horse teams and what seemed like a ranch remuda tied behind.

Doc watched the show for a minute, squinting through the dust. Then he let out a yell. "That's no circus! That's the Earps!"

"What do you mean, Earps? Where? What are they doing here with all that?"

"How do I know? But that's Wyatt handling that team. Nobody else drives like that. Let's go find out."

He set off after the parade, and I ran after, hatless, holding my skirts as high as I dared.

They pulled up in a pasture at the edge of town, and the coach doors opened and out tumbled Bessie, Mattie, and two children, a boy and a girl.

Wyatt set the brakes, wrapped the reins, and stepped down, smiling that half smile that was, in its way, so appealing.

"Well, Doc," he said, ignoring me as I stared open-mouthed. "Ready to go with us to Tombstone?"

"When does my act go on?" Doc cracked. "We thought you were a circus. Hell, man, the whole town thought so." He pointed.

A bunch of wide-eyed kids had followed us. They clung together watching and giggling, and one or two brave boys were approaching the horses.

"Watch out there!" Wyatt shooed them off. "These horses are still green."

I took their hands and led them to a safe distance. "Watch from here," I told them in Spanish. "The horses might hurt you."

Then I went over to Bessie who opened her arms wide. "Kid, it's good to see you. We're on our way to fame and fortune." She looked around. "These are my kids, Hattie and Frank. I'm a proper Ma now."

"What's all this about?" I looked from her to Mattie who was smiling and looked almost pretty.

"Seems there's a big silver strike in Tombstone. Wyatt and Jim and Virge got the notion to run a stage and freight line out of there. You're looking at the running gear. Bought 'em off old Reynolds in Dodge."

I shivered. There was something about the name, a premonition, maybe. "Where is this place? What an awful name."

Bessie nodded. "Sounds kind of deadly, I'll admit. It's

in the desert South of Tucson. We've never seen it, but what the hell? We're pickin' up Virge and Allie in Prescott first."

"I think," I said slowly, "that you're all locoed."

"This family's itchy-footed. I told you before, and I'm as bad, I guess. You think you'll come with us?"

"Me?"

"Sure. Wyatt wants Doc to come. That's why we're here."

"Well Wyatt can damn well get on without him!" I sounded bitter even to myself.

"Look at it this way," she said. "Wyatt wants a man he can trust, and that's Doc. You should be proud."

"Well I'm not." I turned as Doc came up and put his arm around my shoulders.

"Can we feed them?" he whispered. "I hate to hang it on you, but..."

"Don't worry," I answered. In spite of how I felt about Wyatt, I was glad to see the rest of them, even Jim with his bawdy smile and cuss words. Bessie was my friend, more like a sister than Rosa and Mina who'd had it easy while I was fighting for life.

"Come back to the house," I invited. "Chili's in the pot."

"Hot damn!" Jim exclaimed, and Doc said, "You've got that right."

After dinner the men went down to Doc's place, and the women back to camp. "We bed down in those coaches," Bessie said. "Pulled out the middle seats. Plenty of room if you decide to come along."

I didn't answer.

•

"Well?" I asked Doc the next day. "Are we going to do

243

this fool thing?"

"You don't want to."

"I don't, and that's a fact. I've had enough Earps to last me. But what about you?"

He drained his cup and set it down carefully. "I'm thinking about it," was all he said.

Wyatt showed up that afternoon, and I let him in with misgivings.

"Doc's not here," I said.

"I know. It's you I want to talk to."

"Talk then," I said, sitting down at the table.

He began slowly. "Let's call it quits, you and me. Forget about Wichita. It happened, but it's done with, except you won't let go. Why not?"

"I don't know. It just galls me. About Mattie ~ the whole thing ~ like you made fools of us both."

"It wasn't meant," he said. "And I want a man with me I can trust. Somebody good with a gun to watch my back trail. I need Doc, and he won't leave here without you."

Elated, I smiled, and it got to him.

"He's a man, Kate, not a kid in leading strings. Let him go. He won't thank you for holding him back when he's on his deathbed."

"Don't you talk about his deathbed. That's where you'll put him, you and the rest. Thanks to me he's healthy, and I want to keep it that way. All the rest of you seem to know what's good for him. You're full of advice and wants, and what gives you the right? You, especially, with Mattie out there."

"My wants aren't your business," he said. "Remember that, and you'll do fine."

"Doc is my business," I snapped. "Go away and leave me alone. Leave Doc alone to make up his mind. Tell him that.

244

That it's up to him. I'm too tired to fight all of you." And I was. A wave of exhaustion swept over me leaving me shaken.

"I'll tell him."

He stood, holding his hat and looking down at me, and for a moment I thought he was going to say something, something personal between the two of us, and I hoped he wouldn't because it would make him a Judas, a betrayer, and I knew he hadn't been that where Doc was concerned.

But he said nothing, only hesitated and then was gone, and I heard the sound of his boot heels growing fainter and fainter in the dust of the street.

•

In the end we left Las Vegas with them, with the Earps in their coaches, the horses following. The trail was long and arduous; through Glorieta Pass with its Civil War ghosts and the moradas of the Penitentes crouched on the hills; through Santa Fe, city of the clearest light; down the Rio Grande and then Westward into a country of lava beds, desert, red earth, black rock, the brilliant yellow of chamiso, the undulant blue sky.

On. And on. Changing horses, circling mesas that rose before us like waves in a sea, that stretched for miles North and South, and danced in the autumn light, against the smokey blue of far away.

It was country different from any I'd ever seen. The buffalo grass, the tall grasses of the prairie were gone and in their place rock, sand, scrub, tough grasses that seemed to thrive on sunlight and that, in the dry, cool fall weather, had turned to shafts of gold. Mountains rose up, cracking the plain like stone fists, and hawks circled endlessly, wheeling and floating in the updrafts.

It was a raw and aching land, and it suited me, comforted me in a way I didn't bother to analyze. It was naked and tough, and its beauty lay in that toughness, in the distances, in the shadows and the blazing maw of the sunsets.

Whether I approved of our journey or not, I was enchanted by what I could see, and I could see a hundred miles, reaching out to gather in the space, lifting my face to the skittering wind.

"You're nuts," Doc said one evening. He'd followed me out to a dry wash where suddenly euphoria had overtaken me. "You're dancing all over the damn place."

I held out my arms. "Dance with me," I invited. "Come on, Doc. It's so..so fine out here."

He obliged and waltzed me around a stand of chamiso higher than our heads and glowing in the long light of late afternoon; waltzed me as if we'd both gone mad but didn't care.

Maybe that was the night our child was conceived, or maybe on a night just before we left. I've never been sure, and it doesn't matter. We'd been in Prescott only a few days when I miscarried.

CHAPTER Thirty-eight

Allie was at the door to meet us when we pulled in.

"You look just like a traveling whore house," were her first words, accompanied by a grin that stretched across her little face.

I loved her on first sight and never changed my mind; loved her profanity, her wicked sense of humor, her keen understanding of the follies of people. She was the best of all the Earp women, the unquenchable mainstay of the entire footloose, crazy, and courageous tribe.

Bessie got down and shook out her skirts. "Guess we could have paid for the whole expedition, if we'd thought," she said. "This here's Kate Elder, Doc's woman."

Allie shot me a blue-eyed glance that missed nothing.

"So you came? Wyatt wasn't sure you'd let that man of yours loose."

There didn't seem to be any answer I could make, so I simply smiled at her and wondered what else had been said about me.

Allie said, "Mattie here'd like to keep Wyatt tied to the bed post, but it don't work with him, either."

Those tell-tale red spots bloomed on Mattie's cheeks. "He's here, isn't he?" she demanded.

"Not on account of you he aint." Allie held the door open wider. "Bicker, bicker. We could stand here all night squawking like guinea hens, but supper's ready. Come on in and wash up."

A big, jolly-looking fellow slipped his arm around her. "At it again?" he asked.

She tilted her head to grin at him, and her eyes flashed with a blue fire. "Why not?"

He patted her backside, then looked at me, missing nothing. "You must be Kate."

"I am." To my surprise I found myself smiling. He was as different from Wyatt as night from day.

"Virgil," he said. "They call me Virge when they aren't calling me something worse."

"Like horse's ass," Allie deadpanned, and in the middle of happy laughter we trooped in to supper.

•

"Doc," I said later that night when we were in bed, "what's going on? There's more to this than running a stage line."

"What makes you say that?" He propped himself on his elbow and faced me.

248

"I don't know. Just a feeling I have. But you're not going along just to ride shotgun."

"A man's business is his own," he said. "Wyatt needs me along, so I'm here, and I'll do the job as long as I'm able. If there's more, I didn't ask, and he didn't say. And if you're going to nag me to death, you're free to go wherever you want."

He rolled over and blew out the candle, leaving the room dark except for a finger of moonlight that came in and lay across the bed.

"Wyatt, Wyatt. The great god Wyatt! I wish I'd never met a one of them," I said. Then I, too rolled over and lay with my back to him. And sleep didn't come until moonset, and with it a darkness like despair.

CHAPTER Thirty-nine

"**D**oc! Catch her! She's going to faint!"

Allie's scream seemed to come from a distance, at the same time the pain hit, as if someone had come at me with an axe.

When I came to I was in bed, and Allie was there making a bundle of some blood-soaked rags.

"Lie still," she commanded as I struggled to sit up. "You damn fool. Why didn't you say something?"

"About what?" My tongue seemed glued to the roof of my mouth, and it was an effort to speak.

"You were pregnant. Were," she repeated. "And there you came, bouncing all to hell in that coach, and working yourself to death these last days loading up our gear."

The room wavered and receded. I closed my eyes against the dizziness, the pain. A baby! Once again I'd been taken by surprise. The regret that I'd never hold it, see it, stabbed at me and tears slid down my face. "I didn't know," I whispered. "I didn't."

"Better this way," Allie said. "The kind of life we lead."

"It isn't!" Uselessly I clutched at myself, searching for what was no longer there.

"What would you do with a kid, running all over hell?"

"I'd have loved it."

"And Doc?"

"I'd have loved him, too. We'd have been a family. A real one."

"You'd have tied that kid around his neck," she said. "I've been watching you. You think you own that man, but you don't."

"Stop!" I pleaded. "Please."

"I'm sorry," she said. "I shouldn't upset you. You've had enough. But I'm telling you ~ squeeze too tight and you'll kill what you've got. You'll have a man you don't know anymore and don't care about. If he hangs around that long. Doc's a man. That's why you love him." She shook her head. "Here I am running on when you oughta be sleeping. You want to see Doc a minute?"

"No." I closed my eyes against her, against the world.

She patted my cheek, and her hand was gentle. "You'll do fine. You're healthy enough. Maybe you'll have another. But don't grieve. Grief'll eat at you worse than the devil."

Then she left bearing the bundle of rags, her shoulders hunched as if she, herself, had known grief but had hidden it away behind a smile.

Doc was there when I woke in the morning, and he, too,

was shaken by sorrow. He took me in his arms saying nothing, and I held to him, ephermeral though he might be, held to him as the only rock in a treacherous ocean.

At last he said, "We'll stay here awhile. They're going on. It'll give you a chance to get better."

"It doesn't matter. I'm fine. As fine as I can be." Then my control broke. "It was ours," was all I could say.

"Shhh." He stroked my hair. "I'm sorry. You don't know how much."

I nodded. The depths of my pain were too great to bear. I had no comfort for him. He'd have to manage on his own.

Sometime in the next few days I came to a decision. I was going to free us both, how it wasn't clear, but I knew, in the emptiness of my body, that I couldn't go on loving, hurting, scraping my heart raw against those men and their dreams, against a thousand miles of country that called and lured like some irresistable yet poisonous siren. I was going to save myself, and if Allie was right, perhaps I'd save Doc, too.

"I'd like to go home," I said one morning when the Earps had gone, bag, baggage, horses and freight wagons loaded to the bows.

He raised his eyebrow, but didn't speak for a minute. Then he said, "Where's home, Kate?"

"I want to visit my sisters."

"Ah." He searched my face. "Will you come back?" It seemed he held his breath waiting for my answer.

"Yes, I'll come back. I just need to be with my family awhile."

"I'll make the arrangements," was all he said.

Yet when I arrived, when the happy, tearful reunion had taken place, when I'd been petted, hosted, fed, questioned, and my lies listened to with breathless flutterings and genteel exclamations, I found myself longing to be back in the West.

I no longer fit with those people, blood kin though they were. My sisters had become staunch mothers, respectable members of the world in which they lived. Their houses were large, spotless, and typical of the times, filled with bricabrac, antimacassars, ferns, engravings, and fine carpets, and I struggled to breathe in rooms where the windows were never opened for fear of dust.

Compared to where I'd lived, these houses were palaces, but I was as ill-at-ease in them as I'd been at Miramar ~ confined, supervised, constantly guarding my tongue.

Then there were the children, loved, pampered creatures whose presence tore at me, particularly little Lily who reminded me of Michael with her blue eyes and arrogant nose, and who wailed when I clutched her too hard to my breast.

All of them were as alien to me as the moon. When I laughed out loud and freely, they stared at me embarrassed. When I swore, as I did once or twice, I was chastized by Mina.

"I know, dear, that you've led a really different life in different circumstances, but think how you sound! And in front of the little ones! What would Mama say if she could hear you?"

"To hell with her!" I thought but didn't say. I'd become my own mother. My rules were mine, and if they shocked some, they didn't shock the friends I'd left behind.

So I fled back to Prescott and to Doc.

"Well?" he said. "Did they welcome you with tears and open arms?"

"Yes. And I love them. But I'm glad to be back. I don't belong in that world anymore."

"You probably never did. Anymore than I belonged with my family. God knows what they'd think if I went back. Black sheep, Sweetheart, that's what we are, and thank God. You wouldn't really want to live with all those do's and don'ts, would you?"

"That's not living," I said and meant it. "That's like being in jail."

But following the Earps from boom town to boom town wasn't my idea of living either. I was tired of hotels and endless journies. I wanted a home of my own, not like Mina's, but a place in which I belonged, in which children belonged. And I wanted Doc in it.

CHAPTER Forty

It was June, 1880 when Doc and I arrived in Tombstone. It was hot, dry, dusty. The sun blared down out of a cloudless sky, and the jagged peaks of the mountains hemming the San Pedro Valley seemed like skeletons of huge creatures that had died and been flayed by wind and heat.

Still I was awed by the country, the size and raw beauty of it, the power that seemed to rise out of the earth.

The Southern parts of Arizona and New Mexico are split by long valleys running North out of Mexico, and those valleys are separated by mountains, great barriers of rock that at first glance seem impenetrable, but in which, here and there, are canyons like doors in the rock, secret passages for those who know and use them.

255

And in each of those valleys and canyons, though neither Doc nor I were aware of it at the time, were rustlers, outlaws, men full of greed and without conscience who stopped at nothing to achieve their desires; men who stole cattle, robbed stages and freight wagons, who murdered without hesitating, and who terrorized the innocent in town and on the grasslands. These were the men who Doc and Wyatt, a little more than a year later, would meet in the showdown that has become history.

In those valleys were old Man Clanton and his sons, Ike, Phin, and Billy; Joe Hill; Mike Gray; the McLaury boys, Frank and Tom. In those valleys were John Ringo, Indian Charley, Pete Spence, Curly Bill, the so-called "Texas cowboys," who, hand in hand with Sheriff Johnny Behan would soon be robbing the county blind.

Out of this isolation, from domains that stretched as far as anyone could see, a madness had come over these men. They were kings with no one to tell them no. And so the evil grew, and Doc was in the middle of it, a major player, against my will.

But the way I see it we all dig our own graves out of our lives, and Doc was no exception. Awaiting death, he lived as he chose, tempting Fate every day, laughing at it, hating it, trampling it underfoot when he could. I knew all of this, to my torment, for I was helpless against it.

It has been almost sixty years since we caught the stage for Tombstone ~ and found Wyatt riding shotgun. A slim, dangerous Wyatt, burned by the sun, alert as a lion.

"About time you got here," he said, spotting us. "I was going to find out what kept you."

Doc didn't answer, simply shook hands, and I watched them, two men with an understanding that eluded and annoyed me, though it shouldn't have. I'd had the same kind of friendship with Blanche, with Bessie. Perhaps Allie had been right.

Perhaps I did want all of Doc. But who could blame me? The older I got the less I could stand a waste of life, his or mine.

"This is one of my last runs," Wyatt was saying. "I'm taking over the deputy sheriff's job next month. Morg'll be riding guard."

"How's the town?" Doc asked just before handing me to my seat.

"Wide open," Wyatt answered. "Wide open."

His words hardly prepared me for what we saw. I can see the whole scene still, dancing in the summer heat like a mirage. The palo verde trees were in full, golden bloom, and the cactus were crowned with white flowers. Beside the river the mesquites and cottonwoods flourished, and the Dragoon Mountains shone rose pink and lavender in the late afternoon sun. And in the middle of the valley rose a town of planks and tents ringed by holes in the earth where a thousand men labored like moles.

I can hear it. The constant agitation of a mining town; ore wagons, freight wagons, horses, mules, burros; whistles blowing for a change of shift; pistol shots; voices raised in dispute or pleasure; the laughter and constant music from saloons and the brothels on Toughnut Street.

Tombstone never slept in those years, nor did its people. There were too many of them, and they were all busy mining riches however they could. Depending on how you looked at it, Tombstone was the best ~ or the worst ~ of the boomtowns. I took one look and hated it. True to form, Doc stepped out of the stage and fell in love.

We got settled in the Cosmopolitan Hotel, and Doc went off to look around. I called on Allie in the house on Fremont Street.

"Just like a bad penny!" she exclaimed when she opened

the door, then softened her words with a grin. "Come on in. Glad you finally made it. I'll go get Bessie and Mattie and we'll have ourselves a hen party."

We gossiped the afternoon away. Finally Allie said, "I guess you'll be hunting a place to live."

I shook my head. "I'm not staying. Doc doesn't know it yet."

They looked at me startled.

Mattie said, "You're a damn fool."

When a sharp retort rushed to my lips, Allie laid a hand on mine. "Hush!" she said to Mattie. "We all choose what's best. Kate's got her reasons, you got yours."

Then those blue eyes with the lavender edges probed me. "You know what you're doin'?"

"No...yes," I said, and we all laughed. "I just hope Doc will quit this place. We both need a home. We've been running, oh, you know, you've done it. But I'm through. I'm going to settle, and be damned."

"When you tellin' Doc?"

"Tonight."

"Good luck, kid," Bessie said. "You'll need it."

I bided my time. We had a grand supper at the Cosmopolitan - roast pork, applesauce, real ice cream and several bottles of wine. Full of food and laughter, we made our way up to our room.

"Some town!" Doc said, parting the draperies and looking out at the activity in the street.

"At least it cools off at night."

"Not so cool you have to bundle up like that," he said, looking with distaste at one of the lovely nightgowns I'd treated myself to in Iowa. "You make it damned hard with those rags you insist on wearing."

Wordlessly I removed the offending garment, having discovered that the best time to tell Doc ~ or any man ~ unpleasant news was afterwards.

"That's better." He undressed and I watched, loving him, yet with a knot in my throat.

Still, the more I thought, the more sure I became that I was right, that we needed some stability, financial and otherwise. I'd seen too many derelicts, men and women, grown old and helpless before time.

We made love with a passion we hadn't known since before Prescott. I held nothing back, fighting for both our lives.

Finally, as we lay side by side, the flickering light from the lamp washing over us, and the night breeze, fragrant with the scents of the high desert blowing the curtains like sails, Doc said, "What now, Kate? You're as nervous as a whore in church."

I was quiet, gathering courage. Then I whispered, "I can't stay here, Doc. If you have any sense you won't, either. You don't have to keep following those Earps."

"Oh, for Christ's sake!" He got up and went to the wash bowl. "I thought you'd gotten off that horse."

"No." I took another deep breath. "I'm going to Globe. There's a hotel for sale. I saw it on the way down."

He turned, astonished. "Are you asking me for a loan for this lunacy?"

"No. I've saved enough. I'll make do."

"So you're leaving me? Just like that?"

"I was hoping you'd come, too."

"You hoped wrong." He was putting on his clothes. "What would I do in a hotel? Run the desk? Act the part of inn keeper? I'm not right for it. I'm not your goddamned lap dog, either. You may have noticed."

"Of course you're not! Who said anything about that? There's lots to do in Globe. And...and we could be together." I watched him pick up his coat. "Where are you going?"

"Out. Not that it's your business."

"Don't go," I said as calmly as I could. "Please don't. Come with me. I'm begging you."

He fastened his watch chain and picked up his hat. "Go to hell, Sweetheart," he said. "Or to Globe. Same thing."

"Doc!"

He leaned over the foot of the bed. "If you want me to beg you to stay, you're asking the wrong man. We've had our fun, but there's more to be had. And women who aren't shot in the ass with ideas like yours. Good luck, Kate. And goodbye."

Then he was gone. There was no sense going after him. I'd made up my mind, and he'd made up his.

Only Allie and Bessie saw me off the next day. Doc hadn't come back, and my pride wouldn't let me search for him.

"We'll keep you posted," Allie said. "Don't worry."

Bessie hugged me. Her eyes were full. "Take care," she said. "Take care. You've got more guts than I'll ever have."

Guts! What good were guts when I'd cut my heart out? When I'd cut myself in half and left everything that mattered behind?

CHAPTER Forty-one

Tombstone, February, 1881

Dear Kate,

I'd have thought you'd have tired of being cook and scrub woman for a bunch of filthy miners by now, but apparently not. Or perhaps you have returned to your more profitable earlier profession?

I ask simply out of curiosity and because Tombstone is becoming more violent, more twisted than ever. As you probably know, it is now the seat of a new county - named for the Apache chief, Cochise - and it is being run by a gang of thieves worse, even, than those in Griffin. True to form, the Sheriff, John Behan, is right in the midst of them - a sleazy bastard if ever I met one.

In light of all this, should you read of my untimely demise - my health has improved, but I am far from bullet-proof - you may regret your actions - too late. As I promised, however, you are in my will. And as I've been lucky, you'll make out handsomely if undeservingly.

Your obd't servant,

Doc

Damn him! Urging me back in that underhanded, insulting way of his!

I ripped the letter in half and went on chopping cabbage. The day was warm. Spring was on the way, and with it a new influx of travelers. What did I need with Doc's nasty innuendos?

The hotel was paying its way. Once I'd gotten over the initial shock of leaving Doc and being on my own, I'd enjoyed running the place, even though it was the hardest work I'd ever done in my life.

The building had been neglected. It needed soap and water, new paint, carpentry, and a thorough disinfecting. The first weeks I fought fleas, lice, roaches, scorpions and the ever-present desert dust.

I hired two girls to help me, young Mexicans who weren't afraid of hard work once they understood what was required. We washed and repaired the sheets, re-stuffed mattresses, beat carpets, and hung everything in the yard to air and bleach.

In exchange for meals, a down-at-the-heels prospector named Johnny Weed repaired the wood floors and replaced windows rotted out by sun and weather. He painted, tinkered, and became invaluable, and at last I turned the shed in the rear over to him and kept him permanently.

Then I turned my attention to the kitchen. The stove was cleaned and re-blacked, and the chimney cleared of bird's nests. The floors were scrubbed, the walls white-washed. I bought new pots and pans from a traveling man who stopped overnight. Then I went out to explore.

Within a week I'd contracted with Mi Yung, a Chinaman, to supply me with vegetables from his garden and, now and then, a slaughtered pig; with Charlie Williams who owned a goat ranch, for meat, and with a local cattleman for beef.

Then I started to cook, all the dishes I'd learned over the years; gulyas, kaposztaleves, a cabbage soup,pickled cucumber salad from Hungary; roast kid, chili with beans and shredded meat; steaks, potatoes, tortillas and home-baked bread, a good variety.

Within a month people were coming only to eat, and I had to split dinner into shifts. Though I'd cried myself to sleep many a night, hard work and a constant stream of customers put an end to that. I fell into bed and slept until first light.

I was a success, and honestly, too. And though Doc wrote regularly urging me to return in his nastiest fashion, I paid no heed. I was proving my own worth using my mind, my hands, the labor of my back, and the feeling was glorious, especially for me who had always needed someone else, used men - and women ~ to survive.

So, although I answered Doc's letters, writing hasty notes long after everyone else was asleep and sometimes falling asleep myself, I had never gone back to Tombstone, never surrendered to his pleas, his mockery.

Not until Bessie wrote to me in April of that year with the news that Doc had been accused of participating in the Kinnear stage holdup and murdering the driver, Bud Philpot. He was, she said, "released on bond."

263

Kid, she wrote, *he didn't have a thing to do with it, and he has plenty of witnesses to prove it. But without you he's got into bad company, and he's drinking more than is good for any man. You busted something in him taking off like you did. Now, don't misunderstand, I know why you did it, why you needed to do it, but sometimes you got to back off a little.*

There's a badness down here. The whole town's a lit fuse, and our boys and Doc are in the middle. The cowboys and Sheriff Behan want to run us out so they can keep on stealing. And worse than that, Wyatt's taken up with the Sheriff's girl, a real fancy piece from San Francisco, so you can imagine the bad blood between the two men.

Come and visit. It won't do you any harm, and it may do some good, especially where Doc is concerned. He needs you, though it'd kill him to say it. And don't say I told you!

Allie and Lou send their love. Mattie - well, you can imagine. She's never met up with competition like this Josephine Marcus before, and if you ask me, she's going to lose. The girl is plain gorgeous, and Wyatt prances around her like a two year old stud. Can't say as I blame him.

That's my news. Come when you can.

Bessie

That letter caused me a long, hard think. While I hated to leave my new business, it seemed like I had to. Doc was in trouble, partly because of me. I looked around for someone I could trust to leave in charge, and while I was hesitating came the news of the Tombstone fire that had burned half the town to the ground. For all I knew, Doc was dead and without a loving word from me. I called Margarita, Inez, and Johnny Weed into the front room.

"I have to go to Tombstone," I explained. "It's urgent. You'll have to run the place while I'm gone. Do what I do.

Keep the beds changed, the floors swept, the slop jars cleaned out. And no fighting in here. No guns in the dining room or spurs on the beds. Can I trust you?"

The girls nodded.

Johnny said, "I'll see to it. You go on, and rest easy."

So I threw some clothes into a bag and caught the next stage for Tombstone.

CHAPTER Forty-two

"**D**ear God, let Doc be alive!"

I could smell the sickly sweet smell of newly burned wood and wet ashes from five miles away, and I leaned forward in my seat as if I could make the horses move faster up that last, steep grade.

Miraculously, the Earp houses were intact, and I made them my first stop.

"Is he alright? Doc, I mean. He wasn't hurt?" I got out in the midst of a noisy welcome.

"Hell, yes he's alright," Allie said. "It takes more'n fire to roast the devil."

"Be serious!"

She laughed. "I'm telling you ~ it'd take more'n fire to

kill that one. Or any of the rest of us. Stop fussing and sit down. Doc'll wait. We'll fill you in on the details."

There were plenty of those, and when she and Bessie had finished talking, I still wasn't sure I understood.

Bessie took over. "What we're talking about is war," she explained. "There's the cowboys who want to live by lining their pockets off the rest of us, and then there's the rest of us. It's that simple. Right now they'd like to hang Doc because he's on our side. Got it?"

I nodded. What I predicted had happened. On account of Wyatt, Doc's head was in a noose.

"Where can I find Doc?"

"He's moved into Fly's boarding house, but he's usually at the Alhambra. You want to leave your bag here?"

"No. I'll leave it at Fly's."

"You don't figure you'll have to sweet talk him to stay the night?" Allie looked innocent.

"You mean there's somebody else?" I hadn't thought about that, and the very notion gnawed at me.

"He drinks like a fish, but he's no womanizer," Allie admitted. "Besides, with that temper of his, no woman wants him."

"Sometimes I don't either," I said.

"Well, if he don't want you, come on back here. We'll make room and be damned to him."

Bessie frowned. "Shut up, Allie. He wants her. He's just too pig-headed to admit it."

"Aren't they all?"

We went out onto the street. The Dragoons were changing colors in the late afternoon light, and in the valley every tree seemed turned to gold.

"Pretty," I remarked looked out at the astonishing view.

267

"Pretty is as pretty does," Allie said. "This town's a hell hole, and no mistake. I hope we get out of here with our skins."

It was a remark I remembered later, after they'd all fled, carrying their dead with them.

•

Mrs. Fly looked at me with suspicion when I asked to leave my bag in Doc's room.

"Well, I don't know. Is he expecting you?"

"It's a surprise," I said. "I'm Mrs. Holliday. I've been up in Globe running a hotel. I'll just wash up and go find him."

She nodded and left me, and I surveyed the room for signs of a female occupant. Finding nothing, I washed, tidied my hair, and then went out into the noise, the heat, the blowing sand.

"I'm looking for Doc Holliday," I told the bartender at the Alhambra who inspected me closely.

"So's everybody," he said. "Back there." He pointed with his head toward the gaming rooms.

Seeing Doc after almost a year was like twisting a knife in my belly. Right then I'd have given anything to turn the clock back, to never have left him. It wasn't that he looked sickly, far from it, but he was guarded, hungry as a wolf, and not for food but for something other that I couldn't name.

"Doc!" I whispered. "Doc!"

He looked up slowly, blinked as if to clear his head, then smiled, but it was a cruel smile and it didn't reach those eyes of his, like burning coals.

"I'll be damned. What the hell are you doing here?"

"The fire..." I got out. "I thought you might have been hurt."

"A buzzard!" he cackled. "Come to pick my bones!

That's what you look like in that goddamned black dress. Get out of here!"

It wasn't the welcome I'd expected, though with Doc I was never sure just what I should expect. My legs were shaking, and I sat down suddenly.

"I'd like a drink," I said.

He pushed back his chair. "And what else?" he asked.

"You," I said, throwing propriety to the wind.

The others at the table got up suddenly, embarrassed, but Doc stopped them. "Stick around," he said. "This should be interesting. The errant mistress returns."

Shaking their heads, they left. I clasped my hands together nervously, because this was a Doc I hadn't seen, a man driven to the wall and careless of who he wounded.

Someone put a glass on the table, and I took it and sipped slowly, trying to keep my hands from trembling.

"You're in trouble," I said. "Bad trouble. Bessie told me. Then I heard about the fire and got scared. Come back to Globe with me. I'm begging you. Get away from the Earps. Get out of this town while you can."

"Bullshit! You came to dance on my grave! You came for the money. I know you, Kate. You never cared for anybody in your life but yourself."

"That's not true."

"Isn't it?" He emptied his glass and poured another.

"No. And you know it."

"You'd sleep with a priest if you thought he'd hear your confession," he said, and his words fell between us like bullets. "I know all about you, Kate."

"That's not what you wrote me."

"Shit! I was drunk. I've been drunk a lot lately."

"So they tell me."

269

"Who's been talking?"

"The girls."

"Pah! The girls. A bunch of fools. What do they know? Did they tell you I'm out on bail and couldn't leave if I wanted to?"

"No," I said. "Who put up the money?"

"Wyatt."

I downed my whiskey in one gulp. "He'll have you hanged before this is through! And all in the name of friendship. Or they will, those bastards out there, those cowboys, whoever they are. I saved you once, Doc, and by God, I'll do it again."

His eyebrow rose. His mood changed so swiftly I was unprepared. When he spoke again, his voice was soft, caressing. "Ah, Kate. The ever faithful. I remember you on the way up from Griffin. A wild woman. A gypsy. What do you propose to do?"

"I'll think of something." Actually, my head was spinning. I hadn't had a drink in a long time. "I left my bag in your room. Let's go back there."

"Lusty bitch," he said. "I can't forget that." He stood up, weaving a little. "I've missed you."

"Me, too," I said.

We weren't in the room a minute before we were in each other's arms. The old magic was back, tinged as always with fear, as if time was running out, the hounds of destiny snapping at our heels.

I stepped away for a second to unbutton my basque, and he caught my hands. "Quick, aren't you?" he said. "But before we go on, tell me the truth. Who have you been with in Globe?"

It was so unexpected after the passion of his kiss that I simply stood there trying to understand what he meant. Finally

I said, "Nobody. I've been working. You know that. I wrote you."

Then it came, as I knew it would someday.

"I know about you and Wyatt."

How could I answer? I took a deep breath and felt my heart leaping under my fingers.

"Who told you?"

"Mattie."

Of course. It made sense, though what she really knew was anybody's guess. I kept calm.

"Mattie doesn't know everything. She just thinks she does. Since I caught her with my Mama's necklace, she's been after me."

"But you haven't denied it."

"No," I said. "It happened. After Anson died and before I knew about you. I was lonely. Miserable. And it was only once. You can't call it an affair. A mistake is more to the point."

He showed his teeth in a wicked smile. "A mistake! You're goddamned right a mistake! My woman and my best friend, and neither of you with guts enough to tell me."

"What's to tell? If we started telling each other about everybody we'd be here for a month."

"You mean you would." He put his hands on my shoulders and looked down at me. I could smell the whiskey on him; feel anger in the strength of his fingers. I'd be black and blue from the pressure of them in the morning.

"You're a whore, Kate," he said, bringing his face close to mine. "Better than some, but you're still a whore. And you waited until you thought I was dead to come back, didn't you? You thought you'd get my money and my friend into the bargain." He shook me until my teeth knocked together, and it was that that made me angry at last.

271

I wriggled free then hauled off and slapped him with all the strength and pent-up passion I had.

"You goddamned drunken son of a bitch!" I yelled, not caring if they heard me on the street. "You can't tell a liar when you meet one. You don't know gold from shit. I came down here because I was sick to death worrying, and this is what I get." I drew back for another blow, but he caught my wrist.

"Do that again, and I'll break your arm," he snarled.

"And I'll get you for this," I hissed back, meaning every word. "If it's the last thing I do, I'll get you."

I pulled loose and ran out hatless, my bodice unbuttoned, and I stood panting on the corner, not knowing where to go or what to do.

How long I stood there, I never knew. I was wild, crazy, wanting to pull down the whole town on their heads. A whore! That was where life had got me. And love.

"I'll get you, Doc," I said outloud. "I'll make you pay for that."

As I spoke, a gentleman stopped beside me and took my arm. I opened my mouth to tell him to leave, but he spoke first.

"Can I help you, ma'am? Tombstone isn't the place for ladies like you at this hour."

He was well dressed, unlike most of those I'd seen, with brown eyes that sparkled, and in which I, mistakenly read kindness.

All the strength went out of me. I hadn't had a meal since breakfast, and the whiskey I'd drunk wasn't sitting well. "Thank you," I said. "I...I just arrived in town, and I haven't eaten or found a place to sleep. Perhaps you could direct me?"

He offered his arm. "Come with me."

But I held back. Instinct was strong in me not to trust this man who seemed so decent.

"It's alright," he said. "I'm the Sheriff here."

"Oh." I inspected him more closely. On the surface he didn't seem the bastard everyone said he was. But still, there was something.

"Helping ladies in distress is part of my job." He smiled. "Come on. I'll buy you a welcome supper. Where are your things?"

"With a friend." I laughed bitterly, and he bent to me.

"Who? Would I know him?"

I laughed again. "Doc Holliday."

"Ah, yes," he said, "our infamous murderer." He cocked his head. "How is it that a lady like you is acquainted with Doc?"

"It's a long story."

He put on the hat that he'd been holding. "You can tell me over supper," he said, and led me away like a lamb to the slaughter house.

•

When I woke up I was in a strange room lying fully dressed on the bed. My head throbbed, and the light that entered through the curtains struck my eyes like a knife.

I struggled to sit up and then collapsed onto the pillow. What had happened? Try as I would, all I remembered was Doc's face as I'd seen it last, lips drawn back from white teeth, eyes glittering.

Bit by bit I pieced together the events of our quarrel, but what then? Plainly I had to get up, move around, wash. I was a mess, smelling like a bar-room floor.

Slowly I crawled to the edge of the bed. I still had my shoes on. How strange!

The face that looked back at me from the mirror was

ghastly ~ hair loose and snarled, eyes both sunken, the lids swollen, and along my jaw a bruise that could only have come from a blow. It was enough to make me sick, and it did. I vomited into the slop jar, then went back to the mirror.

"Look at yourself!" I ordered. "The dregs. Look! You're disgusting!"

Then I sat down on the bed and wept.

Someone had left my bag inside the door. It must have been him, the Sheriff. I straightened. What had he done? What had I done? My stomach knotted. What had I done?

I washed and put on a new blouse I dug out of my bag. Then I tried the door. It opened and I stepped into the corridor. At least that was familiar. I was in the Cosmopolitan, and thank God. For a moment I feared I'd been kidnapped.

No one stopped me or spoke as I crossed the lobby to the street where the shock of heat and light turned me queasy again. I headed for Allie's, choking down bile. Whatever had happened, she'd know.

She came to the door looking worried, and I soon found out why. When I stepped inside, all hell broke loose.

I'd never seen Wyatt in a true rage before then, and I hoped I never would again. Pity those who had to face him, to look into those eyes behind the barrel of a gun, or anywhere else, either. If I'd been a fainting woman, I'd have dropped right there.

His voice sliced through the others' babble. "Alright, Kate. Suppose you tell me why you did this, and how. And tell the truth, or by God I'll see you in jail where you belong."

"Did what?" I stood there feeling like I was impaled on a spit. "I don't know what you're talking about."

"Signed Doc's life away." He waved a paper at me. "Don't play the innocent. Here's your signature. Here's your

274

confession saying Doc held up that stage and killed Philpot."

The accusation sank in, but made no sense. "How would I know that?" I asked. "I wasn't even here when it happened."

"Exactly. So why this?"

I shook my head. "Where'd it come from?"

"From Behan. Early this morning. He filed it as evidence against Doc."

Then I remembered. I must have staggered because Allie caught my arm and led me to a chair. "Lay off her," she said "She's had a hell of a shock."

"So have I." Wyatt was grim.

"Doc and I had a fight," I began. "He threw me out, and Behan found me. He was...he was kind."

"He's a scum bag," Wyatt said. "Go on."

They were all watching me, a jury of my peers. I struggled to remember. "We went to supper. I hadn't eaten all day. Then..." I closed my eyes trying to pierce through the haze. "He got me drunk. That's it. And then he kept at me and at me about something. About Doc. How he'd thrown me out, and didn't I want to sign a complaint."

I looked up. They stood around me ~ Wyatt, Virge, Allie, Bessie, Morg and Lou ~ only Mattie was absent, and a good thing, too. I'd have torn her apart. They stood there waiting as if their lives hung on my testimony, which in a way, they did.

"He hit me." I touched the swelling on my jaw. "Doc didn't do this. He wouldn't hit a woman. You know that. It was Behan. He got mad at me, I can't remember why, but he did."

"Go on."

But the mist in my head wouldn't clear. I shook my head. "I didn't sign a confession about Doc or any stage coach holdup," I said finally. "Why would I? If I signed anything, I

275

thought it was a complaint, and I don't remember doing it. That's all I know. I'll swear to it in court if I have to."

Wyatt let out a breath. "Good. That's what I wanted to hear." He picked up his hat, and he and Virge and Morg went to the door.

"Stay here tonight," he advised. "We want you in court in one piece."

•

In the end my testimony got the evidence against Doc thrown out of court.

He waited for me outside. "Happy?" he asked.

"Not especially."

"When are you leaving?"

He couldn't wait to see the last of me. I couldn't blame him.

"Tomorrow morning. And I won't be back."

He sighed. "I know you. You'll haunt me till I'm six feet under. How much would it take to keep you away?"

A hot wind blew down the street pushing dust and trash ahead of it. In the mountains thunder rumbled, and I caught the scent of rain close by and coming closer. All that while my pride, my love were shredded into bits and thrown to the storm.

"I don't want your money, Doc. I've never wanted that, no matter what you think. You can't give me what I want. It's not in you. You called me a whore, well I'll tell you something. It's you who's the whore. You took what I had and spit on it. You took my heart like it was trash, but it was all I had."

Then I walked away and left him standing there.

CHAPTER Forty-three

Time passed in a haze. I went about my work without knowing what I was doing, and without caring. My hands and body moved. The rest of me was shut off, closed in, numb. I went on like a shadow. Even Johnny Weed noticed.

"You alright?" he asked.

"Yes."

"You don't look it."

"I'll be fine," I said and turned away from his concern.

That was a rainy summer. It seemed it rained for months, the weather mirroring my despair, and never mind that the desert burst into bloom the way it will, given water. I refused to look at it. How did it dare to lift itself, proclaim life when I was withering?

That was also the summer that Geronimo jumped the reservation and headed South to his beloved mountains and valleys. When I heard the news I cheered him on, hoping he'd kill them all - Earps, cowboys, Doc, Mattie, the lot of them - retake his homeland and rule over it like the chief that he was.

Who were the more barbaric? The white men were no more civilized than the red, plundering and pillaging just as had always been done, and Doc and I were no better. We'd plundered each other, and both of us had lost.

August trickled away, and September. The desert remained green, but it held no peace in its lushness. Never again, I thought, would I trust in love, give away everything with gladness.

And then one afternoon Johnny Weed came to the kitchen where I was sweating over a pot of a Hungarian stew.

"There's a gent out front to see you."

"Who is it?" I drew my arm across my dripping forehead.

"Don't know. City fella. Says it's important."

I untied my apron, wiped my face again. What I looked like had become unimportant. I no longer cared.

Doc was standing at the front desk, and he was smiling that devil's smile while the rays of the sun made a halo around his blond head.

My first impulse was to turn and run across the desert into the mountains, anywhere so as not to have to talk to him. I hated the sight of him, hated what we'd done, what I'd become because of him.

I said, "Get out of here."

He was unfazed. "Not till I say what I came to say. What happened was partly my fault, and I know it."

278

"You're damn right it was. What else do you want?"

"Nasty as ever," he said, but he softened his words with a smile. God! I knew that smile and how it lit up his eyes from the inside out.

"Stop smiling!" I snapped. "Go away!"

He was unperturbed. "Is there a place we can talk? Or do we have to argue in public?" He flicked his eyes at Johnny Weed who was watching open-mouthed.

"Right here is fine," I said. "Johnny, go stir my stew. I'll call if I need you."

He went, grumbling.

"Speak your piece." I faced Doc. "And then leave. I'm full up, so you can't stay here."

"Do we have to stand here like a pair of boobies? Can't we at least sit down?"

He was being impossible. Nobody did that better than Doc. I gestured to two chairs against the wall.

"That's better." He pulled out a cigar, and I lost the last shred of control I had.

"For God's sake, spill it! I've got things to do, and they don't include social calls. Haven't we done enough to each other?"

"We have."

"Well then?"

"I came to apologize. What you said to me when you left got me thinking. Perhaps you were right."

"Of course I was. And what are you doing with that cigar? It's no good for you."

"Nothing's good for me," he said. "What's it matter?"

"It doesn't. Not to me."

"You were the only good thing," he said slowly. "And I shit on you."

279

He wanted me back, for what reason I couldn't determine, but I was sure it was a selfish one. Seeing him, however, had awakened me from what had been a tormented sleep. What we had done was dreadful, but the clash of our differences was, as it had always been, exhiliarating, like fireworks that burst into flame and awaken long forgotten impulses.

"You did, and that's a fact. But I got even."

"Let's call it quits then. Come back with me."

"You're mad," I said. "What do you think I am? Some toy you can move around when it pleases you? Some corn dolly you hang on the wall? Some fool like Mattie moping around waiting for you to crook your finger? You can go to hell in a handcart for all I care."

He threw back that yellow head of his and laughed. And laughed until I stood up and stamped my foot.

"Stop it! Don't you laugh at me."

"I'm not," he said when he'd gotten control. He hesitated. "Then again, maybe I am. You're so direct. You just say whatever's on your mind, such as it is." His eyebrow lifted and he settled more firmly in the chair.

"You want to trade insults? I'll give you a few."

He reached up and caught my hand, pulling me closer. "No, Sweetheart. I came to make up, only between us we've botched it."

"As usual." Oh, but the way he'd said "Sweetheart," had stirred the fire I thought was out. I pulled away. He'd not do this to me.

He was perceptive, and he knew me better than anyone else ever had or would. He stood up and took my face in his hands. "Look at you," he said gently. "Working like a char woman. You deserve better."

"I won't get better from you," I said and heard my voice

shaking. It was the feel of him that finally did me in. Oh, such a weakling I was! Such a fool! No, not foolish, not that. For when you find your place of belonging it's worse to deny it. I'd learned that much shuffling from stove to bedrooms and back, not seeing, not being half alive.

"There's a fiesta in Tucson," he said. "Come with me. Have fun, Kate. You look like you've forgotten how."

"I have." I rested my head in its old place on his shoulder. "Alright. I don't mind going. But then I'm coming back here."

"We'll see," he said, and turning my face up to his, he kissed me. "Go pack your bags," he said when he'd drawn away and was looking at me as if he wanted to take me then and there.

"Go on in the kitchen and get some stew. It's special. I'll be ready in a bit."

In my room I looked in the mirror. What was it that attracted him? I'd let myself go and now had scant time to make repairs. I called Inez for hot water, and she came, her dark eyes wide.

"So handsome!" she exclaimed. "You'll be proud to be at the *baile* with him."

"Well he won't be proud of me looking like this. Get out my traveling dress. No, not the black one, the dark blue." God forbid he should see me in black! "Take it out and brush it while I wash."

I bathed, used the last of my perfume, and brushed my hair until it shone. Thank goddess it was still golden and healthy, rippling around my shoulders like a heavy shawl.

Then I pulled out my pot of rouge and painted youth back onto my cheeks.

We'd go to the fiesta. We'd dance, eat, laugh, make love, and why not? What good had suffering done? Never again, I

281

vowed, because never again would I lose myself in him. I'd learned by being knocked down, torn up, and putting the pieces back together. The repairs were difficult, but in the end, the glue held.

CHAPTER Forty-four

Tucson was a collection of dusty streets and adobe houses clustered together in a natural basin that was ringed by stone mountains and watered by the Santa Cruz River. It was running full because of the heavy rains, and along its banks cottonwoods rustled, and the palo verde trees waved thin, green branches.

It seemed everyone for a hundred miles had gathered for the celebration. There were cowboys on horseback, soldiers, gamblers, respectable women in cascading mantillas, and the madam, Big Refugia, parading her whores in their bright skirts and high heels. There were musicians with silver conchos sewed on their tight-fitting pants, and here and there a priest in somber black as if to remind us that happiness was fleeting.

Street vendors sold everything from menudo and fresh tamales to gorditas and chicharrons, and I sampled them all with an appetite sharpened by several nights of love making.

"For the sight of you licking your fingers like a field hand, I'll buy you five more of those," Doc said. "Or would you prefer my handkerchief?"

"Five more, please," I said. "This is wonderful. I'm glad we came."

"Enjoy it," he said, growing serious. "Things are coming to a head in Tombstone and if they need me I may have to go back."

"If who needs you?"

"Wyatt. Virge. Hell, the whole town! The gang has been itching for a fight, and sooner or later they'll get it. Frankly, I hope it's soon. I'd like to get rid of the whole filthy bunch."

"Don't tell me anymore. I'm sick of it all," I said.

"I won't. We're here to play. Why don't you walk around awhile? There's a game in that tent I think I'll sit in on. When the dance starts, come and get me."

"Alright."

I watched a puppet show for a minute, then lured by the coolness of the river, I made my way there, going downstream away from the crowd. I wanted to think. If there was going to be a showdown, Doc would be in it. Could I go back to Globe and erase the dread from my mind? I doubted it.

I found a flat rock and sat and looked into the water, then up at the Catalina Mountains to the North. Above them one star glimmered in the purple twilight, while to the West the entire horizon blazed, the heart of a dying fire. A breeze danced along the bank, and the cottonwood leaves pattered like rain. The music of the fiesta seemed far away, part of another, different world.

How long I sat I never knew, but the shadows were long, and the river no longer sparkled but had turned dark, mysterious, belonging once more to itself.

Suddenly ill at ease, I shivered. And then I heard it - the dreadful wailing of a woman lost, desperate, betrayed. Dear God what a sound! Where was it coming from, and from whom?

I peered through the darkness, and saw no one, yet the mourning continued like a prayer, on and on until I covered my ears with my hands to drown it out.

Of course I'd heard the Spanish legend of *La Llorona*, the weeping woman seeking her dead children, but as with other fairy tales, I'd ignored it. But this agony couldn't be ignored. It fired every nerve in my body so that I trembled, remembering the rest of the legend. How trouble came to those who heard her. How they were doomed one way or another, with no chance of escape.

Terrified, I picked up my skirts and ran, dodging branches, jumping over stones and ditches. I had to find Doc.

But before I did I bumped squarely into Morgan Earp.

CHAPTER Forty-five

"**W**here's Doc?" he asked without noticing my terror.

"I don't know." I had the ridiculous notion that without my help he'd never find Doc and would return to Tombstone alone.

"Kate, I have to find him. We need him."

Morgan was my favorite of the Earp brothers. He was young, handsome, hot-headed, and that night he seemed like a coiled spring ready to bust loose. I could imagine him charging through the fiesta in search of Doc.

"Oh hell, Morg, he's gambling. Relax and go buck the tiger yourself, or better yet, come dance with me."

A band was playing one of those sinuous old songs from deep in Mexico. I knew the steps, the swaying motions, how to

286

appear demure and flirtatious at the same time. I held out my hand to him.

"No time, Kate. Save me one though, will you?" He flashed his sweet smile before crashing into the tent where Doc was.

They came out together, moving fast.

"Morg and I have to leave," Doc said, and they walked away so quickly I had to trot after them.

There was trouble coming. I'd have known it even without La Llorona's warning. I forgot about going home. If Doc was walking into danger, I was going along to try and stop him. "Not without me," I said when I caught up.

"We're in a hurry, and it'll be a rough trip. Stay here and I'll come back and get you."

"If you can stand the trip, so can I."

"Goddamn it, Kate, do what I tell you!"

"Not this time," I said. "If you're going to Tombstone, I'm going with you, and you can't stop me."

He stopped walking and looked at me, hoping to stare me down. Then suddenly he smiled, a lightning flash that crossed his face and disappeared as quickly as it had come. "Alright. But no complaints."

"You've never heard me complain before. You won't now."

We caught the evening Eastbound train. It was half empty, and we took seats together.

"Get some sleep while you can," Doc advised, and obligingly I closed my eyes. But instead of sleeping, I listened.

"It'll be soon," Morg said. "Marietta Spence told Josie she heard Pete and some others talking. They'd like to get rid of us and Ike Clanton at the same time. They got wind of how Wyatt offered Ike the reward if he'd bring in Leonard, Head and

287

Crane, and the rest of them are on the prod."

"Leonard!" I sat straight up. "Bill Leonard from Las Vegas?"

"Go back to sleep," Doc said.

"Not till you tell me."

"Yes, that Bill Leonard. He opened a store in Tombstone. Probably was melting stolen gold in his back room before he decided to ride with the cowboys."

"I told you he was no good," I said, and Doc looked annoyed.

"Trust you for two things. Intuition and having the last word. Now go back to sleep."

But I didn't. Without shame I eavesdropped, and by the time we pulled in at Benson I had a fair idea of what had happened.

It appeared that Wyatt had approached Ike Clanton and offered him a reward for turning in the real robbers of the Kinnear Stage. Once they were in custody, Doc's name ~ and Wyatt's own ~ would have been cleared. The plan would have worked except that Leonard and Head got killed doing some other dirty work, and Crane, likewise, leaving Ike as a betrayer without a payoff. When the rest of the gang learned about the doublecross, Ike weaseled out by saying Wyatt had made up the whole thing. Logically or not, the gang was forcing him into a showdown to clear his name. And according to Marietta Spence the wife of one of the outlaws, that showdown would be soon.

Behan, of course, was no help. Frank Stilwell, his deputy, and Pete Spence, had held up the Bisbee stage a few months earlier, and had gotten off scot free. The guilty were tracked down and brought in by Wyatt and his posses only to be let go in a matter of hours. Even worse, Wyatt had stolen Behan's girl, a bitter pill for a self-styled charmer like Johnny to swallow. Justice, it seemed, had disappeared from Tombstone, leaving both the town and the new county to the wolves.

The closer we got, the more I could feel evil running loose. I imagined it, like a nightmare out of the Apocalypse, racing the train on iron shod hooves.

I must have dozed, because suddenly Doc was shaking me.

"Wake up. Morg's got a buckboard waiting. And no complaints even if your bones rattle."

I dragged myself onto the station platform. My mouth tasted of dust and metal like I had a bit in my teeth. Doc put his arm around me, and I could feel his excitement. He was ready to shoot, to strike and loving every minute of it, while I ~ I was a nuisance to be pushed aside, made to behave, to watch while he got shot at by a gang of thieves.

"Quit spooning and let's get going!" Morg was holding the reins of a restless team.

I stepped away from the warmth of Doc's body. "Why don't you Earps fight your own battles?" I asked. "Why do you have to drag Doc in?"

Doc took my elbow. "They didn't drag me. It's more like the other way around. Now climb up there." He shoved me up on the rough plank seat and climbed aboard himself.

Nights are cold on the high desert in late October, and the piece of moon that lit the road South gave little light and no warmth at all. I wrapped my shawl around me and huddled between the two men. In the distance a pack of coyotes howled, a wild and lonely echo of the cry of La Llorona.

I felt in my pocket for my derringer, but the feel of the cold metal gave little assurance. If we should be ambushed, what good were two shots against many?

The road wound through sandhills whose weird shapes

showed against the sky, and whose arroyos offered a thousand hiding places. It was a stark landscape, unfeeling, uncaring of any kind of life at all. So I was almost glad when we reached the noise, the lights, the confusion of town. From all appearances it was just an ordinary night in Tombstone.

CHAPTER Forty-six

The next day passed quietly, although to anyone in the know the tension was there, like a rope frayed to the breaking point.

Doc took me to dinner at the Maison Doree, and we'd just sat down when Wyatt came in with a woman on his arm, a woman whose beauty rivaled Blanche's.

"So that's her," I murmured.

"Want them to join us?"

"Sure." I was curious about this Josephine Marcus who'd switched men in mid-stream. And such men! If ever I saw complete opposites, it was Wyatt and Behan.

Close up, she was even more astonishing, huge eyes cut out of dark brown velvet and a complexion any woman would kill for. No wonder Mattie was in such a state. This girl had it all, youth, beauty, and an air of sophistication that put everybody else out of the competition.

I laughed to myself thinking how I'd been planning revenge on Mattie for blabbing what she thought was the truth to Doc. Life, itself, was getting revenge in the person of this girl, so perfect, so poised in her wine-red evening finery, with her chin tilted slightly in my direction as if she expected trouble.

Well, she'd not get it from me. I liked her. She was young and nervous like everybody else, but there was a feistiness in her, a rock-solid determination to hang on to her man. Wyatt had more than met his match!

I laughed again, thinking about it, and she was watching me and probably wondering what it was that made me smile.

She said, "I'm so glad to meet you at last. You're not what I expected."

"What was that?"

"I don't know, but you're not it."

A graceful touch, I thought, and gave her high marks.

"Doc has been very kind to me," she said after a pause. "I guess he's told you about the situation."

"Allie and Bessie did, too," I said, throwing them in to see how she'd handle it.

"I guess they painted me pretty black." She looked down at her hands in her lap. "But it...it just happened between Wyatt and me. I was in love before I even knew it."

"As a matter of fact," I said, "Bessie wrote me some time back and said you were beautiful. Anyhow, why should you care what people say?"

"I don't. Not now. Oh, I did at first, I'd gotten myself in such a mess coming out here engaged to Johnny and then throwing him over for Wyatt. But I won't apologize for doing it. I

292

couldn't have stayed with Johnny. Not after I found him out."

She was honest. She didn't give a hoot in hell for gossip or disapproval. Those huge brown eyes held more than a hint of arrogance.

I liked her even more after she leaned toward me and said in a low voice, "And now I'm scared. Part of this is my fault, and if something happens to Wyatt..." She shivered.

"There's not much we can do about it," I said. "Except pray."

When she spoke again, it was in despair. "I think," she said slowly, "that I've forgotten how."

When was the last time I'd said a prayer? "When the time comes, maybe we'll both remember," I said.

But when the time came, as it did two days later, I was frozen in terror and my mind was blank.

•

What would have made it easier for me, had I thought, was the plain fact that a cowboy rustler gun man just wasn't the equal of Doc, Wyatt, or even Virge or Morg. I'd seen Doc practicing, and I knew Wyatt did the same. I'd also seen both of them in a rage: Wyatt cold as ice and deadly, and Doc his opposite but just as lethal. Together they were invincible.

I went out that fateful day and headed for Allie's, wanting to stir up some trouble of my own. It was petty in view of the situation, but I was restless and couldn't wait to dangle my impression of the Marcus girl in front of Mattie. But I never got to Allie's.

Doc and Ike Clanton had tangled the night before, and Doc had drawn his pistol. Ike, however, was unarmed.

"Go get a gun then," Doc told him. "I'll meet you whenever you're ready."

293

He just wanted it over with. You can live with tension only so long, and Doc had reached the end of his tether. "I'll blow that bastard to hell!" he'd said when he came in. "And the rest of them, too."

Ike was coming into Fly's just as I reached the door; a nasty looking hulk, not handsome like the McLaury boys or self-possessed like Ringo. Wyatt's description of Behan came back to me just as Ike spoke. "Scum bag."

"Where's Doc?" He'd nearly knocked me over but seemed ignorant of the fact.

No manners, either, I thought, eyeing him. "I don't know," I said.

"Tell him I'm looking for him."

"Next time you come smashing into a lady, apologize!" I snapped. "You deserve what's coming to you."

I left before he had a chance to reply.

I repeated the conversation to Doc. He buckled on his pistol under his blond buffalo coat he'd won in a Cheyenne poker game and that he swore brought him luck. "If God lets me live long enough, he shall see me," he said. "Go on to breakfast."

Then he was gone, moving with that light, taut grace that characterized his anger.

He hadn't kissed me goodbye! I hadn't wished him luck! "Oh God, oh God," I wailed, and that was as close as I came to a prayer.

"Stay off the street," he'd warned.

That left me pacing the floor in Fly's house, back and forth, back and forth, expecting to hear gunfire at any minute, and feeling that the walls were pressing in on me.

Finally I went to a window that looked out on the vacant lot between Fly's and the little place where a black woman ran a whore house.

What happened next has lived in my memory for over fifty years. As if looking through a long telescope, I can see five men, Ike and Billy Clanton, Tom and Frank McLaury and Billy Claiborne coming into the vacant lot from the O.K. Corral. I watch them knowing they are waiting for Doc and wondering how I can get word to him. Too late! Wyatt, Virgil, Morg and Doc turn the corner into the lot from Fremont Street.

What they intend is clear. There is a readiness about them to do what they have to do once and for all, as if they've reached the limit of tolerance, all four at once, and are now parts of a whole, moving and thinking unanimously.

What follows happens so fast it seems it is over before I can take a breath. The two factions are ten feet apart when the shooting begins. Frank McLaury is hit, and staggers away toward the street. Billy Clanton is shot almost immediately, and falls backwards against the building, trying to draw his pistol and firing wild before he can pull it from the holster. Ike runs, leaving his wounded brother. He stops and grabs Wyatt's gun hand just before ducking into the passage between Fly's studio and the house. Just like him, I think, all bluff and bluster and yellow as a mongrel cur.

There is a lull of maybe ten seconds before someone ~ I think it is Johnny Behan from the glimpse I get of his big cow hat - fires a shot from the passageway, and the others turn that direction to protect themselves. Then Tom McLaury takes advantage of the distraction and aims at Morg over the saddle of his nervous horse, and Morg, shot through the back, goes down. The horse panics, dragging Tom with it.

Where the sidewalk had been on Fremont Street is a deep ditch. The town is laying pipe, and the hole has been left open. The crazed animal jumps over the dirt and out onto the

295

street, leaving Tom exposed. Doc nails him from no more than ten feet away with both barrels of buckshot. He drops the shotgun and turns toward Frank who, mortally wounded, has somehow staggered out into the street. I don't know who finishes him, whether it is Wyatt or Doc, but he falls, quivers once, and fires one shot before he dies. Doc spins around and falls.

The scream I hear is my own, and La Llorona's, filled with anguish. Slowly then, as if he is stunned or wounded, Doc gets up and stands looking around the battle ground.

It is over. For minutes no one seems to move. The players stand in place like the subjects of one of Camillus Fly's photographs, and I can see them still, and hear the sudden, deathly silence, as if even the town is holding its breath, and the wind, and the mountains under that cold, grey sky. It is a little after two o'clock on October 26, 1881.

At some time during the shooting, a bullet had gone through the window over my head. Though I didn't know it, my hair was full of glass, and my face was bleeding in a dozen places, but my involvement with the scene just played out was so great, I didn't feel anything.

When the town finally shook itself back into reality, I ran out onto the street, my heart in my mouth.

Josie was running up Fremont Street, hatless, her skirts blowing up to her knees. She ran straight up to Wyatt and into his arms, leaving Mattie, who had come out with Allie, Lou, and Bessie, to stand alone, watching while her man publicly proclaimed his choice.

They took Virge and Morg away in a barouche while I watched, and then Doc, limping a little, came up to me, his face registering shock at my appearance.

"What happened? Are you hit?" were the first words he spoke.

I was crying out of sheer relief, and couldn't understand what he meant. "Hit? Why?"

He took my arm. "Let's get out of here," he said and hurried me back to the room.

"This is awful," he said. "Awful! You could've been killed. Look at yourself."

I was bleeding freely from cuts on my cheeks and forehead, and my hair sparkled like a frost had come over it.

"I'm alright," I got out, "but what about you?"

He peeled off his overcoat and trousers. There was a nasty red bruise on his left hip.

"I told you this coat was lucky," he said grimly. "That and my holster saved me."

"Thank God." I sat down suddenly, all the courage gone out of me. "Thank God." I let the tears flow.

In a repition of that long ago night in St. Louis, Doc came to me and gently washed the blood from my face. His hands were deft, graceful; his eyes searched mine.

"We've cheated death again," he murmured.

I didn't answer. I put my arms around him and held on, memorizing the feel of him down to the bones, melting in the heat of the fire of victory.

•

That should have been the end of the trouble, but it was only the beginning. The whole town and half the county showed up for the funeral of Billy Clanton and the McLaury's. And then Ike Clanton swore out a warrant for the arrest of Wyatt and Doc, Virgil and Morgan.

"He can't do that!" I protested. "Everybody saw what happened. It was self-defense."

"That crowd doesn't give up easy," Doc said. "Behan's

297

behind this, sure as you're born. He's been sitting on a gold mine like the rest and isn't about to quit."

"The hell with them!" I shouted. "I'll bust you out again if I have to. You and Wyatt both. And I bet Josie would help me."

"I bet she would," he agreed. "But I want you to go back to Globe. Don't get involved in this or give testimony. They'll come after you simply to get at me."

"Let them try."

He chuckled. "You against the outlaws. I'd like to turn you loose, but there's too many of them. Do what I tell you, and I'll come when I can."

"Promise?"

"I'll try my best," he said and went off to jail whistling.

I returned to Globe, but Johnny Weed had the hotel running as smoothly as ever, so I went back to Tombstone, thinking that I knew every twist and turn and bump in the road after so many trips.

Doc gritted his teeth. "Don't you ever do anything I tell you, even for your own good?"

"Damn my own good. You're not going to hang, and that's that."

"You going to burn the town down like before?" he asked, looking hopeful.

"I will if I have to."

The hearings dragged on. Behan and his cronies swore to tell the truth and then lied through their teeth, even to the point of testifying that the cowboys had been unarmed and shot while surrendering. The honest witnesses, the town people, spoke the truth.

On December 1, 1881, Judge Wells Spicer handed down his decision. I have a copy of it still.

"...When, therefore, the defendants, regularly or appointed officers, marched down Fremont Street to the scene of the subsequent homicide, they were going where it was their right and duty to go; they were doing what it was their right and duty to do; and they were armed, as it was their right and duty to be armed, when approaching men whom they believed to be armed and contemplating resistance....

...It does not appear to have been a wanton slaughter of unresisting and armed innocents, who were yielding graceful submission to officers of the law, or surrendering to or fleeing from their assailants, but armed and defiant men, accepting the wager of battle and succumbing only in death...

...I conclude the performance of the duty imposed upon me by saying in the language of the statute: "There being no sufficient cause to believe the within named Wyatt S. Earp and John H. Holliday guilty of the offense mentioned within, I order them to be released."

Doc was free!

CHAPTER Forty-seven

It wasn't a week before the threatening letters started to come. Everyone got one ~ Doc, Wyatt, Judge Spicer, Virgil, Morg who was still flat on his back and cussing, John Clum the mayor and publisher of the Epitaph, and me.

"How will you feel when Doc is dead?" my letter read. It was printed on brown paper and was barely legible.

Doc's letter, printed in the same crude fashion, said, "Your next."

"Goddamnit!" he exclaimed. "The dumb bastards can't even spell. Looks like we'll have to take care of the rest of them.

"We?"

"Yes, we. Wyatt and I. Not you. You're leaving on the

next stage for home. I'm staying here awhile. With Virge and Morg both laid up there's no telling what they'll try to pull."

"And leave you to face them hoping you'll be lucky?"

"If I have you to worry about, they'll get me that much quicker. I can't protect the whole damn world."

Home. The sound was comforting. Home was a place I'd built with my own hands, a refuge where I could lock the door and sleep through the night without threat or gunfire.

"Alright," I agreed. "But be careful and come as quick as you can. You promised."

But Doc never lived in Globe, and we never shared a comfortable house together, were never a couple talking over the little events of our lives with pleasure and quiet laughter.

You can't domesticate wild creatures. And Doc was a wild thing. Hemmed in, caged, he paced and burned and ate at himself from the inside out. I should have known that from the first, and maybe I did in some small corner of my mind, but that never stopped me from trying. My idea of home was something I hadn't had since I left Hungary, and it was romanticized, vague, composed of longings that had nothing to do with reality.

Doc and I were two different people, and in the end those differences kept us apart.

•

On December 28, 1881, someone, probably Frank Stilwell, tried to assassinate Virgil. The attempt failed, but Virge's arm was shattered, and was useless for the rest of his life.

In February, Ike Clanton called for a re-trial, once again attempting to get the men convicted for murder. But the case was thrown out of court for lack of new evidence.

And then, in March, Morgan, happy-go-lucky, handsome Morgan was shot in the back and killed as he was playing billiards in Hatch's Billiard Parlor.

Doc, who was with him, went wild. Morg had been his friend, his poker-playing, temperamental side-kick, and suddenly, before Doc's eyes, he was dead. Doc kicked in half the doors in town that night looking for Behan, Spence, Stilwell, anyone he could kill, but he found no one.

"I bought Morg a new suit," he wrote to me. "It was all I could do. I wish it was more. But one thing I can do is see that they pay for this, those back-shooting, yellow sons of bitches. Stay close to home, Sweetheart, and pray for us, Wyatt and me. We're all that's left, and we'll need it where we're going."

Wyatt saw his family onto the train, and Morg in his box into the baggage car. With all of them safe in California with the elder Earps, he was free to take his revenge, and he did so, thoroughly, coldly, without any emotion whatsoever; and Doc was at his side.

They killed Frank Stilwell in the train depot in Tucson, and left his body lying on the tracks.

"Frank came after us to try again," Doc wrote. "He just couldn't let it rest, even with Morg lying there dead. Wyatt offed him with a load of buckshot, and I filled his head with lead on Morg's behalf. That's one down and a few more to go."

Within a week Wyatt and his posse had swept the country. Indian Charley and Curly Bill were dead, and Pete Spence had fled over the border into Mexico.

And Wyatt and Doc were wanted for murder, ridiculously, seeing that Wyatt was deputy Marshal, but the fact remained. They'd wiped out most of the cowboy gang and brought peace to Tombstone, but they were fugitives from the law.

Doc wrote me from Denver. "It appears that my promise to join you will have to wait as I'm wanted for murder in

Arizona. Can you come to Denver?"

It was the same old story. Doc on the run and me running alongside panting to keep up. I stayed put and tried to erase the shootings, the killings and threats from my mind.

But Doc came once more to Arizona, in secret, he and Wyatt and several others whose names I never heard and didn't want to know.

It was July, 1882, and I heard horses enter the yard, and low voices of men. Doc came in the back way, and I dropped what I was doing and ran into his arms.

"Why are you here? Who are those people? They'll catch you and you'll hang."

"Not if you don't tell. You and that Weed of yours."

Doc had lost weight, his cheekbones poked up under tight skin, and above them his eyes glittered and danced like those of a hunting and hunted beast.

"We're on our way back to Colorado," he said. "Give us some food, and water for the horses, and wake us an hour before dawn. We got the last of the bastards."

"Who?"

"Ringo. Ran across him on the old road to Galeyville. Maybe somebody tipped him off we were coming and he was running. I don't know. But he's deader than shit. We left him in a tree and took his boots and his horse. Let whoever finds him figure it out."

"Is it finished now?" I asked. "Can we settle down and just live like other people?"

He laughed eerily. "Who knows? I don't. Trouble seems to like both of us. Now get us something to eat, and keep your girls out of the backyard."

"They've gone home for the night," I said. "You're safe." I was stacking a plate with tortillas and beans. "Take this

303

out. I've got a whole pie and some coffee, too. Tell Johnny to water the horses. He'll never talk. He hates the law."

He kissed me. "I told them you'd help. They didn't see you in Griffin like I did." His arm lingered around my waist. "Where's your room?"

"First on the left at the top of the stairs."

We couldn't get enough of each other that night. It was as if we knew we'd not see each other again until nearly the end, as if we had to prove and keep proving what we felt, even to ourselves.

When the sky turned the palest of grey the way it does just before dawn, Doc got up and got dressed. "Don't come down," he said. "The less you see the better."

"Let me get you something to take with you."

"No, Sweetheart. Stay."

"Good luck," I said, getting out of bed and holding him against me one more time. "Let me know when you get where you're going."

And he was gone, they were all gone, vanishing into the mist like apparitions. And had I been asked, which I wasn't, I could have sworn that brief visit was a dream, that the bruises on my lips were imagination, that none of it had happened at all.

CHAPTER Forty-eight

So I stayed in Globe living with memories, and if life lacked the excitement and the breath-taking pace of earlier years, it made up for the lack in its peace and security.

Doc was in Denver, Gunnison, Leadville. He kept in touch, but I felt no urge to join him. I was tired of running, moving, watching my back trail. I was tired of people like the Earps with their friendship, jealousies, trouble-seeking ways.

And then one afternoon I was sweeping the front porch when a wagon pulled up and a woman got out. She moved slowly, carefully, as if she was blind and feeling her way. She came straight to me and then looked up.

"Hello, Kate," she said.

"Mattie!"

We stood staring at each other, ghosts from a mutual past.

Mattie had aged, and not gracefully. What I could see of her hair under her black bonnet was dull and streaked with grey, and her mouth drooped at the corners where lines of despair had cut deeply into her skin.

"What on earth are you doing here? I thought you were in California with the rest."

"I was. Then I left. I went back to Tombstone to sell the house." She looked past me. "Can I come in? It's been a rough trip."

"Of course."

Inside she noticed the carpets, the ferns on stands, the comfortable chairs I'd scattered around the little lobby. "You've done well for yourself," she said, the old envy rearing its head.

"Hard work. But it's mine. I own it. Hell, I deserve it. Come have a lemonade."

"I'd rather have a whiskey."

I brought out a bottle against my better judgement. Mattie showed all the signs of having become a first-class drunk down to her shaking hands. I took her into the office.

"Why are you here?" I repeated, after she'd drained her glass and poured another.

"I waited," she said. "I stayed with them in Colton for almost a year waiting for Wyatt. He never came." Her voice broke. "After all those hard years he took off with that bitch. I haven't seen him since Tombstone, so I went back there. No luck."

Her clinging attitude had always irritated me. "What do you need him for? He left you. So what? Look what I've done, and without any man to help me."

"That's you," she said. "You never loved Doc anyhow."

As always, she got to me. "Don't you tell me about love! You and your lies and your nasty mouth! You're lucky. I could've taken Wyatt in Wichita and left you, but I didn't. Don't make me sorry for that. Just be glad I did love Doc, and shut up."

"That's a lie." She gave me that bulldog look of hers.

"Is it? I wouldn't bet on it. But then, you'll never know because Wyatt isn't around to ask."

She drank some more, and shuffled her feet, acknowledging the truth of that. Her shoes were scuffed. They looked like she'd hiked a hundred miles, and the sight of them aroused that old pity in me. She was stupid and stubborn, but I had to give her credit. She never backed down, even in the wrong.

"So what are you going to do?" I thought I might get her moving in a direction that wasn't so clearly downhill.

"I'm going back to work," she said, and she lifted her head defying me to contradict her.

"You mean...?" I couldn't finish, the notion was too preposterous.

"What else do I know how to do?"

She was old and had lost her looks. She'd be lucky to get fifty cents a trick.

"You're out of your mind!" I snapped. "Stay here and work for me. Meals are free and you won't have to pull up your skirts for the customers."

"Maybe I like doing that," she retorted. "Maybe it makes me feel good. What do you care anyhow? Nobody else does."

I corked the bottle and stood up, my patience, my charity at an end. One thing I've always hated is a crying drunk. "I've got work to do," I said. "Let me know if you find a place."

"Still the same, aren't you? Snotty. I should have

known."

"Still a damn sight smarter than you, too," I said. "You know how you'll end up? Dead in one of those cribs on the line. Beaten. Robbed. But what the hell, it's your life as you say, so go do it. The quicker the better."

She stood, too, and her eyes were glazed. "Wyatt was my life. Now it doesn't matter," she said.

She walked out, still moving with caution, not because she was blind, but because she was drunk and feeling her way in a haze.

"Mattie!" I called after her, but she shook her head violently and kept on going, down the street and around the corner to hell.

CHAPTER Forty-nine

June, 1887, Glenwood Springs, Colorado

Dear Kate,

You always said you'd dance on my grave, and the way things look you should soon have your wish. There is a sanitarium with mineral baths here, and I go every day, but with little or no improvement.

You'll say I should have stayed with you in Arizona where I was healthy instead of running around Colorado. Knowing you, you'll say a lot of things, but save them. The bugs are winning, so pack your dancing shoes and let's say a proper farewell.

Doc

I read the letter three times, knowing from the sight of the shaky handwriting that Doc's time was running out, and that the two of us, for whatever twisted reasons, had denied ourselves the last five years.

I dried my tears and packed my bag, telling the ever-faithful Johnny Weed to mind the store and giving him my brother Alexander's address in Carbondale.

Thank God for Alexander! Carbondale was up the Crystal River from the confluence of the Colorado and the Roaring Fork where Glenwood Springs was located, and I had the vain notion that at his farm I could bring Doc back to some kind of health.

He was, of course, gambling every night and drinking more than was good for him, as if fiendishly trying to hurry his end.

When I found him, it was all I could do to keep the shock off my face, and I didn't entirely succeed. He looked like a scarecrow, thin, stoop-shouldered, a feverish flush beneath the dark circles under his eyes. And his blond hair was streaked with grey that, rather than making him look distinguished, only emphasized the fact that the flame of life was flickering and about to go out.

"You see?" were his first words, and then he hunched over coughing and sounding as if pieces of his lungs were rattling in his throat.

I stood back, afraid that if I touched him the way I longed to do, I'd only make him angry.

When he'd finished, he folded his handkerchief and stuffed it in his pocket. "Come and kiss me, Sweetheart," he said, "or are you afraid it'll get you, too?"

"I'm not afraid." What in hell did I have to be afraid of then - that I'd die, too? I'd have welcomed it.

The world without Doc loomed large, empty, black as one of those mine shafts sunk in the ground. I rushed into his arms, felt his hot skin and the bones that were all that was left of him.

"We're going to Alexander's," I said. "We're going to get you well." I had little hope, but he needed hope more than I did.

"Too late, Kate," he said. "A couple months'll do for me."

"We're going to try."

"Still the same." There was admiration in his expression. "You'd take on God, Himself, wouldn't you?"

"God, the devil, or anybody else," I said. "Now can you pack your things, or should I do it?"

"You do it. I'll watch. Like the old days."

"I wish we could have them back," I said, surprised by the wave of longing that came over me. "I wish we could ride the cattle trail again just one more time. On good horses. The two of us young and not giving a damn."

He didn't answer, and when I turned to look at him, saw that he'd fallen asleep.

I tried, Alexander and his wife Mary tried, to save him, laying out a regimen of good food, fresh milk, plenty of sun and air, and decent hours.

Doc and I took walks, short ones, his strength wasn't up to anything severe. We went down to the river daily and sat, often in silence, watching it slip over the rocks the way life seemed to be slipping faster and faster through our fingers.

What Doc's thoughts were as we sat there side by side, I didn't know. Sometimes a look of terrible grief swept across his face and he grew morose.

Sometimes he was angry and turned on me cursing. "Why do this to me? Why drag it out? Let me go, for God's

311

sake. Leave me in peace to die."

I didn't answer. His rages came and went, and I was simply a convenient scapegoat. It was life and the fact of death that he hated, beat against with his failing strength, not me. Usually my patience only irritated him more.

"Always there, aren't you? Waiting for the end. I know you. You're a bitch in heat and always were. You can have your pick of men soon, I'll be gone. And you'll dance and laugh and I'LL BE GONE!"

"And there will be a hole in my heart I'll never fill," I responded quietly. "We've had our troubles, our fights, but they were part of us, too. I love you, Doc. I haven't said it enough. I was always scared you'd use it against me, but it's true. I love you and I always will."

He felt for my hand. "I know. Who else would have put their neck in a noose for my sake?" He laughed, a breathless sound that stabbed at me. "What I remember best is you standing there holding a pistol aimed at Larn's head. The look in your eyes, and you no bigger than a cat, fighting mad."

"I wish it could have been different," I said, thinking about the wasted years, the child we'd lost. "I wish we could have been like other people."

That took him by surprise. "Why, Kate," he said, "I thought you'd figured it out. If we'd been like other people none of this would have happened. Think what we'd have missed! By now we'd have been bored to tears with each other and with life. As it is..." he spread his hands, "we've got a hell of a lot of living to remember. And maybe we've made a difference somewhere, left our mark. Who knows?"

I didn't, and I didn't care about leaving a mark. I only cared about Doc, and he was slipping away a little more each day. My feelings must have been obvious because he drew me close and stroked my hair.

"Don't feel bad, Sweetheart. It's been fun, and I've lived a lot longer than anyone expected. Mostly due to you. I have no regrets." He paused a minute, and I felt his hand warm on my neck. "Except leaving you. Try not to get in too much trouble when I'm gone."

•

In late October Doc and I returned to Glenwood. My attempts to cure him had failed. He had had several hemorrhages, and was so thin that even I could lift him. Still he held on, and every once in awhile the old devilment shone in his eyes. Not often, and not for long, but it was there, an echo of what had been.

We didn't talk on the trip to town. Doc slept under blankets and his lucky buffalo coat, while I watched the mountains, great hunks of purple stone crowned with pine and aspen. The aspens had lost most of their leaves, but here and there one still trembled on a branch, golden, fragile as a tear.

The sky that November morning was cold and brooding, and the air tasted like snow. Everything, the fickle wind, the purple mountains hunched above the river, seemed to be waiting for the angel of death.

Doc knew. I knew when he asked me to sit with him. "Give me your hand, Sweetheart," he whispered in that dreadful voice that was all he could manage.

His hand was already cold. I held it between my warm ones, and he lay back on his pillows and closed his eyes. "That's good," he said. "My Kate. Always there fighting."

But I couldn't fight death. No one ever wins that battle.

He looked at me a final time, out of eyes like tarnished silver, and he spoke with effort. "Just so you know....I loved

313

you. The whole time...since you were a river rat on the run and scared."

I bowed my head over our hands, not wanting him to see my tears, and he groped weakly until he found my hair.

"Don't...wear black," he rasped. "Not for me. You'll look like hell when you dance."

Then there was silence broken only by his ragged breath. A long silence before he said in a tone of surprise, "The damn bugs have got me after all."

"Not yet," I said. "Not yet."

But they had. When I looked up he was gone, all the brilliant, dancing light snuffed out.

EPILOGUE

The paloverde tree in the yard was an umbrella of golden blossoms when I returned to Globe. It reminded me of that first visit to Tombstone seven years before; the same arch of blue sky, edges framed by mountains, and in the valleys the fierce blooming, the buzzing of bees, the sweetness in the air.

It was that sweetness that did me in. I sat on the porch and wept as I'd been unable to do during the long, frozen winter I'd spent at Alexander's.

Johnny Weed came out and wisely went back in again, leaving me to spill my sorrow. As I'd foreseen, the world without Doc was an empty place, bereft of laughter.

All I had left was myself, and I had to go on as those left behind always do, though I couldn't know then that I'd go on for more than fifty years; that I'd see more war, the coming of the automobile, electricity, telephones, the astonishing motion picture. What would Doc have said to it all?

What would he have said had he been in Globe the day Wyatt and Josie blew into town looking prosperous and truly happy?

They came straight to me to offer condolences, Josie wearing her favorite wine red, with a tiny hat perched on her heavy hair and looking even more beautiful in maturity, and Wyatt dignified in a business suit, although still with those remote blue eyes.

"I miss him," I said. "I always will."

"So will I. He was one of a kind." Wyatt looked like he feared tears from me and was anxious to change the subject.

"You've made a nice place," he said. "Will you stay, do you think?"

"I don't know. Sometimes I think I will, and then again..." I shook my head. "It's like I've been cut loose, slipped my mooring. I can't decide what to do."

Josie laid a hand on my arm. "Wait awhile," she advised. "Don't do anything yet."

Out of curiosity, to see what would happen, I said, "I see Mattie pretty often."

They both looked startled. "Where?" they said in unison.

"No place you're liable to see her. She's working in a crib over in Pinal, but she's in and out of town."

"Good God!" Wyatt looked sick, and Josie blushed crimson.

"Can we help her?" she whispered. "Does she need money? Anything?"

"She won't take it. I tried. But I thought I'd warn you

316

about her." I felt guilty seeing the crack I'd put into their happiness. "Come on in the dining room and have lunch," I invited. "This is the best restaurant in town."

Josie slipped off to wash, and Wyatt pulled out a wad of bills. "How bad off is she?"

"Bad," I said. "She won't last much longer. Booze, drugs, the usual thing."

"Damn it! I didn't mean it to happen this way!" he said, coming as close to admitting his feelings as I ever saw.

"You knew Mattie," I reminded him. "What did you expect? That she'd hook up with a banker or run off and sing opera?"

"Hell, no. I didn't expect anything. I just wasn't thinking about it...about her. There was Josie, and all that trouble in Tombstone and after. I was on the run, and I kept running. Away from her as it turned out. Can you blame me?"

"Yes," I said. "And no. I know what she was like maybe better than you. Anyhow, you've got yourself a real lady now. Treat her like she deserves."

He didn't ask me what I meant. Probably he knew. He handed me money. "Keep this for Mattie. Use it if she needs anything."

"She won't take it if it comes from you."

"Then don't tell her," he said and stood up as Josie came back.

I didn't tell Mattie. I didn't have a chance. I used the money to pay for her funeral when she died in Pinal a week later, and to ship her trunk with its pathetically few contents ~ a quilt, a bible inscribed to Wyatt, a few photographs ~ back to an address I found inside.

It was funny that she'd never mentioned family, and that none of us had ever asked her about her past. But then, that was

317

typical of Mattie who never spoke about the things that mattered most, and who died clutching the emptiness that was all she ever had.

She'd seen Wyatt and Josie in town, had watched them, taking in every detail; how they looked at one another; how they dressed in the height of fashion; how Josie walked, sleek as a Persian cat, earrings flashing, arm in arm with Wyatt. With Mattie's man from that long ago time.

Poor, demented, stupid soul! She raged. She drank. She finished off a bottle of laudanum and fell asleep forever in that shack that measured ten feet by twelve while around her the desert stretched itself in endless perfection.

And I? I sold the hotel and wandered. Back to Tombstone in search of old memories, to Bisbee, that little mining town perched on the slopes of the Mule Mountains. I even married again for what foolish reason I can't now remember. It was a brief union. George Cummings drank too much, and when under the influence he was violent. With a blackened eye and a dislocated arm I stood in court and divorced him, and went on my way alone.

But life still held a surprise or two for me. One day in the Spring of 1900, a gentleman in the mining community of Dos Cabesas placed an ad in the Tucson paper requesting a housekeeper. Being out of a job and in need of income, I applied. He hired me and came to pick me up, this John Howard, driving a wagon pulled by a splendid matched pair of sorrels.

He took off his hat exposing a head of grizzled hair that had once been red. "I hope we suit," he said. "And I hope you won't mind living out of town aways where my claims are."

"I won't," I assured him and climbed on the seat where I studied the horses and watched Howard's hands as they nimbly took hold of the reins. He had good hands, capable ones. The horses leaned into their collars and off we went towards another adventure.

The Sulphur Springs Valley stretched ahead of us, blue in the distance where it spilled into Mexico, and the Chiricahua Mountains, home of Geronimo, Cochise, a thousand unnamed warriors, rose starkly and suddenly from the valley floor to that peculiar, double-topped formation that gave Dos Cabesas its name, "two heads."

Something nagged in memory, and I peered down the spiral of years trying to catch hold of it. But try as I would, nothing surfaced, and at last I looked sideways at Howard who was humming under his breath and holding the team to a ground-eating trot.

"Those are good horses," I said.

He gave a delighted grin. "They are at that. Up for anything, they are, both of them."

He had a trace of an English accent that intrigued me. "How long have you been out here?" I asked.

"Too long, I think sometimes. I left home as a youngster. Went to sea. Came to America and saw the country, then settled here finally. I have a few good claims that bear working. And watching." He sounded grim, but when he turned to me his blue eyes were youthful. "You know how to shoot?"

"Of course," I answered, knowing in that instant who he was and where I'd seen him.

"You had a paint horse named Gidran, didn't you?" I asked.

He pulled in the team reflexively. "How the devil did you know that?"

"I sold him to you. In Texas. That kid with the big hat and worn out boots was me."

"I'll be damned," he said, chuckling in his beard. "I'll be damned. The best horse I ever had. Kept him til he died of old age. I promised you, didn't I?"

He had. And he'd kept that promise. I liked a man who lived up to his word. Life wasn't going to be so empty after all, I thought, and leaning back in the seat, I took a deep breath of the clear desert air.

~

Mary K. Cummings, born Mary Katherine Harony, alias Kate Elder, Kate Fisher, Mrs. Doc Holliday, died at the Arizona Pioneer's Home in Prescott, Arizona, on November 7, 1940, a week short of her ninetieth birthday.

Afterword

Shortly after the publication of "Doc Holliday's Woman" in 1995, I received an astonishing letter from one Mark Horoney. The letter concluded with the sentence, "Ms. Coleman, I beseech you to get in touch with me." What writer could refuse such a request?

As I found out, Mark and his father, Michael, are descendants of Kate's youngest brother, Louis, the one member of the family whose descendants Glenn Boyer had never been able to locate in his search for Big Nose Kate.

From Michael I learned much that had puzzled me during the research and writing of "Doc Holliday's Woman." Perhaps most puzzling was Kate's own statement in her autobiographical letter sent to her niece, Lillian Raffert shortly before her death, that she she had married Silas Melvin, a shoe clerk in

St. Louis, and that both he and their son had died in an epidemic.

Certainly there is a Silas Melvin listed in the St. Louis census, but that census shows him married to a Mary V. Bust. Not *our* Mary Katherine. Still, in writing the novel, I decided to take Kate at her word. Why, after some seventy-five years, would she have remembered this man's name if he'd meant nothing to her?

From Michael Horoney I learned too late that our Mary Katherine had gone by the name Mary May in St. Louis, and had actually written letters home signing herself as such. A second search of the census turned up "Mary May . . . widow" and a William B. May who is listed as the owner of a shoe store but married to someone other than *our* Mary. The shoe store seems the obvious link, but how?

I infer, however, that Kate invented her marriage to Melvin whom she obviously knew, and that she was somehow attempting to cover-up or white-wash a past indescretion as so many Victorian ladies did after they became respectable. The question of what she actually did or who she was with in St. Louis remains, at this time, unanswered.

Michael Horoney also sent me a copy of the Horoney family coat-of-arms dating from the mid-17th century, and the information that Hungarian names that end in "ny" denote land owners and members of nobility. The original spelling was changed after the family arrived in America, an "e" being inserted making it Haroney. In some cases, the name is spelled Haroni or Haronyi.

Most interesting of all is that Michael Horoney through Csaba Harony ~ a relative in Hungary and Slovakia, has discovered that Big Nose Kate's father, Mihaly, was Professor of Toxicology at the Teachers Training College at Nove Zamky and

322

a practicing physician near Debrecen where he met and married Kate's mother, Katharine Boldizar.

There is no record of him or his family after 1859 which is obviously when the Haronys left for the New World. The fact that Mihaly was not only nobility but a toxicologist and physician lends credence to the family traditon that he and his family actually were in the service of the ill-fated Emperor Maximillian who, significantly, had an avid interest in botany and the medicinal properties of plants.

The possibility also exists that the Horonys came first to Davenport, Iowa where there was a large Hungarian colony, and then went to Mexico, returning after the Revolution started. The timing here still needs to be verified.

Writing historical fiction is always fascinating, never simple. It is a bunch of tangled threads waiting to be unraveled. Kate's story is harder than most, but not impossible. Thankfully, I have been supported and encouraged from the first by my husband, historian Glenn Boyer who turned over his extensive research to me.

Among the documents, family letters, taped interviews, and photographs in his collection, I especially treasure those written by Kate herself in her own hand. They show her to be far different from the illiterate, drunken prostitute Hollywood and so many writers have made of her. These letters are thoroughly literate and grammatical, proving that she had an education superior to most of the women of her era.

Through these documents, I discovered a courageous and determined woman who did what she had to do to survive, who reinvented herself when necessary without ever losing her personal pride. A woman who loved Doc Holliday until the day she died.

There is no doubt that they were star-crossed lovers, due mostly to his ill health and the circumstances in which they found each other. But neither is there any doubt that two such passionate people had frequent angry quarrels. That Doc ever laid a hand on Kate, however, is almost impossible to believe. No Southern gentleman, which Doc Holliday certainly was, ever beat a lady ~ which Kate certainly was, and knew it. She would not have tolerated such a thing.

As Dr. Bork told me, "She was very much a lady of quality background who wanted the record set straight."

I hope she approves of what I have done.

Printed in the United States
52349LVS00003B/71